Ribbonwood

Ruby Landers

RUBY LANDERS

Cover design by Cath Grace Designs

ISBN: 978-0-6486402-9-5

First edition 2024

This book was written on unceded Jinibara and Gubbi Gubbi lands. I acknowledge the traditional custodians and storytellers of the lands on which I live and work, and where this book was written, and I pay my respect to Elders past, present and emerging.

To all my single mamas. I see you x

Content Warnings

If you would appreciate content warnings please visit my website rubylandersbooks.com for a full list

Australian Language Glossary

Akubra - an iconic Australian version of a cowboy hat.

Blak - preferred spelling for Aboriginal Australians

Chook - chicken

Doona - duvet/quilt

Ethnic - a "polite" term used for literally anyone who isn't of Anglo-Saxon heritage

FIFO - Fly In Fly Out. A method of working in remote areas, often a few weeks on, then a week off.

Jinibara - the Aboriginal people of the Blackall Ranges, the traditional owners of the real and unceded land upon which the fictional town of Ribbonwood is located

Neighbours - a famous, long-running Australian soap opera (which gave you various Aussie stars including Margot Robbie; you're welcome)

SES - State Emergency Service

Ute - utility vehicle/pick up truck

Roo bar - a metal bar on the front of the car theoretically designed to keep you safe if a six foot tall bunny rabbit (Kangaroo) suddenly jumps onto the road in front of you

Wog - a racist term for Italian/Greek migrants. Sometimes used for Eastern European nationalities and frequently used affectionately by Mediterranean migrants and their descendants for themselves. Yes, Australian racism even manages to extend to other white people, it's a real talent.

Prologue
Ribbonwood

There aren't too many small towns that would band together and say a woman deserved to be widowed, but Ribbonwood was that town and Lara Bennett was that woman.

Lara had been too good for everyone else by the time she turned seventeen. Her long blonde locks swaying down her back, blue eyes shining, her body a grown woman's since she'd hit Year Nine and you bet she knew what to do with it. No time for high school boys, she seduced Josh Rees right before everyone's eyes and he was a man of twenty-eight and already engaged to marry Jessica Webb. What kind of a girl does that?

Addie Armstrong said her boyfriend had heard from his mates on the football team that Lara had boasted she could suck a man's soul right through his dick and didn't that just tell you everything you needed to know? Josh Rees - Ribbonwood's golden boy though he might have been - never stood a chance in the face of those batted eyelashes. As for Jessica, she was so heartbroken she had barely turned around before she was married to Stephen Westerson and we all know how *that* turned out.

Lara gave Josh the runaround; quite the dance she led him on. You've never seen a man so hung up, it was like she'd cast a spell. Three years later she was married to him: twenty years old and a bride so fresh-faced and pretty it was unnatural. Still, it seemed a bit like telling a lie in everyone's faces that she'd dressed for her wedding in white. *That,* whispered Dottie Parsons as Lara passed by her in the aisle, satin and lace snuggling up to her indecent curves, *is no damn virgin.*

Of course, it was no wonder Lara had turned out the way she had, with no mother to raise her and no one but her half-drunk father to keep an eye on her. Phil Bennett was gentle enough but quite hopeless, on that Ribbonwood was clear, and honestly, it was a good thing when you thought about it, that Lily had died before she saw the kind of girl her only daughter had become. Lily had always been the sweetest of angels; it was mystifying to see how far that particular apple had fallen from the tree.

But life moves on and for a while, Lara Rees *née* Bennett passed by under the radar. Josh's little home down the paddock from his parents' big house was not good enough for her of course, and some said it was her pestering that had him take out that oversized bank loan, the one that bought them a farm of their own. She worked him hard, day and night, always wanting the finer things in life. You'd see him down at the pub, exhausted, barely able to stand up straight, the poor man. Some men just aren't built to farm macadamias, but did she care about that? Not one whit.

. . .

In all that time, what did she even do? No one ever saw her outside of glimpses here and there, pushing a shopping trolley over in Silverbloom or flirting with Nate Kerr at the mechanic shop to give her a free service. *Oh, I'll bet she got serviced alright,* Albert Sanderson claimed down at the Ribbonwood pub, his white bushy eyebrows raised high over his beer glass.

They'd been married five years before she even deigned to pop out a child for Josh, and by then he was already thirty-six years old. The man had been dying to be a father his whole life, but just like always, she made him wait until it suited her. And *then*, oh lord, if you thought she'd had airs *before*. You'd think Matilda Rees was the first damn baby ever born on this planet. The way she snuggled and cuddled and coddled that little girl? Kylie Burgess told Crystal Berry that she wasn't even sure if two-year-old Matilda could walk on her own, Lara held her so tight.

And as for Josh, he may as well have been last week's leftovers, she discarded him so fast. There he was, down at the pub, night after night, lonely as all get out and no wife whatsoever to comfort him. She was all wrapped up in the baby; barely gave him any attention at all after she'd got her child from him. All he had was his mounting debt, his struggling business and his loneliness. When his car left the road one night, after an evening of drinking away his sorrows, and was found wrapped around a tree, his broken body flung free from the wreckage, all of Ribbonwood knew the facts: the whole thing was Lara Rees' (née Bennett's) fault.

. . .

If she had just started having her babies earlier and made him a proper family man when he was ready for it; if she'd just made him feel wanted instead of forcing him out into the cold; if she hadn't insisted on that big bank loan that had him working day and night; if she hadn't seduced him in her damn *school uniform* in the first place.

After that, of course, Lara lay low. Played the grieving widow, or perhaps, more likely, didn't dare show her face around town. Because, after all, maybe she'd gotten what she'd wanted all along? The insurance payout was enough to buy her home and a little corner of the macadamia farm outright, while she sold the rest to pay off the bank loan. She was independent, set for life, and now she had Matilda. She'd always been a schemer, that woman, you could tell by the look of her, even way back when. Too good for high school boys? Oh, she'd always had a plan.

And then came the real icing on the cake. Lara Bennett - she changed her name back, can you believe the nerve of her? The man had barely been gone for four years - up and bought the Ribbonwood General Store. Her daughter was at school, and now - *now* - she wanted to work. At least, that's what she told Myra Jenkins when she popped her head in to see what the hell was going on, brown paper covering the front windows of the store and the doors temporarily closed to the public.

Ribbonwood's population was only 907 people at last count (906 *now, Lara Bennett?*) and that's far too small a town to hide from your crimes. Who, precisely, did she think was going to buy from her?

. . .

The Michaels were the previous owners of the general store - Michael Webster and Michael Patterson, that is - boyfriend and boyfriend if you can believe that, but nice enough fellas and people shopped at the store because it's important to support locals. The Woolworths over at Silverbloom was a hell of a lot cheaper however, and just a thirty-minute drive, so Lara was dreaming if she thought she could keep that business afloat.

But to everyone's shock, when the brown paper came down off the windows, Lara had rebranded. Sure, you could still buy your tea bags and a loaf of bread, but there was a clear tilt towards the tourist market: free-range organic eggs at double the price - as if everyone's chickens around here weren't damn *organic* - overcharged jams with exotic ingredients, locally grown coffee beans and artisanal cheeses you'd have to re-mortgage your home to afford. All the weekend tourists up from Brisbane, staying in yurts, going glamping, or holidaying in Airbnb's on Myra's or Crystal's or Albert's or Jessica's property all *flooded* through the doors.

Typical Lara Bennett, still too good for the locals. *I'm not saying she deserved to be widowed,* whispered Amber O'Brien to Kimberley Evans, *but doesn't she look like she secretly enjoys it?*

Chapter One

The problem with flying from Melbourne to Brisbane was always the outfit. When Ollie had left her home in Brunswick at seven a.m. that morning, it had been eight degrees. She'd ducked from her front doorstep to the Uber, wrestling her wheeled suitcase and trying pointlessly to dodge the shards of tiny raindrops flung up by the breeze that sliced right through her puffer jacket, carefully stepping around puddles in her leather boots.

Now, as the plane began its descent, glaring sunlight bounced through the portholes and the pilot announced the ground conditions with sudden brightness in his crackling voice: *thirty-three degrees and sunny*. A few passengers actually cheered, ready to holiday. Ollie looked down at her tight black jeans and winced. There was no way to win.

It wasn't until she stepped out of the terminal that it really hit her: a wave of humidity so hot and sudden it was like walking smack into a wall. She actually felt the moment the moist air hit her lungs, a warm mist filling her breath like a bath. This, she supposed, should feel like home.

It didn't though.

The hire car was a gleaming little Toyota Corolla, a hybrid, swift and quiet. She didn't need the navigation system to find her way to the highway north; she'd moved from the state seventeen years ago, but the road to home was written in her veins.

Sunglasses protecting her from the glare and the air conditioner blasting, she still felt the heat baking through the windscreen as she travelled up the Bruce Highway. The view wasn't much, just scraggly trees and oversized petrol stations, but there was still something so *Queensland* about it all in the occasional burst of bright red or purple flowers popping through the foliage, or the low scruffy spikes of a pineapple farm at the roadside. Always something chaotic, teeming with unstoppable life. Even with six crammed lanes of traffic surrounded by the ever-present roadworks, there were glimpses of an almost decadent lushness battling to survive against the concrete.

She passed a plastic sign planted on the road verge. *Koala Killed Here,* it read, with a cartoon of a fuzzy creature crying. She winced. A tradie in a ute tailgated her needlessly; she was going a hundred and ten in the centre lane and the right was empty. She was tempted to tap her brakes to make him back off, but the likelihood of a methed-up twenty-two-year-old behind the wheel made her sigh and indicate into the damn fast lane, letting him speed by unchecked. He must be going a hundred and forty. A brief image of a screaming, crumpled and impossibly small body flashed into her vision and she gritted her teeth until it passed.

She drove past billboards featuring the ever-present smile of Steve Irwin cuddling outsized crocodiles as she passed the zoo, then turned off, up into the hills. Here the lushness took over: wild bamboo, grasses higher than the car, unstoppable trees that leaned across the road, creating green tunnels of rainforest briefly obscuring the sky. The road wove up the mountain, slipping through bustling tourist towns, along the range, past buffalo farms, macadamia groves, strawberry fields and banana plantations, before dipping back down a winding back road of lush forest. Road signs warned of wildlife she hoped still existed, but equally hoped existed well away from her car tyres. As the sky widened beyond the trees, she saw a pair of eagles slowly circling above an empty field.

A strange sensation opened up in her chest as the road began to climb again. She was almost home! She was so far from home. The cognitive dissonance almost split her in two: Dr Gabrielli, thirty-five years old, the sophisticated, urbane Melburnian; Ollie, the grubby-kneed, backwoods, Queensland country girl. She rounded the bend and saw the road sign. *Welcome to Ribbonwood, Winner of the Hinterland's Cleanest Town 2003!*

She didn't drive into town. Vintage awards for cleanliness or not, she almost never did. Ollie's visits stayed short and sweet - at Christmas, if she could wing it on the roster - and Ribbonwood itself held no draw for her. Instead, she turned left almost immediately after the sign, driving the single-lane winding road out into the lush wilderness, rainbow lorikeets swooping and screeching above the car. Ten minutes later, she reached her old mailbox, where the school bus used to drop her. With her heartbeat escalating, she took the long gravel road up through the sun-filled olive grove, trying not to ping too many rocks into the rental car's previously pristine paintwork.

A motley collection of farm dogs raced out to shout at her as she pulled up before the house; Ollie counted four. A wily-looking Kelpie, a mouthy collie, an authoritative yet miniature Jack Russell and - quite ridiculously - a dachshund?

"Who the heck are you?" she asked over the sound of aggravated barking as the small, sleek sausage jumped up to put his dusty paws on her black jeans. He eyed her seriously while the others circled and blustered.

"I could ask you the same thing," came an outraged voice from the wide wooden porch. The screen door banged open and out stepped a harried-looking woman with grey-streaked hair, flushed cheeks and a t-shirt splattered with something red. "Viola Gabrielli, I will murder you *dead*," her mother announced before she swept down the porch steps and wrapped her arms around her in a fierce hug. "Shut your mouths!" she blasted the dogs, the volume blaring directly into Ollie's left ear.

Ollie closed her eyes, tears leaking from her lashes. Her mum's hug was almost smothering in the ridiculous heat of the middle of the day, but she didn't want her to let go. She smelled of fresh herbs and also herself, some indefinable scent that the primal part of her brain still recognised as *mama*. Her mum was crying too as she pulled back.

. . .

"How *dare* you?" she said, her eyes blazing. "I should have known you'd pull something like this."

"I didn't want you to fuss." Ollie rolled her eyes. "I knew you'd drag everyone down the bloody mountain and make a big deal at the airport and it's totally unnecessary."

"Unnecessary? Listen to you! You're only our youngest child, living on the other side of the world, driving all this way on your own. Anyone would think nobody loved you!"

"Melbourne isn't the other side of the world." A smile sneaked from the corner of her lip despite herself. "It's a two-hour flight."

"What is that, a rental car?" Her mother looked at the gleaming vehicle like someone had dropped a turd on her kitchen table. "How much is that costing you? Who did you hire it from? Your father and Matty can drop it at Hertz back down at Caboolture this afternoon for you. What a waste of money. You can drive the ute."

"It's fine, really-"

"It's unsafe! Look how small it is! There's not even a roo bar-"

. . .

"Those things don't work, Mum, they actually make the car more unsafe-"

"Tell that to your father! He's only alive because of that bar. That bloody kangaroo was bigger than a horse, he said, and if it had of went through his windscreen-"

"That guy is full of horseshit," interrupted a gruff voice behind her and Ollie whirled around to see a wiry figure with a cloth hat covering what was once a fine head of hair, huge hands streaked with soil.

"Dad!" Ollie hugged him.

"You came," he said quietly. He hugged her back firmly, his arms hard and strong.

"Of course I did." Her eyes stung again.

"Well," he said, "now you've done it. She'll be so pleased to see you, she'll never bloody die now."

Ollie's jaw dropped. She met her father's wet eyes and they both burst out laughing.

. . .

"You're both as bad as each other!" her mother scolded. "Any minute, one of you is going to get struck down by lightning, and you'll deserve it. Help her with her bags, Vanni. Make yourself useful."

Inside the house, it *could* have been blessedly cool. There was ducted air conditioning for god's sake - top of the line, the best deal possible - her father had insisted; he knew the guy. But to Ollie's deep dismay, instead the windows and doors were all open, as if a non-existent breeze was about to drift through the screens and cool the house down.

"You've gotten soft," her dad scoffed when she protested. "We don't turn on the air-con until it gets to thirty-six. Waste of money."

"*Dad.* I'll pay your power bill myself. Please can we cool this place down?"

"Pay it? We've got the money," he bristled. "It's the principle of the thing. Besides, it's bad for the environment. Thought you Melbourne Greenies were all about that kind of thing."

"Go and get changed, for goodness' sake." Her mother put her hands on her hips, surveying her jeans with judgement. "I'll come with you," she added, her eyebrows suddenly shooting to her hairline. "I haven't made up your room yet since you told us you were coming *tomorrow.* It's in a state-"

"Mum. It'll be fine. Let me dress myself, would you?"

. . .

Ollie trailed along behind her father, who insisted on lugging her suitcase for her, all the way around to the back of the house to her childhood bedroom.

"Thanks, Dad." She practically had to shut the door in both her parents' faces as her mother followed along behind, fretting about dusting and whether there were enough coat hangers. She sank down on the bed for a moment, trying to get her bearings.

The room was stuffy with heat but as neat as a pin, just as she'd known it would be. Her mother would have been prepping for her visit for days. Gone were the band posters and athletics trophies that had scattered the room, but her parents still referred to it as hers. The bed was a snug double with a slightly too shiny doona cover, about eight too many pillows and there were knickknacks on the bedside table she couldn't even begin to understand, but she could still see it the way it had been when she was a child, staring around at these same four walls.

She pulled herself to her feet and flung open the windows. It only let in a wave of damp heat, but at least it was fresh, the scent of hot earth and green leaves. She gazed out at the view. Her family home was a big old Queenslander - large, wooden and up on stilts, ready for the Summer rains - with a wide wraparound deck on three sides. Her room was in the back corner, with no deck, just a drop down to the ground and a view over the hills. She looked out at the neat rows of vines, *Sémillon, chardonnay, shiraz, merlot,* the source of her family's livelihood, along with the olives in the front. The family business.

. . .

Sweat trickled down between her shoulder blades and she turned and pulled off her jeans, gasping in relief as she shed the clinging denim from her clammy skin. She opened her suitcase and sought out a pair of small linen shorts and a light cotton singlet. It felt weird seeing her legs free after a Melbourne winter that seemed to go forever, even now, in what was supposed to be the middle of spring. Neither state seemed to know what it was doing.

She was putting her clothes on hangers and into drawers when she heard the dogs beginning to shout, the crunch of gravel under car tyres, her brother Matty's voice cheerfully bellowing for the hounds to *shut the hell up* and she smiled even as she shook her head. She'd been home all of ten minutes and the family was already starting to arrive as if it were an emergency to see her.

Ollie leaned her hands on the windowsill and took in a deep breath of the subtropical air, her lungs now adjusting. She steadied herself. Then she slipped out of her room and down the hall. She was too late; she could already hear her mother's voice drifting out of the room two doors down.

"Stop fussing, Alessandra," she heard her saying, "let me get the wheelchair and bring you down-"

"I don't need that thing-" came the frail but irritated response and Ollie blinked back tears as she smiled. She stuck her head around the door to see that her mother was the one fussing and the elderly lady in the armchair was looking on in exasperation, clearly ready to leap out and try to make a run for it. Both women looked up as if with a sixth sense for her presence.

．　．　．

"Hi Nonna," she said softly.

"Viola." Her dark eyes lit up. "All I had to do to bring you back home is start dying, huh?"

Chapter Two

Eva Sinclair felt cold as she strode down the road, her hands gripping her son's stroller ahead of her. The day dripped with heat, but the coldness that spread through her came from within. She had failed him. She was failing him now, even in this instant. How could she have let this happen?

Her son's wails were slowing as if the hot air was smothering him. She checked over the top and made sure the canopy was shading him from the glare of the relentless sun. The agitated speed at which she was going seemed conversely to be calming him. Two years old: tantrum city.

Not that she could blame him. Honestly, right now she envied him; she too wanted to drop to her knees and howl. What choices had she made to get them here? What choices did she have left to fix it? Was there a fix? Was there a choice?

. . .

She gritted her teeth and tried to get it together. The car was toast. It had taken her an hour from home to walk this far and it would be twice as long back as the heat of the day arrived in force. She'd packed three bottles of water, one with a sippy straw for Spencer, still clutched in his hot little hand. What was she thinking, bringing him out like this? But what else could she do?

She hit the main street of Ribbonwood and ground her teeth, trying to calm herself and think rationally. She pulled up her phone to check her bank balance - an act of desperation - as if the number on the screen was about to change. $18.03 it still read, as it had every day for the last four days.

She did mental calculations. Milk was the priority, the only thing that would calm her son. She knew she should wean him from the bottle he still had first thing in the morning and last thing at night, but it was the last little comfort of babyhood that he had left. God knows she didn't have the capacity right now to deal with the meltdowns that would ensue if she tried to take it away. Then, perhaps bread? Not the most nutritious thing, but then again, toddlers never ate anything bloody good for them anyway. At least it would fill their bellies. Maybe a tin of beans for some protein, maybe there'd be enough left over for an apple, perhaps even two? You could live off that, right? Just until...until...

A flash of cold terror hit her and again she pressed *call* on the same number she'd been dialling for the past week. It rang out again. *That bastard.*

. . .

For a moment, her vision faded to black. When she blinked her eyes open, she was at the front door of the general store. Taking a harsh breath in, she turned and used her back to open the door, pulling the stroller in, containing her now silent child. The small bell tinkled as the door swung shut and she cursed, hoping Spencer didn't wake and start to scream. A beat. Blessed silence.

The store was cool, which should have been a relief. Instead, Eva felt herself start to shiver. She glanced up, just briefly, toward the counter. There she bloody was, Lara Bennett, cool as a cucumber, gazing down on her like a queen from her throne, eyes impassive, like Eva was a bug in her shadow. Eva scowled at her and tugged the stroller around the shelves.

She stared wide-eyed at the produce. *Organic local* began every label, before a price tag that made her eyes swim. Pomegranate, dragon fruit, lychees, not one damn apple. She found the milk fridge and blinked. The largest bottle of milk took up almost half her budget, though that wasn't abnormal, the supermarket was the same these days. She found the bread and almost laughed. There were *artisanal rustic* sourdough loaves priced at an arm and a leg next to a small stack of plastic packaged, white, sandwich bread. One product for the tourists, one for the locals. Lara sure knew what she was doing alright. Eva was basic lousy white bread, and she felt every crumb of it.

A sudden flash of rage hit her. Imagine it. *Imagine it.* Swanning into Ribbonwood, cooing over the rainforest from your oversized SUV. Flashing your credit card over *finger lime compote* and *maple smoked organic bacon* before you drifted into some glass-walled daydream with a plunge pool overlooking the coffee plantation and posted the view on Instagram. That's who shopped here. Not desperate, sweating locals with bare cupboards and blistered heels.

Her hand shot out, and she grabbed a wedge of *ash brie* and shoved it under the nappy bag in the bottom of the pram. She looked up. Nothing. A pang of vengeful glee hit her. *Swipe,* a handful of heirloom cherry tomatoes. *Slip,* a tin of smoked salmon.

She grabbed the stroller, about to turn into the next aisle, when an icy feeling sideswiped her with its suddenness. Lara was standing beside her, quite still, her eyes calm and watchful. Eva's vision suddenly wavered. The glee turned to sickness. Instead of a goddamned sandwich, she was going to get served the humiliation of *Lara Bennett's* rightful sanctioning. She felt so tired she almost collapsed.

"Here," said Lara after a beat that seemed to last forever. "You look like you need this."

A bottle of cold raspberry lemonade was pressed into her hand. She stared at it, dizzy and confused. Lara took it back and unscrewed the cap like she was a child, handing it back to her.

"Drink it," she pressed. "I don't want you passing out on my fucking floor," her tone was brusque.

Eva blinked. She drank. It was cool and sweet. As the sugar slowly kicked in, she became aware of the heat pouring off her skin like she'd been baked alive out there. Lara watched her for a beat, then turned her back, stalking away down the aisle, confiscating Eva's basket as she did. Eva stood there, uncertain. She drank half the bottle, partly because Lara had been right; she was low on blood sugar and hot as hell. She had the wherewithal to check on Spence. He was napping peacefully, his cheeks flushed but out like a light.

Finally, she steeled the nerve to slowly press her way back to the counter and face her fate. She pulled out her stolen items from the stroller and put them in front of Lara, forcing herself to meet her sharp blue eyes.

"That's all, I swear," she said dully. "I'm sorry."

Lara picked them up without a word. She put them into a shopping bag on the counter. Eva swallowed. She couldn't afford this, and she was damn sure Lara knew that. Was this her punishment? Having to flee the store without even milk for her boy?

She held her debit card between her fingers, awkward, prepared to bargain, tears of humiliation threatening at a low prickle. Lara was watching her. Was she enjoying this? Then she coolly picked up the bag on the counter and handed it over to Eva. It was heavy. Eva spotted a dozen eggs, a head of broccoli and some crackers amongst the items she'd picked and those she'd tried to steal. She held it in surprise, her mouth opening in confusion.

"I can't afford-" she started miserably, but Lara held up her hand, cutting her off.

. . .

"Dan's away again, huh?" she said evenly.

Eva felt her face flush red. She nodded, avoiding her eyes. There was a silence. When she finally looked up, Lara met her gaze.

"You know, we're having a bonfire tonight. At mine. A few of the girls. You should come."

Eva blinked. The words didn't line up in any way that made sense.

"I can't," she said, like Lara was slow. "I've got Spencer. Plus, my car won't start."

"Bring him," shrugged Lara. "He can nap in the spare room. Sadie will pick you up; she lives out your way. I think you need to get out of that house for a bit, don't you?" Eva just stared. Lara nodded at the bag still clutched in her sweaty hand. "You okay to get home?"

It was only when she found herself back out the door, blinking in the bright light, a full bag of food stowed under her sleeping child and a half-drunk bottle of artisanal soda in her left hand that she realised she hadn't managed to say thank you. Lara hadn't given her the chance.

———

True to Lara's word, just after tea time when Eva had coaxed a little omelette into her son's mouth, Sadie O'Malley arrived at her front door, her daughter in tow, a lanky ten-year-old named Frankie who hung back and stared.

Sadie looked at her too, assessing. Eva was too tired to even care as Sadie glanced around the messy kitchen and piles of laundry on her couch. Going out seemed ridiculous. Impossible, even. What was happening here, exactly?

"Okay," Sadie said. "Here's what we're going to do."

Eva found herself organised into bathing her son and putting him in his pyjamas while Sadie lugged the car seat out the back of Eva's useless sedan and wrestled it into her station wagon. Frankie hovered over the edge of the bathtub, making Spencer squeal and giggle, then bounced with him on the bed while Eva ducked into the bathroom to comb her hair, put on her damn bra and a swipe of lipstick. Then all four of them piled into Sadie's car, a bottle of warm milk satiating Spence, making him drowsy.

Eva looked sideways at Sadie as she drove. They'd gone to school together, technically. Technically in that they'd been in the same year, but Sadie was a lone wolf, by virtue of being one of only two Aboriginal kids in the school, the other being her brother Dave, who was in the year below. She'd been a skinny kid back then, with thick wavy hair and dark skin, large wary eyes and an unwaveringly serious disposition. Eva could feel a hint of that same wariness as they sat side by side in the car, only now it seemed to her to be balanced by a bone-deep calmness. Sadie was at home in herself in a way Eva suddenly craved. Just imagine being that self-possessed.

"How do you know Lara?" she asked, by way of conversation, less comfortable than Sadie was with the silence.

Sadie darted a wry glance sideways.

"Well," she said, "we went to school together. Ribbonwood High. You know it?"

Eva rolled her eyes.

"I mean," she corrected, "when did you become, like...friends?"

"Oh, you mean White Barbie and Blak Barbie?" Sadie smirked. Eva winced. "She's my best friend," Sadie shrugged. "We go way back. Her bonfires are legendary."

Eva stared out at the dense rainforest as they wound through the back roads, single track now, moving onto dirt, her son sleeping peacefully as the car wheels scuffed over the gravel. What was this secret Ribbonwood world where Sadie O'Malley and Lara Bennett were friends and Lara hosted something *legendary*? She thought of Dan, imagined what he might be up to right now, how she'd left her phone at home on the kitchen counter. *Let him just ring,* she thought, as the beginnings of sunset coloured the sky. *Let him wonder.*

. . .

Sadie turned down a long drive, then bumped her car up over the grass next to a modest wooden villa. Eva blinked. It wasn't the mansion she'd heard Lara had scored in her ill-gotten gains, but it was lovely. It was carefully painted in bright tones, like a little jewel on the grassy plain. The macadamia orchard swept out in front of it.

Softly she gathered her sleeping son, following behind Sadie and Frankie who had scampered ahead in the lead to loudly shush the grownups whose voices were ringing out from inside. There were six other cars parked beside them, but when Eva and Spence made it to the door, the other inhabitants of the house had tumbled out the back door, their voices disappearing up the paddock and it was only Lara Bennett who smiled at the sight of the flushed-face sleeping child on her shoulder and silently crooked a finger to lead the way to an expansive spare room, a single mattress made up on the floor next to the king bed, ready for her child to be tucked away.

Eva hesitated as she covered her little boy with a blanket. She couldn't leave him here, alone, to head out god knows where. Lara anticipated her worry, handing her a small electronic device.

"Baby monitor," she whispered. Eva met her blue eyes and found herself smiling.

Sadie put her to work carrying a case of beer while Frankie skipped off ahead with Lara's daughter Tilly, heads bent together, one dark one light, whispering and conspiring. Lara carried a basket, bottles of wine sticking out the top.

. . .

Eva saw the smoke and smelled the scent of charring meat even before they rounded a corner in the trees into a huge clearing and saw the fire. She stopped still and stared.

The fire was an immense leaping pile of flames, sending bright sparks up into the darkening sky. Several feet away was a whole separate BBQ, a woman with her back turned manning the grill, a bottle of beer dangling from her fingers. There were eight or nine other women, sprawled on picnic rugs and beanbags, drinking and chatting. Eva recognised them *all*.

The woman at the grill turned to see them arriving and Eva's jaw dropped. It was Esme Walker. Everyone in Ribbonwood knew she and Lara were sworn enemies. Esme ran the small tuck shop directly across the street from the general store, her livelihood dependent on the country kids bussed in from all over the district to the high school. A modest affair, it sold pies and fresh doughnuts, icy poles and bags of sweets.

When Lara had taken over the general store it had been barely months before she too was offering cold drinks and mixed bags of sweets displayed prominently in the front window. The town was outraged at this blatant attempt to sabotage a much-loved local business. Esme was sweet, demure and hard-working. How *dare* that woman? Stern instructions were issued to school kids and parents picking up their children marched pointedly across the road to Esme's tuck shop, Lara's temptation all for nothing. Esme and Lara had glowered at each other across the street ever since, one vanquished, the other gratefully still in her rightful business.

. . .

"Ez," called Lara now. "Put another steak on. This one looks like she hasn't had red meat in six months."

Esme laughed and nodded, toasting the new arrivals with her beer. *Ez.*

Around the fire, her own beer in hand, Eva gravitated back to Sadie.

"What the fuck is *that?*" she gestured at Esme and Lara bickering companionably over the grill, a haze of smoke wafting up between them, Lara pushing back her golden hair with a peal of laughter. Sadie glanced over in question.

"Oh, you mean the *feud?*" she raised her eyebrows. Suddenly, a blinding smile swept over her features. Eva realised she'd never seen her smile before. It was as bright as the sun and twice as lovely. "You didn't believe that, did you?" she asked. "Esme's business was struggling, Lara puts up a bit of competition and the whole town throws themselves wholesale behind Esme? Convenient much?"

Eva stared at her. She looked over at the two women piling food on plates together like they were about to feed an army.

"Oh," she said dumbly, watching on as Ribbonwood rearranged itself before her eyes.

Sadie just nodded.

28

. . .

"Yep."

"So," said Lara Bennett, half an hour later as she sat herself down next to Eva in the grass, licking the remains of the meat juice from her fingers, her golden hair glinting in the firelight. Eva looked up and saw the other women were all watching quietly, ready to hear her. "Tell us what's going on with Dan."

Chapter Three

Ollie awoke to a wet nose in her face.

"What the-" she spluttered, her eyes snapping open on melted chocolate eyes gazing back into her own and a quick lick to her nose. "Ugh!" she lifted her head abruptly. "How did you get in here?"

Rocco the dachshund blinked at her, his expression serious. She looked up and saw her bedroom door open a crack. She knew damn well he hadn't done that himself. She suspected her mother; the bloody dogs ran this house. She tried to stretch her legs and found the blanket pinned tight to her feet. Pushing herself up she saw Portia, the oversized ancient moggie glaring at her for disturbing her restful nap. *And* the bloody cat as well.

By the time she'd showered and dressed the day was already heating up.

. . .

"Morning arsehole," greeted Matty where he lazed on the front veranda, thick dark coffee in his hand. Her eldest brother lived with his wife and three kids barely three minutes' drive away and Ollie strongly suspected he was here not so much to be early for work but to escape the chaos of his household, and so his mother could cook his breakfast for him like Ollie was pretty sure she did every day.

"Morning fuckface," she ruffled his hair and he dodged. She sat down on one of the wooden deck chairs beside him and took a sip of her own cup. Even in Melbourne, home of good coffee - home of *Italian* coffee - there was nothing quite like drinking freshly roasted beans that had grown a hundred yards from where they sat.

"Hayley didn't come up with you, huh?"

She flicked her eyes over his face but the question seemed innocent.

"We broke up," she said. "Six months ago."

"Shit Ollie, I didn't know," he sat up straight, staring at her. "Jeez, did the grapevine blow a foo-foo valve or what? I didn't hear a thing."

Ollie snorted. She and her siblings liked to joke that if you sneezed in a church three thousand miles away, their mother would hear about it within eight minutes flat and that was on a bad day. Privacy between family members was not a thing her parents believed in.

. . .

"Mum only found out last night," she admitted.

"How are you alive right now?" Matty looked at her in wonder. Deep creases were starting around his heavily tanned face and a sprinkling of grey in his thick dark hair. It suited him - a solid hardworking guy, with a life he loved - but Ollie could still see the reckless young foot-baller he'd once been, teaching her how to tackle in the backyard by bowling her into the grass so hard she'd had the wind knocked out of her and her dad had put her on concussion watch.

"Oh, I'll pay, don't you worry," she shook her head, watching a kookaburra swoop from a tree branch with incredible speed, down into the grass and fly off with what looked like a hapless frog in his beak. It was a perfect analogy. Her mother would bide her time and swoop when she least expected it. "She'll be trying to marry me off to a friend's cousin's farmer's daughter within the week."

"Watch out," Matty grinned like a little boy, "there's that many eligible bachelorettes in Ribbonwood just waiting to get swept off their little gay feet by a hotshot Melbourne doctor. Just don't get anyone pregnant or you'll be stuck here for life like the rest of us."

Ollie laughed.

"I think I'm pretty safe on all counts," she promised.

. . .

"Seriously, Ol. Are you okay?"

"Yeah, I'm fine." She clearly wasn't particularly convincing because Matty kept watching her face.

"How long are you here for?" he asked.

She hesitated.

"A while." He didn't drop his expectant gaze. She sighed. "I've taken three months off work," she admitted.

"Holy shit," he said, his eyes widening. "What happened?"

"I mean Nonna is dying, Matteo. Jesus, isn't that enough?"

"You wouldn't take three months off work even if *you* were dying," Matty accused her. "Plus you flit in and out of this place as if your head's on fire. You haven't been here longer than a week since the day you left. Three *months?*"

"Listen," she lowered her voice to just above a whisper. "It's nothing to jump up and down about - okay? - but the head of my department told me to take a sabbatical. I'm...I might be a little burned out."

. . .

"Shit kiddo," he leaned forward, his elbows resting on his tanned hairy knees, his big hands clutching his cup. "I'm sorry. What happened?"

"Nothing happened," she said truthfully. There was no big traumatic event to disclose, just a thousand perfectly regular ones. She was a paediatric emergency physician; if you were someone who loved a child, she'd seen your worst nightmares and she'd seen them every day. She'd witnessed countless catastrophes visited upon tiny bodies and after coping with it again and again, one afternoon, she'd suddenly...stopped. "I just hit a wall," she summarised neatly for her brother's sake. "And two weeks into it, Dad called me and told me about Nonna." She gazed down at her own hands, not soil-stained and large like her brother's, but capable all the same. Or so she'd thought. She looked up. "Oh shit Matty, you can't fucking *cry*," she said in dismay.

Her brother burbled out a laugh, his eyes wet, and she immediately burst into tears while laughing in horror at herself. She loved that her brother had always been both absurdly masculine and completely comfortable with his emotions. He had a barrel chest and arms like a bodybuilder and he would cry freely if the moment hit him. Jesus, she'd missed him. He stood up and grabbed her in a hug, both of them weeping and laughing.

"For fuck's sake," came another voice. "It's not even eight o'clock in the morning."

Nico, her other brother stuck his head out the screen door and looked at them both in disbelief. That just made her laugh harder. She pulled out of Matty's hug, picked up her coffee and took a big gulp, wiping her eyes. Nico shook his head like he was disgusted, stepping out into the light.

"She hasn't even been home twenty-four hours and you're already making her cry. Thought you'd grown out of that big brother bullshit."

"Come here and I'll make you cry too, you little pansy," threatened Matty good-naturedly.

"Oh really, homophobic slurs?" Ollie glared at him. "I really am back in Queensland."

"Pansy's not homophobic." Matty looked startled. "It's a bloody flower."

"Oh my god." Nico and Ollie exchanged disbelieving stares. "Mate, it's a gay slur," Nico shook his head. "What planet are you from?"

"Wait, are you serious?"

"Jesus *Christ-*"

"Enough of the language!" their mother's voice called from inside, making them all straighten, three grown adults suddenly widening their eyes and closing their mouths. "Come and have some breakfast before you put your Nonna in an early grave."

"Did she actually just say that?" Nico mouthed, all three of them swallowing appalled giggles as they filed in the door to eat.

———

Nonna refused the wheelchair so between herself and her mother they practically carried her out into the garden. Together they sat down on the wooden bench beneath the massive Moreton fig that overlooked the lush sprawling vegetable patch where her grandmother had once reigned. It wasn't particularly hard to move her; her once solid Nonna was now as light as a sparrow. It seemed quite possible that she'd just get lighter and lighter until she faded away from them altogether.

"Don't look at me like that Viola," her grandmother frowned, as the thought made her blink back tears. "I'm not dead yet. Now, sit here and tell me why you're single again. Hayley was such a lovely girl."

"She was Nonna," Ollie agreed, swallowing down the part of the story where lovely Hayley found someone she thought was lovelier than Ollie and let the timelines overlap *just* enough to make the whole thing seem pretty damn grey. It hadn't felt especially lovely to Ollie in the moment.

"Are you going to try to get her back?" Nonna's big liquid eyes gazed back at her.

. . .

"Oh, no. No thank you," Ollie told her firmly. "A bit of single time will do me for now."

"Well, you're getting a bit long in the tooth for ideas like that," her mother interjected.

"Mum! Oh my god-"

"You're in your mid-thirties. You'll run right out of time to have children with that kind of attitude."

Ollie and her mother exchanged a meaningful glare right over the top of Nonna's head. Her mother was well aware that Ollie didn't want to have kids. Not in her job, not now she'd seen the things she'd seen. Her mother, on the other hand, wasn't having a bar of that nonsense. *Love is risk,* she'd argued vehemently when Ollie had first disclosed the news, years ago now. *Love means fear and loss and pain, that's what makes it love.* Ollie had stared at her mother. *Wow, you're really selling it, mum. Sign me up.* They both knew Ollie was too chicken-shit to argue this one in front of her grandmother. No one was going to die today, be it an elderly woman of dismay or a doctor in her prime receiving a solid whack to the back of her head.

"Are these nice old ladies pestering you?"

. . .

Ollie had never been so damn glad to see her older sister in her life. She jumped to her feet and hugged her as if it were for the first time in months, rather than just since their reunion dinner the night before. Also, she'd be hard to hug for much longer, with the giant baby bump she was sporting.

Pia was an English teacher at Ribbonwood High, a career choice that made Ollie shiver every time she thought about it. Pia loved it, the weirdo, but with this being her third pregnancy she was wrapping up early at just thirty weeks. *I'm big as a house*, she'd groaned to Ollie over dinner. *My classrooms are all running wild because they know full well I can't be bothered to get up from my desk and sort them out.*

Ollie doubted this last part was true. Her sister was warm, caring and made of sharp-honed steel. When she reached the end of her calm nature and her dark eyes flashed, Ollie was sure even the most troublesome of teenagers would sit the hell down and listen. She was only four years younger than Pia and even she knew not to cross her.

Then Ollie's eyes lit up.

"Aunty Ollieeeeeeee," came the cry and two small girls came flying down the lawn towards them. Sienna and Rosa were six and four, and both desperately excited to see her, poor Natasha - Matty's wife - relegated to the boring aunt now their novel Melbourne-based aunty was within reach.

"Niblings!"

· · ·

Within five minutes she was lying in the grass having fairy crowns made for her out of wild clover and dandelions and feeling very much like the next generation of Gabriellis were far more relaxing than the ones who came before them.

She closed her eyes in the sunshine, just for a second. A bloodied image flashed behind her lids, ripping the breath from her lungs before she quickly jerked them open. The girls were still there. Still whole, still healthy, both giggling: safe. She breathed in slowly and smiled at their little glowing faces. She lay back to let herself feel the sunshine, but she didn't close her eyes again.

Chapter Four

Like it or not, her mother seized control of the rental car situation and by day two a brisk return had been arranged and Ollie was without wheels. Well, practically without wheels. She'd eyed the battered old ute she'd been offered and decided it was lucky she was planning on staying put at home.

A full week went by. She took Nonna out into the garden in the early part of the day before the sun got hot. When it rained, she sat at her side and watched her favourite Italian soaps with her. Her grandparents had migrated to Australia in the 1950's and hadn't owned a television for at least a decade after that, but Nonna insisted that *Un posto al sole* - which as far as Ollie could tell was the Italian version of *Neighbours* - was an essential part of maintaining her heritage. Ollie was pretty sure she remembered the same storyline from the last time she'd visited.

. . .

She cooked with her mother, who kept up a running commentary on her knife skills, and weeded the vegetable patch, picking cabbage moth caterpillars off by hand, feeding them directly to the trio of runner ducks that lived in the garden for exactly such purposes. She hung out with her nieces and nephews and took them yabby hunting in the dam. She helped mulch the grape vines and watched Nico man the cellar door on the weekend.

She said a polite *no thanks* to her dad's invitation to come down to the Ribbonwood pub for a cold beer on a hot afternoon and a firm *another time perhaps,* to her mother's suggestion she join her on her trip to town to meet up with her friends from book club. It wasn't just the prospect of getting stuck in long gossip sessions with the older generation - a strong likelihood for both invitations - that made Ollie recoil. It was Ribbonwood itself.

Growing up there had been hard enough. Some kids thrived in a small town; queer kids often didn't. Ollie had fit in relatively seamlessly during her school years - she'd been athletic and acceptably pretty enough after all - but she'd always known there was something about herself she had to hide. Hiding wasn't her strong suit it turned out, and the high school mean girls were smart enough to be dangerous. It was all Ollie could do to pretend their little hints and barbs weren't entirely accurate until she could get the hell out of there.

Leaving Ribbonwood was the best thing she'd ever done in her life. In Melbourne, girls were always stoked to find out she was gay; it took barely a handful of kisses from pretty women in queer nightclubs to vanquish most of her lingering internalised homophobia. Still, there was no part of her that held a fondness for small town life. As far as she was concerned it was all gossip, no privacy, and every single person knew your damn mother.

Eventually though, as the days wore on, the mother in question shooed her out into town with a list of errands. With a sigh she turned the key in the old ute and managed, eventually, to get the engine to turn over. Nico snickered at her as she drove out the gate. The ute was a bit of a family joke. Her siblings had their own slick vehicles and her parents shared a "town car" and a "farm car." The ute was the farm car and as both the baby and the non-local of the family, Ollie was granted exclusive use of it while she was home. She doubted there'd be much competition for it.

The speedometer was broken so her father had wired in a digital one that looked like a shitty alarm clock. She was already convinced it was accurate no more than about forty percent of the time. The muffler had a hole in it so the engine roared like an earthquake every time she shifted up a gear. Oh, that was another thing: it was a manual. Ollie hadn't driven one of those since she was in high school. In the rear-view mirror she saw Nico almost fall over laughing as she bunny-hopped almost immediately out the gate.

By the time she'd gotten to town, she'd hit her stride, her gear changes a little clunky but no stalling. *Look at that, practically a country girl.* She parked outside the tiny hardware store and jumped down from the front seat. Almost instantly she felt sets of eyes on her. She wasn't sure if they were really there, or if it was just the teenage part of her brain convinced everyone was staring at her, a self-conscious tic that perpetually reactivated whenever she found herself in her old hometown.

. . .

In the hardware store she recognised Jenny Mason's dad, though by the way he looked at her with bland politeness she knew the recognition wasn't returned. She imagined she was very different these days. Eighteen years ago she'd been a lanky jock, always in her soccer kit or athletics gear, and an ever-present ponytail. Today, she was a touch more sophisticated - golden-brown instead of sunburned and grass-stained, her long body finally proportionate, her ponytail traded for sleek dark locks.

"Oh my goodness, I'd know that face anywhere," piped a voice to her left. Ollie's shoulders dropped. *So much for that fantasy.* She smiled though, when she saw who the voice belonged to.

"Mrs Lowe," she put down the basket of miscellaneous goods her mother had deemed necessary. "How lovely to see you."

"Honestly Ollie," Mrs Lowe chided gently, "I think you can probably just call me Robyn, now you're grown and I'm retired, don't you?"

"Oh. Sure, Mrs...Robyn," Ollie tried, and winced.

Mrs Lowe smiled at her. It felt hard to see her older, hard in the same way watching her parents get old was hard. She'd been the high school biology teacher who'd encouraged Ollie to focus on something broader than just sport. Other teachers had tried detention and censorious family meetings to try to get Ollie to think about her schoolwork. Mrs Lowe had tried another tack and simply talked to her like she wasn't just some soccer-obsessed moron. She'd encouraged her and inspired her to see the purpose of education beyond passing exams and getting her teachers off her back. She'd activated Ollie's fierce work ethic and competitive streak in a whole new arena in life and Ollie knew full well Mrs Lowe was the only reason she had the career that she did now.

Sometimes, she reflected, as they chatted their way to the register, being known in a small town wasn't entirely horrible. Mrs Lowe already knew about her career and glowed with pride on her behalf. She also knew about Ollie's grandmother and had just the right words to say. By the time they'd parted ways at the front door, Ollie felt a warm glow in her chest. Her years in Ribbonwood hadn't been all bad.

She walked down the road and consulted her list. She crossed over at the corner and stepped into the General Store. Wow, this place had changed. What had once been a musty and dull experience had been transformed by little golden spotlights beaming on chalk black shelves filled with fresh produce, bright jars gleaming like jewels, luxury chocolates and fresh flaky ciabatta. Bon Iver crooned quietly from hidden speakers. The vintage floorboards creaked but glowed with polish. It smelled divine, like beeswax and fresh basil.

She approached the register, a basket full of luxurious nonsense that absolutely wasn't on her list and her stomach dropped right out of her body. Fucking *hell* that was an attractive woman.

The woman behind the counter was distracted, poking at the vintage looking till, her long blonde locks swept up and held back by a rosie-the-riveter style red bandana knotted around her head. The soft nape of her neck was mesmerising and the slope of her delicate shoulders *did* something to Ollie. There were knockout curves that followed from there but it was something about the set of her spine that made Ollie's teeth ache just to look at her: vulnerability and strength in equal measures. The woman was staring down at the register, the profile of her lashes lush and intensely feminine, neat white teeth sinking into a firm pink lower lip.

Her lashes raised and the blue eyes that met Ollie's flickered immediately from frustrated to arctic cold. Ollie's mouth dropped open, momentarily struck speechless.

"Lara." She found her voice. "Lara Bennett."

In an instant Ollie was whipped back in time, walking the corridors of Ribbonwood High in her soccer uniform and scuffed sneakers, her backpack slung over one shoulder. Lara Bennett swept up the corridor towards her, her gold locks bouncing, a scattering of mere mortals in her wake. Their eyes met, and both sets narrowed: the queen bee and the sporty tomboy. Natural enemies. Lara tossed her a look so scathing that Ollie felt the sharpness of the slight without her needing to utter a single word. *Airhead,* Ollie muttered as they passed each other. *Oh stop asking,* Lara bit back, her voice louder for those at the back, craning her neck to flash those blue eyes at her as she walked, *I won't be your girlfriend, god.* Ollie stopped still and widened her eyes. *How are you not pregnant already?* She tossed the words back, not waiting to see them land as they both stalked away in a huff.

. . .

Ollie cringed as the memory flooded her senses. It had been the early 2000's; all they'd had to wield at each other was the rampant misogyny and homophobia in which they all swam. *What times.*

Now though, adult Lara looked at her with a studied blankness.

"I'm sorry," she said coolly. "I can't seem to place you."

Flabbergasted, Ollie pushed her basket onto the counter with a slight jolt and met her gaze.

"Ollie Gabrielli," she said flatly. "We were in school together."

Lara shrugged. There was just enough hostility in the action that Ollie knew for sure that her next words were a lie.

"Doesn't ring a bell. I'm sorry."

"You're literally going to pretend not to know me," Ollie said, a smile of disbelief at the woman's pure brazenness sneaking out despite herself. It was ludicrous. There'd been no more than forty kids in their entire graduating year.

Lara's eyelashes flickered.

. . .

"You're perhaps vaguely familiar," she relented since Ollie was clearly going to press the point.

Ollie found herself laughing out loud.

"Wow, you're something else," she said drily, which was quite honestly the truth. Had Lara Bennett always been so *hot?* The girl in her memory had been beautiful, but in a completely impersonal way, like a pretty painting you'd stop and admire. Never tempting flesh and blood in the kind of way that made Ollie's fingers twitch. Oh *fuck.*

Lara was pretending not to watch her right back as she rang up her items and placed them neatly in a brown paper bag. Ollie however, was paying unwillingly rapt attention so she noticed her slip up and place the last two items in without even scanning them.

"You missed the pink chocolate and the ginger gummies," she said, her tone coming out *exactly* that of a smug seventeen-year-old arse-hole pointing out that the queen bee had a run in her tights.

"Sophisticated taste in snacks you have," Lara said, in a tone that could slice you to death as she fished around in the bag for the items and scanned them. "That's one hundred and eighty-three dollars and thirty-five cents," her soft curved lips pronounced.

"They're for my grandmother," Ollie defended herself. "And these prices are highway robbery," she said through clenched teeth, handing over her credit card.

"I'm sure you can cope, *Dr Gabrielli*," Lara made a show of reading off the card strip. Her lashes flicked up and she studied Ollie's face. "What kind of an ego do you need to have to make sure that even your credit card lets everyone know you're a doctor?"

"It's a professional title," Ollie snapped, snatching the card back after Lara had tapped it. The tips of their fingers brushed and she felt the electricity tingle low in her spine.

"What, did you change it by deed poll too? Do you need it printed on a t-shirt? Maybe a cute little cap?" Lara's eyes gleamed as she leaned on the counter towards her, the action neatly highlighting the shape of her breasts - perhaps deliberately - and Ollie couldn't for the life of her prevent the quick once-over her pupils automatically leapt for. There was an almost smirk on Lara's pretty mouth and Ollie felt it all the way through her body.

"God," she said, grabbing the bag of groceries before she could say or do something regrettable. "It's so comforting how some things just never change."

"Mm," agreed Lara, watching her back away. Her eyes did a deliberate sweep of Ollie, from head to toe and back again. "Some things do though."

. . .

Ollie stumbled back into the outdoor world, her mind spinning as to *what the fuck* that was supposed to mean. Had Lara just *flirted* with her? Was that a come on? There was just enough of a sharpness to her tone though that it didn't quite seem right. Lara was mocking her somehow, perhaps by pointing out that the thing that had changed was Ollie's newfound desire to hungrily ogle her. Her cheeks burned. One thing was for sure, Lara Bennett was still an Olympic level expert in getting under her skin.

Chapter Five

"Hey, watch it kiddo!" Ollie's breath escaped her in a huff as her nephew barrelled directly into her abdomen as she balanced an over-sized bowl of salad on her way out the door. He squealed as his older sister chased after him, escaping out into the evening air, his dad bellowing after them to slow down.

Family dinner was shaping up to be as epic and chaotic as always. Ollie had imagined that after the buzz of her returning home had faded, everything would quiet down. After all, her siblings had their own homes to run and their own dining tables to gather around, even Nico who as a single bloke shared a house with two of his old mates from school. And yet, every other night it seemed, her parents hosted *everyone*. Her brothers and sister, her brother and sister-in-law, as well as their accumulated five children (six, if you counted the one kicking Pia in the ribs) would all join in to gather around the huge wooden table on the west side of the deck and eat a feast while the sun went down.

. . .

There was still a very specific gender split in her family that made her wild. Her mother in the kitchen, her father outdoors. It was a split her siblings had replicated, the women arriving with food - more food - and the men all relaxing back with beers and conversation as the food was placed before them, then their plates cleared after they were done. Ollie wasn't sure if it was because she was gay, the youngest, or because she just wasn't a small-town girl anymore but she was the only one it seemed to really bother.

She didn't shirk her own responsibilities to help out because she was also the only one on holiday, but it irked her to see her brothers happily accepting being served while the women rushed around attending to everyone's needs. She was pretty sure that if Nonna still had her legs under her she'd be up fussing too.

"You need to sit down," Ollie finally snapped, watching Pia juggle a complaining child around her knees while she placed a loaded serving bowl on the table. "I'll take her," she gestured to Rosa. "Or better yet, her father could help out." She glared at her brother-in-law. James instantly leapt into action, quickly the doting dad and the helpful husband but it made her nuts knowing he had to be asked. "Mama, sit *down*," she said in exasperation as her sixty-eight-year-old mother bustled back and forth. "Nico, go and get the bloody salad spoons."

Her brother gave her an exaggerated salute as he got to his feet and her family all exchanged obvious glances. Ollie rolled her eyes.

"So," said Matty, his tone over-the-top casual. "How was your day, Viola?"

. . .

Ollie glared at him.

"It was lovely, thank you, Matteo. And yours?"

"Wonderful, thank you for caring. I worked my arse off in the hot sun. What did you do with your day?"

"Chores," she bit back, "and errands." She blinked and blurted out, "I saw Lara Bennett at the general store."

"Ah," piped up Nico as he returned to his seat. "That explains your mood."

"What does *that* mean?"

"You always hated her, right?"

"Plus, she's a real piece of work," added Matty's wife Natasha, picking up her wine glass and sipping to emphasise. "Enough to ruin anyone's day."

"That store," her mother huffed, a clear signal she was on her way up to a soap box. "Eight dollars for a bottle of passata? It's almost like she doesn't want any locals buying from her at all! You know I was there last week," she lowered her voice conspiratorially, "and I overheard her telling Kimberley Evans that her husband running off to Sydney on her was her own damn fault. What a thing to say! She and Lara used to be friends, but I'll tell you what: there's a lot of women in this town who say you can't trust your husband around her."

"That's true enough," Nico's grin spread, his eyes going bright. "Remember that bar fight over her? There was a full on brawl down at the Ribbonwood pub after that bloke from the school tried to hook up with her."

"He was the high school principal," Natasha explained to Ollie, "and married with kids."

"I mean," Ollie scrunched up her face, "he sounds like a real charmer."

"He got arrested after that brawl. Lost his job as well as his wife," her father chimed in solemnly, his eyebrows lowered.

"Let that be a lesson to him." Her mother gave him a threatening look as if her adoring husband of forty-five years were about to leap up from the table to join a bar fight over a woman half his age. He scoffed at her and her eyes softened. "That's not the only marriage Lara's wrecked either." Her mother wasn't doing a great job of hiding her glee as she geared up to breathlessly detail yet another scandal.

. . .

Just like that, the table erupted into Lara Bennett stories. As the blazing pink sunset settled around the hills, the delicious meal shrank and the tales flew. Lara Bennett had ruined the general store, she'd seduced married men, she'd bite your head off as soon as talk to you, she'd ruined Robyn Lowe's life, insulted Myrtle Jenkin's elderly husband, plus she'd basically killed a man.

"Wait, *what?*" Ollie interrupted. "What did she do to Mrs Lowe?"

"There's a lot of gossip in this town," her mother said primly as if she wasn't one of Ribbonwood's most active participants, "but that one was the worst of it."

"What happened?"

"Poor Robyn," her mother shook her head woefully. "It was years ago now. Lara took against her - no idea why - but she told everyone who'd listen that Robyn was carrying on out of town having an affair with a younger man. Her husband was humiliated," she sighed. "He up and left her, just straight up abandoning her and her two children, just like that. And then," she paused for dramatic effect, "it wasn't even *true*. She'd been in Silverbloom Hospital the entire time, the poor woman. Sick in hospital and completely unable to defend herself."

"Wow." Ollie shook her head. Lara really was a piece of work. God, but what a devastatingly attractive one all the same... *No, shit, Ollie, think of Mrs Lowe's sweet face.* Mrs Lowe had looked so much older than her years, deep creases on her face that Ollie didn't remember from back when the kind teacher had taken the time to change Ollie's life. Was it simply the natural progression of ageing or was it something else? What would possess anyone - even Lara - to do something like that? As she licked the last of the sauce off her fork, she realised her accusation back in the general store had been correct: some things never did change. Once a mean girl, always a mean girl

A child's shriek broke her from her thoughts and her head jerked up. She turned sharply toward the corner of the deck where the kids had all scampered off to play. Her spine stayed stiff while Pia heaved herself to her feet to go and investigate. Ollie made herself stay in the chair until she heard her sister's calm voice soothing over a squabble.

"Not so fussed on the *killing a man* part of the story?" Matty asked, his eyebrows raised. "That tracks."

Ollie snorted.

"I mean that one definitely sounds like an exaggeration," she scoffed.

"No, she basically did," Nico piped up. "Josh Rees was a stand-up guy. She might not have actually murdered him but it was a death from a thousand cuts kind of situation for sure."

Ollie rolled her eyes. She knew enough of how her brothers saw relationship dynamics to recognise a specific viewpoint when she heard one. Plus she'd heard about that back when it had happened. Josh Rees chose to get behind the wheel while drunk. It was a terrible tragedy but it was on him and him only and the only blessing was that he hadn't taken anyone else with him.

"It just goes to show you," Matty said, his tone grave, "that she was like that from the start. You were a good girl in high school, Ollie; you recognised her for what she was. A real-life femme fatale. Seducing a grown man, that's not a normal thing to do, is it?"

"Oh for fuck's sake!" Pia returned to the table. "Sorry, Nonna-" she hastily apologised. "But that's a load of bull. Lara Bennett might be a lot of things, but back then she was a *child*. And that man took advantage of her."

Silence rang out. Ollie felt her fist grip tight around the stem of her wine glass, the sound of a fork clinking against a plate absurdly loud in the night air.

"She was hardly a child-" Nico started.

"Oh yes she bloody well was," Pia snapped. "Sure, she was technically the age of consent - barely - but I work with seventeen-year-olds every day and I'm telling you, they are clear as mud, *children*. What kind of adult man would go after a high school girl?"

Ollie's stomach clenched. She too worked with adolescents and her sister was right. She remembered the rumours, the snide insinuations, the names Lara got called. Some of them from her. All the nasty words, the blatant stares, all directed at a seventeen-year-old girl, not the adult man who-

"He groomed her," Ollie said slowly.

"Of course he did," Pia bit out. "These days that's what we'd call it. Back then, she was just a precocious *slut*."

"Pia!" her mother protested. "That's enough-"

Pia's eyes flashed.

"No," she said. "What if that was Aria?" she asked Matty, watching him flinch as she referred to his ten-year-old daughter. "Would you say an adult man who tried to sleep with her in just seven years' time was a *stand-up guy?*"

The table fell silent. Both Matty and Nico looked violently unsettled. Matty glared out towards where the children were playing and Nico took a solid swig of his beer.

"Yeah, that's what I thought," Pia's voice was sharp. "She no more 'seduced' him, than I bloody did. He was a straight up predator. She also didn't kill him, but if she had, I'd have backed her."

. . .

"Keep that one in mind, Jimmy," Nico tried to joke to his brother-in-law to lighten the mood, but no one laughed. The word *predator* and everything it entailed seemed to ring in the quiet night.

"Why didn't we see that?" Ollie's tone was low. "We all blamed her. We treated her like a pariah-" her voice faded out. In her mind she saw the set of Lara's spine in the store earlier that day. Defensive.

"And she still is, isn't she?" Pia raised her eyebrows.

"I mean-" Natasha started, then stopped. She picked up her wineglass and put it down again. "She's still pretty nasty," she said quietly.

"Some women need armour," came a voice that made every single head turn. Her Nonna, tiny in her chair. She looked pale and immensely tired. "If you make a girl an outcast, what else is she going to do?"

———

That night Ollie lay awake, sheets kicked off, listening to the geckos barking from the window eaves. She couldn't get those sharp blue eyes out of her mind, replaying over and over the moment that Lara Bennett had seen Ollie and her gaze had frozen. If back in high school Ollie had looked at a teenage girl in trouble and only seen a *slut*, what had Lara seen when she looked back?

. . .

God, this was why Ollie hated coming back to Ribbonwood. It wasn't flattering, understanding herself so fully. She felt queasy, seeing herself through Lara's eyes. She'd been so young back then, floating thoughtlessly along on the same cultural currents that had made her hate herself as well as Lara. Ollie knew better now and she damn well did better, on that she was sure. But if they'd all been wrong about Lara back then, were they wrong about her now? The world might be changing, but had this tiny town changed one bit?

She thought of her brothers, so easily accepting women's service without ever seeming to notice, of the way they had to be instructed to put their own young niece and daughter into Lara's shoes before they were able to empathise. She thought of her mother, happily engaging in salacious gossip about another woman while simultaneously denouncing that same woman for gossiping back. God knows they all had a point of view. After everything she'd heard that evening, Ollie wondered if she'd learned anything at all. Because who *was* Lara Bennett really?

She stared up at the ceiling and tried to tell herself that it wasn't just the hot stab of desire that made her want to find out.

Chapter Six

Goddamnit, Lara was early. Normally she tried to time it better but today she'd been fired up, turning what should have been a slow saunter in the afternoon heat into a quick determined stride. She'd been too distracted by her own thoughts to realise her pace, until she'd looked up and found to her chagrin that she'd made it to the school gate with ten minutes to spare.

Ribbonwood Primary School was a mere freckle on the map, a tiny country school with two whole handfuls of children to keep the doors open. There was absolutely no reason to act as though it were a gauntlet.

Lara looked at the collection of other mothers already clumped together at the gate and held in her sigh. She straightened her spine and tossed back her hair as she arrived alongside them.

. . .

"Afternoon ladies," she injected just enough steel into her tone to remind herself exactly how few fucks she gave that the next ten minutes of her life were about to make her feel like they were the ones trapped in the playground again.

As per absolutely usual, Lara was greeted with a full round of silence. A couple of the women exchanged sideways glances like the audacity of *Lara Bennett* greeting them was beyond their belief. Addie Armstrong gave her a solid glare to which she returned a broad glowing smile. Lara kept walking and took up her usual position, leaning back against the opposite gate post from the rest of the group and neatly crossed her bare legs at the ankle. There was a subtle rearrangement of bodies, closing her out.

"Hi Lara," one soft voice ventured back. Lara blinked. Natasha Gabrielli didn't normally deign to speak with her. She was tall and willowy, a perfectly put together wisp of a woman, married to the eldest Gabrielli brother. She'd been no fan of Lara's at any point over the past half-decade that they'd had their daughters in the same class. Lara gave her a short nod, unclear as to what the fuck had brought that on, then turned her attention to her phone.

She texted Sadie. Mum life was far easier when her best friend was at her side.

> Where are you? Gang's all here

She added a photo of a flock of screaming seagulls. Her phone rang immediately.

"I'm running late," Sadie said as soon as she picked up. Lara felt several sets of eyes close in on her as she held her phone up to her ear. She hesitated.

"Okay baby," she made her tone go sultry. "I'll be waiting for you."

There was a pause, then Sadie spluttered out a laugh at the other end.

"Can you stop fucking with the fine mothers of the PTA long enough to pick my daughter up too?"

"Oh, stop being so *bad*." Lara tucked her hair behind her ear. "Your wife might overhear us," she stage-whispered. She heard a gasp of outrage from across the gate as she wrapped a long strand of blonde around her finger, her teeth sinking into her lower lip.

"You're such a shit." Sadie groaned. "Listen, can you please just take Frankie back to the store with you? I'll be there in twenty minutes. Play nice with the grownups for like, a minute, for fuck's sake."

"Mm, I can't wait," Lara breathed and Sadie snorted and hung up on her.

. . .

Lara looked up at the other mothers, not a one pretending they hadn't been leaning in and trying to listen to Lara Bennett's sexy phone call. She delivered them all a solid wink and the smile that fell out of her was genuine. God, this whole thing was so ridiculous.

Addie was just opening her mouth to snap something when everyone's attention turned to the arrival of a newcomer. Lara swallowed excess saliva all of a sudden. This one was adamantly not a Ribbonwood school mum.

"Well, hey everyone," the cause of Lara's annoyed distraction on her walk to the school that afternoon announced her presence. Ollie was slightly breathless, her olive skin glowing in the sunlight and her dark hair tumbling down her back. For fuck's sake; *more* Ollie Gabrielli was absolutely the last thing Lara's week needed. "Long time no see." Ollie's tone was cheerful and friendly. As the mum squad all turned to coo and greet her, Ollie clocked Lara. Her easygoing gaze sharpened slightly, fixing on Lara's face like she was taking in every single element. "Hey Lara," she added, her warm brown eyes holding fast to her own.

Lara cocked her head slightly in short acknowledgement and to absolutely everyone's surprise, Ollie separated from the group and came to stand beside her.

"How old's your kid now?" Ollie asked conversationally, like they were friends. Lara just stared at her, expression flat. Why was this happening exactly? She and Ollie Gabrielli were not now and never had been *friends*. "You've got a daughter, right?" Ollie pressed on. For a second Lara fought competing urges. Did she freeze out her biggest high school enemy or simply enjoy the befuddlement of the pack of wolves at the other gate?

"Actually, I've got eleven children now," Lara decided to pick both. "They've all got different fathers. At least, most of them anyway. Right, Addie?" she smiled sweetly. Addie flushed red at the insinuation. She had a habit of clutching her husband possessively whenever they crossed paths with Lara, which...had Addie even seen her husband? Lara was *not* interested - had tried to tell Addie that - but the belief had been enough to make Addie bristle and freeze her out for years.

"Wow, you've been busy," Ollie's voice was awed. Lara saw a little spark in her eyes as she leaned into the story, her elbow resting atop the stone gate post Lara leaned on. "Kept your figure though," she raised her eyebrows, her voice studiously casual. Lara gave her a sharp look. Ollie's gaze might have passed as innocent to the other school mums but Lara knew better. It had been barely twenty-four hours since the golden girl of Ribbonwood High had last run her eyes over Lara's body.

She had to admit to herself that it had been satisfying, seeing hunger flare in the eyes of her old nemesis. How extraordinarily *delicious* to be the one to get under her skin after all this time. It was a lot to balance though. Lara had felt it like a punch to the stomach yesterday afternoon when she'd looked up to see Ollie Gabrielli, of all people, less than two feet away in the middle of her store, stock still and staring at her. Ollie had appeared nothing less than gobsmacked, as if it were her and not Lara who'd been quietly minding her own business only to get slapped in the face by the past.

Ollie had been both instantly unmistakable and wholly changed at the same time. She'd stood there, all long tanned legs and long toned arms, still holding her easy athleticism into her thirties, only now she looked *expensive*. Gone were the ponytails and sports kit, instead her glowing skin was offset by a tiny pair of linen shorts and a short-sleeved white button-up that looked both soft and casual as it fell from her body. Lara estimated the ensemble at approximately the price of a full fortnight's pay for most folk in Ribbonwood. With her gleaming dark hair effortlessly tangling around her shoulders she'd looked like she'd wandered in from an Instagram marketing campaign for luxury leather boots, all fake country and natural beauty. God, how infuriating.

She looked equally good now in the afternoon sunlight, practically exotic amongst the drearily familiar Ribbonwood faces and Lara was relieved when the bell sounded and children began streaming from the two classrooms.

Tilly and Frankie took their sweet time, her daughter too grown now to run and fling herself into her arms, the way one of the small, dark-haired Gabrielli girls did to Ollie. The little girl giggled and glowed as Ollie hugged her. Another squeal of excitement rang out, this one adult, as Audrey Coleman arrived at the school gate and also flung herself into Ollie's arms. Lara tried not to wince. Aside from Sadie, Audrey was one of her few school-gate allies and something of a friend. It grated to see her so warm and familiar with Ollie, tactile in a way she'd never be with Lara.

. . .

Of course, she belatedly remembered, Audrey and Ollie had been best friends back in high school, both of them sporty and academic. For a moment Lara felt dizzy. This moment, right here, could be transplanted back in time by something like *eighteen years* and be completely unchanged: Audrey and Ollie giggling together; a gang of girls off to the side gossiping and freezing her out; and Lara, standing on her own. It quite literally took her breath away.

For a sharp, sobering moment, Lara quite despaired. Her high school self had held on by imagining this was all one terrible blip in what would soon be a whole new life. To think that she could experience everything she had in almost two decades and somehow *nothing* would change?

"Hey mum!"

Lara blinked to clear her vision and her daughter grinned up at her. The neat braid Lara had given her that morning was in disarray, there were stains on her previously clean school uniform and she was dwarfed by the giant backpack she was wearing, like an absolute nerd. Lara had never seen anyone so perfect.

"Hey kid," she remembered how to smile as she cupped her daughter's face. Frankie bounced up behind her and whooped when Lara gave her the news she was coming with them and Lara's *real* life - the one that existed completely outside of what Ribbonwood's eyes saw - kicked back into gear. She remembered, as she walked out the gate, that when it truly came down to it, she didn't give a fuck. Not a single one.

. . .

"You off?"

Lara's head snapped up. Ollie Gabrielli had paused her chat with Audrey to catch Lara's eye.

"Yes?" Lara apparently had to answer the fucking obvious as she tried to leave. Audrey smiled and gave her a goofy little finger wave, still bright with the joy of reuniting with Ollie. A small flash of anger hit Lara's bloodstream. If Ollie Gabrielli hadn't materialised back in Ribbonwood then Lara wouldn't be having full-on flashbacks to high school right now. She made her mouth smile back at Audrey and started following her daughter into the street.

"Lara," Ollie spoke again and god help her, Lara stopped. She raised her eyebrows questioningly, waiting to hear what Ollie had to say. Ollie looked back at her, her eyes curious, like she was working out a puzzle. Then she grinned, her mouth almost a smirk at her satisfaction with making Lara wait. "See you round," she said warmly.

Lara shook her head. Nope. They weren't doing this. She looked Ollie dead in the face and rolled her eyes. Head held high, she walked away.

Chapter Seven

Joe Armstrong was pumped. He looked at his reflection in the full-length mirror hanging on the inside of his wardrobe door. Black shiny leather boots. Pants with a sharp crease up the front. The belt, heavy and satisfying, weighed down with the tools of the trade. The lapels on his sky-blue cotton shoulders. The *hat*. He grinned at himself. Then he quickly furrowed his brow, practicing his serious face, the one he'd use when he got to say words like *you're under arrest*.

"Bye mum," he called as he ducked out the front door, moving fast to avoid the breakfast she'd been trying to push down his throat and the kiss goodbye he knew she would aim for. He was twenty-three years old and as of today he was a goddamned *police officer*. She was bloody embarrassing, that's what she was.

He got into his car. It felt weird driving the old Honda in his uniform. He was looking forward to getting around in a real squad car again, this time as a fully qualified officer. It was a great feeling: watching the heads snap up from the footpath at his presence, the other cars around him slowing down, people everywhere suddenly on their best behaviour knowing he had his eyes on them. The beat-up maroon model he was in right now didn't quite seem dignified somehow.

He checked his watch. He was due at the Silverbloom Police Station at nine a.m and he'd planned to drive straight there. He'd arrive early, but that was the right thing to do on a first day, showing he was good and keen. But now, with his stomach was churning with hunger and nerves, he wished he'd eaten what his mum had made him. After all, he was a country copper; who knows where he'd find himself by lunchtime? Catching sight of the Ribbonwood General Store he pulled in and parked.

As he approached the entrance, he groaned inwardly. The sign on the door said *closed*. He stared at it in dismay, but just as he turned to leave in defeat he saw movement within and the sign get flipped to *open*. With a grin of relief - today really was his day - he pushed the door.

"*Jesus christ,*" came a sharp voice from mere inches away and Joe nearly had a heart attack. A woman was staring at him, wide-eyed, her hand resting on her...spectacular upper chest. *Oh fuck,* Joe stared back. He'd heard talk of Lara Bennett, had even glimpsed her a few times before, his mates in high school slapping each other on the back and nodding towards the older woman as she passed them by at the Ribbonwood Fair. This was the first time he'd seen her up this close and he swallowed hard. She was legendary for a reason, he realised with a flash of dizziness. She was *stupidly* hot.

. . .

"Uh, hi! I mean, good morning." Joe quickly deepened his voice. He was a *police officer*; a man in uniform. Women liked that. He'd done okay before, but *now*... well, Joe's whole life was about to change. He gave Lara a suave grin. She stood quite still and watched him. Joe let his chest puff out. "I didn't meant to give you a fright," he said generously. She was so petite and pretty and Joe was a *cop*. He wanted to impress her but he didn't want to intimidate her with his presence.

"Late for a doughnut were you?" Lara raised her smooth eyebrows, recovering her equilibrium surprisingly fast. Joe frowned. She gave him a guileless smile and for a second he was lost in the sky blue of her eyes. He decided not to take offence. He also decided not to buy the chocolate milk he'd been planning on.

"Uh no," he stood his ground, taking her all in. "Just a quick breakfast before a busy day."

"Mmhm," she said. "Take your time then." He watched Lara walk away down the aisle, the sway of her hips just...*obvious*. Blood rushed to his crotch and he diverted his gaze quickly before his pants could tighten. Overeager teenage boy wasn't the look he was going for, after all. He cleared his throat and made his selection carefully. A banana. A fancy protein bar. An iced coffee: much more manly and grownup than the chocolate milk he actually wanted. He sauntered up to the counter, the creak of his new leather boots satisfying as he crossed the wooden floor boards.

Lara was behind the counter now. She looked up at his approach. He couldn't quite read the look in her eyes, but he was pretty sure she was impressed as he laid his selection next to the register.

70

. . .

"Find everything you needed?" she asked him, her eyelashes rising, and *fuck* was she hitting on him? There was just something about her; everything she said sounded so sexy. She was older than him for sure, but he could look past that on this one occasion. He'd heard it said that older women were *wild* when you got them into bed. Grateful, right? Joe wasn't exactly that experienced but he knew he could show Lara a good time. A fit young stud like him? A police officer? Fuck, he loved that this was his job.

"Almost," he said back, his gaze teasing.

"Oh?" She had to look up to meet his eyes and he liked it.

"Just need your phone number and I'm good." He raised his eyebrows challengingly, proud of himself for the smoothness of his approach. He sounded confident as hell and he liked it.

Lara cocked her head, a lock of her silky hair falling over her shoulder.

"Oh honey," she said softly, "I'd break you. Stick to girls your own age." There was a sass to her words. She was playing hard to get, clearly. *Break him?* He wasn't entirely sure what that would entail, but he very much wanted to find out.

. . .

"I can handle myself," he insisted, deepening his voice further. She laughed. He looked at her slightly closer. Suddenly he understood that it wasn't a flirty laugh; it was like she was she laughing *at* him. He flushed. "Give me your number." The words came out abrupt, almost angry. It covered his embarrassment at least.

The last remnant of Lara's sparkle vanished.

"Is that supposed to be an order, *officer?*" Her voice was calm but he felt the accusing note.

"Hey, wait a minute-"

"No, you wait." Her voice had gotten even softer and for some reason all the more intimidating because of it. "How long have you been a cop? Five minutes?" His face went redder, all but confirming the accusation. She watched his expression almost sympathetically. "A little advice? Just because you're wearing the uniform doesn't mean you need to be a bully as well."

As well? Wow. He could see what she thought of police officers, loud and clear. Offence swirled tightly in his gut, despite the gentleness of her tone. Where did she get off being so condescending? He was here to protect and serve, goddamnit! She might find herself needing to call ooo one day and you know she'd expect help just like the next person, even as she stood right there, mocking the police to his face. He wasn't going to stand for this. Start out the way you intend to progress, right?

.   .   .

"Listen here," he started, "that's-"

"Honey," she interrupted him. "We're done here. Off you trot." She gave a little flick of her fingers in dismissal and he heard a titter behind him. He jerked his head and saw Millie Robinson, his brother's ex-girlfriend standing there with a bottle of milk in her hand, her eyes amused. He felt his blush turn to dark red.

"That's enough," he snapped, at Lara, at Millie, at every woman who'd ever laughed at him. He shrivelled, anger welling up inside him.

"Or you'll arrest me?" Lara raised her eyebrows. "Well that's just adorable." She shot an exasperated look over his shoulder at Millie and unable to take it any more he turned and stormed out of the store. He gunned the car down the main street, hurtling towards the back road, towards Silverbloom, toward his destiny. He was going to get some power in this fucking town and Lara Bennett would regret the day she laughed at him.

Goddamnit he'd forgotten his chocolate milk. Iced coffee. *Fuck!*

Chapter Eight

The next afternoon Lara timed it better. She'd been forewarned that Sadie had a meeting and she knew that on Wednesdays Audrey worked in Brisbane, so her nanny was on pick-up duty. She made it to the gate at bang on 2:59pm, one minute before the bell rang.

"Hey mum!" Tilly arrived, her face bright and distracted. She was struggling out of the straps of her school bag, dumping it at her feet. "I just gotta-" her daughter ran over to the playground after Frankie and a couple of girls from her class.

Lara sighed. She followed over towards the playground.

"Tilly," she called, "come on, we've got to go."

. . .

"Five minutes, mum!" Tilly's eyes were beseeching as the small knot of kids gathered around some creepy high-tech talking toy Lara would never let into her own house.

"Nope," came a low voice just over Lara's left shoulder. She looked up to see Ollie approaching again, her eyes on the kids. "That's a nope from me. I'm pretty sure that thing reports directly to our overlords."

Lara almost laughed. She swallowed it quickly and flat out refused Ollie the win. She realised now that the child holding the toy was Aria Gabrielli, a pair of equally dark-haired children jumping up at her heels.

"You're on pick-up duty for the whole family now?" she asked. She didn't remotely care about the ins and outs of the Gabrielli family schedule but she wanted advance warning so that she didn't keep finding herself so *surprised* by Ollie, everywhere, all the time.

"Seems like it," Ollie told her, her eyes on her nieces and nephew. "Just this week," she clarified. "Pia's about to go on maternity leave and I figured I'd help her out with the school run until then. And if I'm here for one, I might as well be here for all." She shrugged. "Natasha can lay back and have a wine, or whatever it is mums with toddlers at home do with their spare time."

Lara stole a glance at her and caught the wry smile on her face. She found herself distracted by Ollie's ridiculous glossy locks. How the fuck did Ollie comb all of that? It was almost curls but kind of waves, perfectly tousled as if Ollie had sauntered to the school gate directly from the beach. Lara's palms itched and she looked away, right as Ollie turned to look at her.

"No kids, huh?" Lara said, purely to cover her stare. She could feel Ollie's eyes on her and she refused to meet them. God, why was she making conversation with Ollie Gabrielli exactly?

"Good lord no," Ollie told her. "I definitely don't have the constitution for that."

Lara huffed. She didn't care if another woman wanted kids or not, but it always irked her to hear motherhood spoken of as if the women who did have them were somehow mystically stronger, instead of just plain tired and doing their damn best, no more talent and skills than the next person.

A small Gabrielli boy burst into tears and flung himself at Ollie's legs. Ollie ducked down to hug him, her voice low and soothing and barely a minute later he was chuckling and running off to fling himself back into the fray. Ugh. Aunty stakes were always so much lower, she told herself, vastly annoyed by the wild display of competence.

"She's cute," Ollie said, after she straightened up. She was looking over at Tilly who was giggling wildly and whirling in a circle, arms akimbo. "Like a mini-you."

. . .

The thing was, Tilly *was* a mini-Lara: same colouring, same eyes. It was joyful and terrifying all at once. It wasn't remotely the first time people had commented on the resemblance but it was the first time it had made Lara's cheeks heat. She was furious at herself *and* at Ollie. Ollie was making perfectly appropriate playground conversation - again, as if they were *friends* - and yet just like the day before, Lara felt sure she could read deeper intention behind her easy words. If Ollie wanted Lara to know she thought she was *cute* - not an adjective most people used about her by the way - it really meant nothing to Lara whatsoever.

"Tilly, Frankie, it's time to go!" She studiously ignored the woman beside her and both girls looked up and groaned. Lara's tone broached no argument however and they dragged their feet to go and grab their bags. Lara turned to follow, at the exact moment Ollie stepped forward toward the playground. Lara stopped abruptly with a sharp intake of breath, their bodies barely an inch apart, Ollie's hands flaring at her sides like she was ready to grab Lara's hips to stop her stumble.

"Sorry," Ollie apologised as Lara quickly stepped back. They looked at each other for a beat of confusion, Lara flustered, Ollie surprised. Lara opened her mouth and closed it again. They hadn't even bumped into each other, Lara zealously guarding her personal space, but she felt the collision like it had happened. "You good?" Ollie asked her, her expression curious at the heat Lara could feel rushing up her neck. Ollie's lips were slightly parted and their bodies still way too close. Lara quickly unfroze. She whirled on her heels and walked away, extremely aware of the eyes on her back as she did. *Jesus Christ.*

. . .

The next day, Lara was fully prepared. Ollie found her attractive, that was manifestly evident. Lara *was* attractive; it was her most blatantly obvious feature. Who didn't like long blonde hair and a cup-size that made men stupid? Ollie was gay, Ollie was into it, Ollie would be as easy to ignore as the rest of them, once Lara got over her surprise at the flash of heat between them. Because that's all it was: Ollie's interest, Lara's surprise, the sudden proximity and the old tension between them, all combining into one strong zap of electricity.

It was fantastic, actually, Lara decided, after she'd thought about it for perhaps slightly too long. What better revenge after all this time than Ollie Gabrielli wanting something and Lara getting to be the one to deny it to her? Lara stalked into the schoolyard the next day, chin high, eyes for no one but her best friend, she and Sadie laughing together because this was *not* Ribbonwood High. Lara had an ally, a daughter, a business, a whole world of her own and Ollie had *no* impact on her now. She was wholly insignificant in the scheme of Lara's life and Lara wouldn't reward her with a single scrap of further attention.

Lara knew she looked good; knew because she'd checked her reflection in the store's bathroom mirror before she'd left; knew because she'd dressed this morning knowing she was going to be looked at. It might not be ethical exactly, but as Lara reflected on the last two years of high school she felt entirely justified. She remembered another stab of feeling she'd discovered back then: the power that came with being wanted but out of reach. *Slut,* she remembered. *Cocksucker, stuck-up bitch.* Boys had wanted her despite all that, maybe because of all that, who even knew? But girls were the ones who'd truly hurt her.

. . .

78

Ollie...well, Ollie hadn't really been the worst of them, objectively Lara knew that. She wasn't even sure that Ollie had used any of those words, at least not to her face. She didn't have to. No, Ollie had tortured her simply by holding herself up as Lara's polar opposite and making her deep disdain crystal clear.

If there were high school archetypes then she and Ollie had each represented one. The blonde, sexy, bad girl and the sporty, brunette high-achiever. The nasty slut versus the good girl who stayed away from boys. Lara had only found one chink in Ollie's perfection, the one thing that might turn the approving teachers and swathes of friends against the girl who had everything. She'd watched Ollie wrapped up in her female friends as if oblivious to the existence of boys - both privileges Lara sorely lacked - and put two and two together. It wasn't her fault Lara had turned out to be right.

Still, Lara was not remotely above using any of this in her favour now. The unseasonable hot weather was the perfect excuse for the miles of bare skin she'd left on show, her hair loose and flowing, her move-ments sensuous and languid. Sadie tossed her an odd look. It wasn't out of character for Lara to put this exact armour on against the school mums but she knew her energy today was different; she could feel it herself. She kept up the pretence of total carelessness, all the way into the schoolyard and out again, but just as they disappeared out the gate, she cracked. She couldn't help but look to see how this version of herself was landing.

Ollie was leaning on the school gate post, surrounded - as always - in women. Her eyes were sure as hell locked tight on Lara though. Lara had meant to brush her gaze over Ollie as though she was mere scenery, inconsequential to Lara and absolutely not the focal point to all of this. But at the look in Ollie's dark eyes, her breath hitched. Ollie didn't look wrung out with desire or lessened by the weakness of wanting what she couldn't have. Oh no. Ollie looked *knowing*. Her eyes reflected a clear hit of lust, that much was true, but she also looked solidly amused.

Lara flicked her hair over her shoulder and jerked her eyes back to her daughter, calling to her not to run, instantly a harried mother, no time for games with Ollie Gabrielli, but inside she was fuming. Why had she *looked?* Why did Ollie always get to fucking win?

———

The following afternoon just as she was getting ready to cash up the register and close for the day to go and retrieve her daughter, Lara heard the store's front door bell jingle. That was a good thing, she reminded herself. One more sale for the day, another handful of dollars to keep the whole show on the road.

She heard purposeful footsteps down the aisle and looked up to see none other than Ollie Gabrielli, dark eyes fixed on her, a packet of ginger gummies snatched in her fist. Lara almost laughed at the sudden win. Ollie didn't drop her gaze the whole way to the register.

"That's quite the sweet tooth you've got." Lara raised her eyebrows, the remains of her annoyance helping keep her expression thoroughly unimpressed.

"You've got no idea," Ollie said softly, her voice low.

80

. . .

Lara narrowed her eyes. There was no way she'd let such an obvious line hit her anywhere that mattered. She let Ollie set the bag down on the counter and rang up her purchase as perfectly calmly as if she were any other wealthy, interstate tourist customer briefly crossing her path.

"Sightseeing?" she asked blandly. Lara managed not to let the victorious smile slip out as Ollie flushed very slightly pink. Score one for Lara, *finally*. She might be a single mother and a shopkeeper but at least part of her had been right: the overly blessed town princess really couldn't seem to take her eyes off her.

"Lara-" Ollie didn't budge from the counter, even though her purchase had been made. "I wanted to..." Her words petered out as she seemed to struggle with herself. She changed tack, her chin raising, eyes on Lara's. "High school was a long time ago. It was a different time."

"Not around here it's not," Lara stated the blindingly fucking obvious, her tone cool.

Ollie nodded. She chewed on her lip and watched her.

"We should go for a drink."

. . .

Lara couldn't help her smile then. Ollie was so *serious* with her big brown Bambi eyes, her jaw set with determination. Lara leaned towards her, watched Ollie's lips part, just a breath. She bit her own lower lip, heard that breath catch.

"Olivia-"

"It's Viola, but you know that."

"Ollie," she raised her lashes. "There is not a single chance in hell."

Chapter Nine

"Hey," said Sadie, pausing to wipe her sweaty brow as she banged in the corner post. "Did you see Ollie Gabrielli at the school today? I didn't know she was back in town."

Lara sighed, her own hammer dangling from her hand. She was sweaty too as the sun beat down mercilessly. They'd waited to start this bit of the job thinking the heat would dissipate but it really didn't feel like it now.

Eva looked up from where she was struggling to unpick the end of a roll of wire. It had been Sadie's idea to set her up with a chicken coop to help keep her food bills low and to kickstart a real vegetable patch, but honestly right now Lara would rather just give the woman a lifetime of overpriced eggs and silverbeet from the store and be done with it.

. . .

"Huh. I wonder what she's like these days." Eva tucked a lock of sandy hair behind her ear. "She was always so smart and funny."

Lara scoffed. Both women looked her way.

"First of all, she's not *back*, she's just passing through like the tourist she is," she said shortly. "And she's exactly the damn same, only worse. Still thinks she's better than everyone else, whole life on a silver platter."

Eva and Sadie exchanged a glance.

"That's right," Sadie remembered, "you two always hated each other."

"I didn't hate her," Lara defended herself. "I barely thought about her."

"Mmhm," Sadie agreed. "Clearly."

Lara ignored her, picking up her hammer again and thudding it against the post.

"You've spoken to her," Eva observed, "since she's back."

. . .

Lara nodded. She found she didn't want to elaborate. Each interaction had felt slightly more complicated than the last and Lara felt no urge to process any of them, thank you very much. The sooner Ollie jumped back on a flight to Sydney or Melbourne or wherever it was she belonged, the happier Lara would be. Up until this week she hadn't seen her old tormentor since high school and that, quite frankly, was fine with her. What the hell was Ollie doing back in Ribbonwood anyway? She had big city written all over her.

She certainly couldn't imagine Ollie out here in the bush, sweating. Especially not now she was a goddamned doctor. Lara would bet her last dollar that Ollie had her own cleaner. And a dog walker. And a guy who mowed her neat little city lawn for her and probably cleaned her pool too. Meanwhile Eva couldn't buy food to eat while her erstwhile partner worked FIFO in the mines, leaving her and her child stranded out here with no supports, no car and apparently, no access to his pay-check. They'd hatched a decent enough plan around the bonfire last week but it made her crazy thinking how easy some women had it compared with others, by pure accident of who they were born to and what unfair talents they were gifted.

It was only the thought of Ollie's face falling when Lara blew off her pick-up-disguised-as-reconciliation attempt that kept her warm at night. She wondered how often women turned Ollie down these days. Probably not many now she was rich and successful and looked the way she looked. It was intensely satisfying to know that Ollie Gabrielli couldn't get *everything* she wanted. Even after all these years Lara wasn't going to give her a damn thing.

———

"Come on kid, we gotta go," Lara called to her daughter.

. . .

"Mum, no! It's early," Tilly protested. She and Frankie were playing some kind of complicated game in the corner of Eva's yard involving a lot of whispering and then shrieking. Lara had been up since five and her head was starting to ache. The coop was almost finished and all three women had prepared a meal together, Lara quietly slipping more ingredients than necessary into Eva's fridge just to tide her over another day.

"It's seven o'clock. The mosquitoes are biting and it's a school night. You'll see each other tomorrow," she reminded her daughter as she and Frankie clung to each other like they were about to be swept apart at sea.

"Frankie's going home to bed anyway." Sadie appeared next to her in the blessed coolness of the dark night. Both girls groaned, trading scathing glances and rolling their eyes at the unreasonableness of their inane mothers. Lara tried not to smile. Sometimes ten-year-olds were like toddlers, other times like world-weary forty-year-olds, exasperated by the pitiful ways of the world.

"*Now*," she told Tilly, who sighed and wandered up the grass towards her. She slung an arm around her daughter, squeezing her narrow shoulders and a hum of warmth hit her chest when Tilly hugged her back. That wasn't always a given anymore, now that her baby girl was practically a pre-teen. They walked up to the car together, calling out their goodnights to their friends. This, at least, was something she could give her daughter: community and chosen family. She always wanted Tilly to know that belonging was a thing she could create for herself.

. . .

She drove home, the car winding around the dark track, Lara taking every bend cautiously. There were roos everywhere and all kinds of small wildlife scattering before their tyres, not to mention the grubby-kneed creature in the seat beside her.

The whole way home she experienced that feeling - the one she labelled *motherhood* - where she would have died a thousand deaths for the small girl in the passenger seat, but she also couldn't wait for her child to please *please* fall asleep so she'd finally stop chatting and just give her a moment of peace. And yet an hour later, when Tilly was tucked up reading in bed, barely registering her mother's goodnight kiss, Lara started to miss her. Ridiculous.

She moved around her house in steps that were so rehearsed it was like an endlessly repeating dance, rescuing stray cups, wiping up dinner preparations, throwing clothes in the washing machine. It was all so mundane and mind-numbing that it took a good half an hour for her to shake herself out of the mood she was falling into.

Yes, her life was filled with predictable drudgery sometimes, but that was precisely the gift she'd longed for. This was the privilege of comfort, of safety, of having the power to choose exactly who she did and did not let through her front door and into the sanctuary of her home. Even this, she thought, as she scooped up Tilly's damp towel from the bathroom floor, this little moment of peace was a gift.

She let herself out the back door, an almost full moon lighting up her garden, glinting off the leaves of the macadamia trees. She shoved her feet into boots - doing a quick check for stray wildlife inside them first - then wandered out over the soft dark grass, making sure the automatic coop door had closed and her own flock of chooks were secure. They were. She heard a little bristle of clucks from inside as the girls shuffled on their perches. She soothed them with a goodnight.

She leaned on one of the fence posts, gazing out at the moonlight reflecting off the dam. An owl shrieked and swooped and she could hear the flying foxes chattering to each other in the trees. Her phone buzzed in her back pocket, making her jump, disturbing the peaceful night.

It was Eva, her voice shaking but strong. As she listened to the woman speak, Lara knew the plan they'd made was going to have to change.

It was time for another bonfire.

Chapter Ten

Lara looked across the road as she put her keys into the front door of her store the next morning and saw Esme arrive at the same time. She glowered at her. Esme shook her head disapprovingly, her shoulders drooping before she flung open her front door with a snap. Lara was tempted to give her the finger while she was at it but that might be going over the top. She heard a tsk in her direction as Kylie Burgess walked by her.

"Come on honey," Kylie grabbed her thirteen year old daughter's hand, all but dragging her away from Lara's toxic influence. Her child looked embarrassed so Lara shot her a friendly wink and her jaw dropped. She stared at Lara as they crossed the road and her mother glanced back and shot her another dirty look. Kylie reached Esme and rubbed her arm comfortingly. Lara smirked and walked into her store, turning the closed sign to open. Another day.

. . .

It was a Friday, always her busiest day as the luxury SUVs began to flood up the mountain. Lara was friendly to them all, just enough. They were mostly couples here for a romantic break and Lara knew full well that being even baseline friendly to the husbands never worked in her favour. Instead she focussed on the women, smiles and flattery, tips for good massages and day spas, places she never ever went herself, though she'd never betray a hint of that to her customers. It was all part of the fantasy, wasn't it? The rainforest hinterland, full of lovely locals living the dream. Her bottom line depended on it.

The day sped by in a rush, a haze of polite smiles and light chit-chat - the new line of boutique infused coconut oil she'd stocked just flying off the shelves - before she finally closed up the shop and picked up Tilly. She stalked past Ollie with barely a glance, her power neatly restored now that Ollie had made a play and lost. Lara was more than happy to know it was hopefully their last school gate encounter according to the timeframe Ollie had helpfully provided her. No more overthinking about what the hell to wear each day: normality restored.

Tilly was filled with excited chatter for the evening ahead and the weekend beyond. Once home, Lara put her to work, tidying the living room and peeling potatoes, and, in accordance with the magic of bonfire night, Tilly didn't even complain.

By five p.m. the women started to arrive, Frankie jumping out of Sadie's station wagon with a squeal and a smile, little Spencer toddling amongst everyone's knees, ignoring his mother's every attempt to get him to eat the cheese toastie she'd grilled for him, Esme and Chloe out in the back paddock piling up the logs.

. . .

The flames were just licking at the wood, the sky going from deep blue to gentle lavender when the last straggler - Audrey - finally arrived.

"Oh my god, *hi!*" The voices around the fire rang out. "You look *amazing!*"

Lara turned to see if it was a new haircut or a great dress, ready to smile and agree, when she stopped still. Along with her, Audrey had brought Ollie fucking Gabrielli. To Lara's *home*. To bonfire night. A sharp wedge of betrayal sliced through her. Bonfire night was hers. It was all but fucking sacred. Bringing *her* here? She straightened her spine.

A hand gripped her arm, just as she started to open her mouth. Sadie had her eyebrows raised.

"Oh come on," she said, her voice low. "Are you going to tell her there's not enough room in this town for the both of you?"

Lara narrowed her eyes, but let out a small huff.

"She's at my *house*," she emphasised.

. . .

"No," Sadie reminded her, "she's in your back paddock. I think you can probably survive that."

"For fuck's sake," she muttered. She looked up and found Ollie's eyes on her. She didn't drop her gaze when she saw Lara look back. Lara toasted her, sarcastically, with her wine glass and Ollie smiled widely. God, she was so damn smug. Lara looked away.

Chloe was on BBQ duties that night, but Lara found all of a sudden she'd rather not mingle. She helped with the cooking and let the wine take the edge off her annoyance. When the cooking was almost done, her glass was empty.

"Here," came a low voice, just above her left ear. "Let me refill you. This one's far better."

Ollie was pouring her something crispy cold and golden, a *Gabrielli* labelled bottle, of course.

Lara rolled her eyes.

"Thanks," she said, keeping her tone practically dead.

Ollie smiled, her eyes flicking to hers for a beat.

. . .

"You're welcome," she said, as if Lara had been actually sincere. Then she melted back into the group.

Ollie held fucking *court*. She was the new face but also an old face, and a popular one at that. The women flocked around her, Lara only able to watch in helpless fury as her bonfire night became an Ollie Gabrielli welcome party. She did her best to ignore the woman and talk instead with others but every break in the conversation she could hear a breathless voice asking about Melbourne, or Ollie's warm tones talking about her nieces and nephews, her mother driving her nuts or a dog called Rocco.

"Um, actually," she heard Ollie pause, "I'm back for three months. My grandmother is dying."

Lara felt an uncharitable urge to roll her eyes. Here we go, the sob story, let's all feel sorry for the princess of Ribbonwood High. Predictable sounds of sympathy echoed around the fireside.

"Oh no, it's okay," Ollie added. "Old people die. It's kind of their thing."

Lara found herself cackling in surprise, just slightly too loud and Eva looked at her, appalled. Ollie looked over at her and grinned too.

"Sorry," Ollie added wryly. "I love my Nonna. I don't want to lose her." For a second her voice cracked, but then she rallied. "But to die at ninety-one, living at home with your family and your grandchildren and great-grandchildren...it's hardly a tragedy. We should all be so lucky."

Ugh. That was even worse than a sympathy ploy; now she was a fucking philosopher. Everyone was nodding meaningfully.

"Alright," Lara interrupted. "Thank you for the beautiful life lesson, Ollie, we're all so glad you're here." Eyes widened around the circle at her dry tone but Ollie just imitated her toast from earlier, an almost pleased smile on her face at her irritated interjection. Immediately Lara was annoyed at herself. She really was playing right back into her hands, Ollie still the golden girl and Lara the sharp-tongued outcast. God, three *months* did she say? She remembered why they were all here. It wasn't for Ollie Gabrielli. It wasn't for her either. "Shall we get down to business?"

She reached over and squeezed Eva's arm, handing the spotlight to her. Eva hesitated, but then told them the latest, murmurs of outrage slowly building. Lara waited until she'd finished and the silence rang out for a beat. Then all the eyes around the fire turned to her.

"I think," she said calmly, "it might be time to escalate things. Don't you?"

The discussion fired up: wild ideas, comedy revenge, tentative suggestions. Ollie sat, open-mouthed, quiet, letting the words swirl around her. Lara tried not to waste time wondering what was going through her mind. She didn't care. She really didn't. After about twenty minutes of silent listening, the newest - temporary - member of bonfire night finally spoke up.

"I have a cousin in the mines up there," she said softly.

Lara felt her eyes light up.

"I think," she said, her gaze on Ollie's - just daring her to back out now - "that maybe we have our plan."

Ollie looked back. This time when she raised her beer at her, her face was serious. A pact.

When the details were in place and the buzz died down, the formality of the evening broke. Small conversations resumed, some women louder with the buzz of alcohol in their veins, others quiet and thoughtful. People milled about, easy gossip, comforting murmurs. They could have let the fire die down but by unspoken agreement they kept throwing logs on, just enough to keep the flames holding the darkness at bay.

Sadie went up to check on the girls, to make sure they were tucked up in bed - not sleeping, there was little chance of that - but safe none-theless.

Lara was propped up lazily against a cushion and gazing into the fire when she found her glass was empty again. She wasn't drunk but there was a pleasant warm haze floating in her bloodstream that made her a little too comfortable to want to move. She was just about to heave herself up and go grab another drink when Ollie Gabrielli materialised, plonking herself down on the picnic rug beside her, wrapping long graceful fingers around the stem of Lara's wineglass and pouring her another one herself, meeting her eyes with a provoking smirk. Lara suddenly realised she'd been waiting for this moment all evening, though for the life of her she couldn't say why.

Ollie looked more than comfortable reclining right there next to her, watching Lara with her steady warm gaze. It was as if Lara had never rebuffed her at all, let alone barely three days ago. The confidence of this woman was other level.

"I have a question," she said, apropos of nothing. Lara readied herself for another come-on, shrugging her assent, ready - pumped, in fact - to shoot her down again. Ollie held her eyes, the firelight glowing off her skin. "Are you all witches?" she asked. Lara choked on her wine. As she wiped her mouth, Ollie was grinning. "I mean, it's a fair question, is it not? Here you are out at night, burning fires, in a circle under the full moon, plotting men's downfalls. Seems witchy as hell to me."

Lara found herself laughing, faintly delighted at the image despite herself.

"Do you really think I'd tell you, if we were?"

. . .

"Oh, I won't tell anyone," Ollie said sincerely. "I think it's fucking hot."

"Apparently you do because you've just sold your soul to us."

"Mm." Ollie toyed with the label of her beer bottle, then flicked her eyes back up to Lara's. "I suppose I have."

"You shouldn't be here." Lara wasn't about to let her off the hook. "Do you have some kind of memory loss about the fact I said we wouldn't be going for drinks in this lifetime?"

"Huh," Ollie said thoughtfully. "From what I recall, you said I had not a single chance in hell of that happening," she reflected. She bumped her beer bottle gently off Lara's wine glass, mere inches away. "Cheers, by the way," she smiled victoriously.

Lara's jaw dropped. She snatched her hand away, the glass with it.

"This doesn't count-" she protested, thoroughly peeved.

"Oh, I think it does," Ollie argued. "There's your drink, here's my drink, and here we both are." She leaned back on her elbows and stretched out her long legs, wiggling her toes luxuriously in her stupid, stylish, expensive looking ankle boots. "It's quite cosy, actually."

. . .

"Can you *leave?*" Lara tried. "Like honestly?" Her tone was unconvincing, even to her. Ollie was extremely aggravating, but her genuine smugness at just getting to drink next to her was - okay, *fine* - kind of flattering.

"You're still the Queen Bee, aren't you?" Ollie raised her eyebrows at her. "Still in charge after all these years."

"*That's* what you thought?" Lara found herself gaping.

"Sure." Ollie shrugged. "The blondest, the most beautiful, the coolest, the most coveted. There's one in every high school. You were ours."

"Oh, fuck off Ollie." Lara couldn't believe this shit. "That's rich coming from you."

"Me?" Ollie looked genuinely confused. Lara wanted to toss her wine in her face.

"*Yes* you. The prize-winning athlete, the one who topped every exam, the one who won every award there was to award. Princess of Ribbonwood, then and now. The pretty, popular one. The *good* one." She hardened her tone to stop her voice from cracking over the last point. Lara, it was well documented by the whole town, had not been *good.*

. . .

Ollie's jaw dropped.

"I was a nerdy tomboy," she said flatly. "And the class lesbian as you so astutely told everyone. Not to mention a wog."

"Oh yes, that's right, I forgot, also the beloved youngest daughter of a wine dynasty. Really rough stuff you were going through."

"Lara," Ollie sat up. Her face was suddenly serious. "Lara, I was a piece of shit to you. We were all shit to you, in the end. We were wrong. You didn't deserve-"

"Oh, save it!" Lara did not want to hear this. There was something about it that made her feel slightly panicked, like all these years later she actually might want to cry to hear this from Ollie Gabrielli of all people. "Please, Ollie, fuck off with this shit-"

"I'm sorry, are there two grown women over here arguing about *high school?*" Sadie sat down next to them both with a thump. She looked straight up amused. "The same high school we went to - what - *twenty years ago?* When we were all fucking morons who didn't know shit from a shovel?" She looked from one to the other. "Except me, of course. I was better than all of you which is the only reason I had no friends, not because every last one of you was a racist cunt."

Silence rang out.

.   .   .

"Oh christ," said Ollie. "I just thought you hated me. I didn't-" She looked devastated, her mouth opening and closing, searching for the right words.

Sadie burst out laughing.

"I did hate you!" she snorted. "No need to turn on the white fragility routine. I thought you were a knob actually. Both of you." She shrugged. "Turns out, *things can change* in twenty fucking years. I swear to god, if you don't put a lid on this shit yourselves I'm going to sit here and prod you until you kiss and make up."

"Oh please," Lara interjected, rediscovering both her steady voice, and her pride. "We all know Ollie would enjoy that way too much."

"Don't worry," said Ollie, her eyes back on Lara's. "I know there's not a single chance in hell that would ever happen."

Chapter Eleven

"Your head's in the clouds," her dad said, arriving next to her on the front porch steps, ever-present coffee in hand. Ollie looked up at him in surprise.

"Huh?"

"Just said your name eight times," he announced, taking a seat beside her. "Thought I'd better bring you a top up, just in case you were unconscious." He handed her a fresh cup of her own.

She blinked in the morning light.

"Thanks," she said. "I was just...daydreaming."

. . .

Wasn't that the truth? She'd been in her head ever since the night of the bonfire. Thinking about high school, about privilege, about relative morality. About sharp blue eyes and the sudden flash of genuine pain she saw in them when Lara spat the words *the good one* at her. She thought of Sadie's perfectly warranted accusation and her very generous retraction. She thought of how in both cases her attempt at apologising only made things worse. Some things couldn't be fixed simply by saying sorry.

"Some daydream," her dad interjected. She raised her head.

"You have no idea."

Another day went by, and another after that, and Ollie found she still had no answers. She went and lay out in the shady hammock by the dam, gazing up at the tree canopy, listening to the whip birds crack and the catbirds yowl from the leaves.

She felt, if anything, even more conflicted about the person she'd always believed she was. She'd long thought of herself as a kind of underdog, the nerdy, gay farm kid made good, and yet here Lara was, calling her a *princess*, along with a solid reframe of who Ollie was that made her head spin. Because everything Lara had said about her high school self was true: she was academically gifted, athletic, popular, from a comfortable background, with a supportive family. She'd been teased for being a wog, but that was laughable compared with what Sadie faced in Ribbonwood, or just about bloody anywhere in Australia for that matter. As for the barely veiled jabs at her sexuality that teenage Lara had led...well Ollie was seeing them in a different light now. The kind of light that said *if they're looking at you then at least they won't be looking at me.*

Lara Bennett. When Audrey had invited Ollie to what she described as more or less a *secret society* bonfire at Lara's place there'd been no way Ollie could say no. *Oh please,* Audrey had said, when Ollie had teetered, pointing out Lara's solid dislike for her, *that's just Lara.* The way Audrey described it, Lara was prickly on the outside and soft in the middle. Far from convinced, Ollie had taken that as a goddamned challenge; if there was a way in through the thorns she was going to find it.

She'd figured it as her one and only last chance to figure Lara out. Because if Lara didn't want Ollie's amends then that was her right. But Ollie had only walked away from the bonfire even more confused than before. She and Lara had kept sparring, but she'd seen the flash of enjoyment in Lara's eyes, and oh how Ollie had relished making her laugh. At times Lara had looked straight up disarmed.

On top of that, *this* Lara, the one hosting bonfires, surrounded in women who clearly admired and cared for her, all scheming and plotting together on behalf of a spurned ex-girlfriend? If Ollie had thought Lara was superficially gorgeous standing there behind the till of the thriving business she owned... well *this* Lara was shockingly attractive.

Apparently Ollie hadn't been remotely subtle in her reaction either since after Sadie had defused their escalating squabble about high school, she'd grinned directly at Ollie with that *kiss and make-up* line, her eyes smug and knowing. So that had happened. The hit of pink in Lara's cheeks that followed, had that been from the emotion of the argument, or the directness of Ollie's response? Because the tension between them felt knife-edge, like it could flip on a dime from a fight to a kiss at any second - either felt completely fucking possible - and she was pretty sure that wasn't all coming from her side. Lara's eyes seemed to blaze with it, with a heat that felt palpable. And that wasn't even taking into account her actions at the school that past week. Ollie smirked every time she remembered Lara's almost breathless demeanour, every aware flicker of her gaze saying *are you looking at me?*

Because oh god, Ollie *was*. Lara was hard to take your eyes off at the best of times, let alone when she was trying to make you look. Lara Bennett did not have to fucking *try* and it made Ollie a very complicated combination of endeared and aroused to know that Lara apparently very much cared to make Ollie stare.

Thirty-four was perhaps too old to be so hung up on a girl you used to fantasise about slamming up against the lockers - and not in a hot way. This whole crush she seemed to be growing felt slightly regressive, pushing Ollie back into a time she'd really rather forget. But something was nagging at her; something about the friction between them wouldn't let her rest. She wanted to resolve this feeling, one way or another, with an urgency that seemed entirely out of proportion with simply running into an old classmate, even one as fascinating as Lara Bennett.

She wondered if she was letting herself get stuck on this exquisitely prickly conundrum because it was easier than her other conundrum, the one she really should be focussing on. What the hell was she supposed to do with the fact that the job she loved was giving her

PTSD? She wasn't stupid. The hyper-vigilance, the flashbacks... she didn't have all the symptoms, but there was enough to leave her lying in bed at night staring at the ceiling, a cold fear growing in her belly.

She'd worked so hard to get to where she was, the point at which her whole damn life was this job. There should be another thirty years in this career for her; there was no way she could stop now, not after everything she'd sacrificed to get there. But dealing with it felt impossible. Every time she contemplated looking at the problem directly, she felt like a woman in a horror movie investigating a strange noise in the attic. *Don't go upstairs,* her brain screamed at her. And so Ollie wouldn't. Overwhelmed, she closed her eyes and lay back, listening to the sounds of the winery and the rainforest beyond, and thought again about blue eyes.

———

By the end of the week she found herself walking down Ribbonwood's main road like she was magnetised, pulled irresistibly inside the doors of the General Store. Lara was right where she expected her to be, behind the counter in the middle of her work day, and yet Ollie felt slightly winded at the sight of her, shoulders bare beneath her casual, sleeveless dress, her hair twisted up with soft wisps escaping down the nape of her neck.

This time though, Ollie wasn't the sole customer. Lara's eyes flickered over her briefly, not outwardly registering her presence, as she spoke to a tall, solidly built man at the register. His back was to Ollie, but his voice sounded familiar.

. . .

"Come on, Lara," he said, his tone wheedling, just a hint of irritation. "Give me another chance. I won't fuck up again, you know I won't."

Ollie's ears pricked up from her way down the aisle. Another grown puppy with a crush? God, this was really humiliating for both of them.

"Adrian." Lara's voice was silky soft, like a caress. "You know I want to." Ollie peered at her over a shelf of fresh produce, torn between feeling curious and surprisingly miserable. "The problem is, I have another supplier now. That's what happens when I put in orders and you don't deliver."

Ollie's relief at realising that it wasn't a romantic encounter she'd stumbled onto was straight up troubling. Adrian Wills was from a local family that grew bananas and lychees. He was also, she knew from Nico, quite the stoner. He sounded less than chill right now though.

"For fuck's sake!" His voice got hard as he gripped the edge of the counter and glowered at Lara, his knuckles turning white. From years in emergency departments, Ollie recognised the signs of a man right on the verge of an aggressive verbal outburst. Her spine stiffened, ready to step in, a response both professionally and personally second nature by now. "You're not *listening* to me-"

"Honey, I am." Lara's voice got even softer. She leaned towards him, her breasts angled just so. Ollie swallowed. So did Adrian. "You know how much respect I have for you," Lara said coyly. "You're always number one to me. It's just -" her eyelashes floated down slowly over his torso, like she just couldn't help herself, like she was barely able to hold herself back, "- it's just business. You wouldn't hold that against me would you?" She gazed up at him, her lips moving into a gentle pout.

Adrian defused faster than a pricked balloon.

"Jesus Lara," he said. "I mean, you're really killing me here-"

"Oh, I'm just small fry," she stopped him sweetly. "You've got much bigger retailers to worry about - real money - a successful guy like you. I wouldn't expect you to be so gentlemanly, pretending like my little store was something you even noticed."

"You know I'd look after you," he said meaningfully, his hands moving from gripping the counter to resting pressed up to her delicate forearms. Lara didn't flinch.

"Oh I *know* you would," she said, with a breathless giggle. "Now run along home to your wife like a good boy," she scolded him teasingly and pulled away. Ollie held her breath until he disappeared out the door. She popped back out from amongst the shelves.

"Wow," she said. "That was masterly."

Lara shrugged, her eyes growing cool.

. . .

"It's who I am," she said cuttingly. "Right?"

"You're resourceful," Ollie said carefully. "And wily as hell. Lucky he's dumb as a bunch of rocks though, since that's not remotely the way you flirt."

"Excuse me?"

Ollie drifted closer.

"No," she said plainly. "You don't do that breathy, giggly, baby-girl shit when you actually mean it."

"I don't?" Lara looked borderline confused at how to deal with this line of conversation and Ollie was living for it. Jesus she looked good today, her hair gleaming in the warm light, the swoop of her kitten eyeliner deployed to perfection. Ollie focussed.

"If you were actually flirting with him you'd be mocking him mercilessly." She shrugged. "Making fun of his grocery items, even his credit card. Pretending not to notice him at the school gate, making him sell his soul just to get a drink with you."

To her absolute shock, Lara's cheeks flushed, just slightly. Oh *fuck,* she had her. Ollie had been merely making a stab in the dark, based on nothing but her growing suspicion. Lara's mouth was hanging open, ready to argue and coming up with *nothing*.

"That's not-" she managed.

"Oh, I think it is. You know, I'm pretty sure I've figured out by now that hate-fucking is your love language." Ollie smiled at her sweetly.

Lara stared at her, her blue eyes wide. For a second Ollie thought she was about to throw her out of the store. All of a sudden Lara began to laugh. It was a laugh Ollie had never once heard from her, both surprised and delighted and completely taken aback. Her cheeks stayed flushed and her eyes sparkled and oh my *god* Ollie could kiss the mouth of the woman who laughed like that.

"You're delusional," Lara denied, struggling forcefully to wipe the smile from her lips.

"Oh, there you are, doing it again." Ollie smirked. "God, it's like you're obsessed with me."

"Please." Lara recovered herself. "You wish I was."

"You close the store on Mondays, don't you?"

Lara sobered fast, looking mutinous.

. . .

"So?"

"Sunday night dinners are kind of a thing with my family," Ollie told her. "Everyone's there. My mum's an incredible cook, plus, as you know, we're a wine *dynasty*," she reminded her with a faint eye roll. "You should come."

For the second time in less than two minutes Lara seemed completely lost for words.

"I'm not... I don't..." she started. She gripped the edge of the shop counter, examining her own knuckles for a response. "I don't have a babysitter," she eventually said. "It's sounds like a family thing?" she hastily added. "Your mother wouldn't want me there," she bit out, perhaps getting to the real point, her cheeks reddening slightly. "Your family won't-"

"My family will fucking love you," Ollie said, clear-eyed, holding her gaze. "Bring Tilly with you. Frankie will be there anyway."

"Frankie?" Lara frowned.

"I invited Sadie too. She said she'd drive, so you can pretend not to enjoy the family wine again even though it's fucking *excellent*."

. . .

"I..." Lara stared at her. "No, I-"

"What, you have to wash your hair that night?" Ollie jumped in, desperate to sidetrack her. "There's a shower at mine, if you want." Lara narrowed her eyes at that and Ollie grinned, unabashed. "Worth a shot." She shrugged. "What is it? Pet dog you can't leave at home? Bring him too, we've already got four. Wait - a cat? Why not? The more the merrier."

"Ollie," Lara finally showed her some mercy and cutting her off. "This level of begging is embarrassing, even for you. If Sadie is going and I get free dinner in a winery with my best friend then I suppose I can tolerate your presence. Just as long as you don't, like, sit next to me or try to talk to me or whatever."

Ollie felt her smile stretch wide.

"Wow, it's like you can't even *help* flirting with me," she tossed over her shoulder as she turned to leave, before the Lara could gather herself and find a reason to change her mind. "Have even a little bit of chill, Lara."

"You've never once even *asked* me if I'm queer," Lara said suddenly. Ollie turned back to look at her where she stood, stock still behind the counter. "Your ego is just... stunning."

"Oh," said Ollie. "I thought it was obvious."

. . .

Lara balked.

"What?"

"I mean, your whole life is built around women," she said. "And I know who you flirt with, and who you don't. Even if no one else does."

Lara looked at her for one full, shimmering, sparkling moment. Ollie recognised the look in her eyes. It was indisputably a look of wonder.

"See you on Sunday," she added. Then she slipped out the door and into the light, wonder of her own sparking in her chest. She'd finally figured out the key to Lara Bennett and it was heartbreakingly simple: actually just *seeing* her.

Chapter Twelve

"Why exactly are we doing this again?" Sadie asked her as Lara locked her front door that Sunday evening. Most people who lived in the middle of nowhere didn't bother to lock their houses when they went out, but Lara always did.

"I have no idea." Lara trailed reluctantly down the porch stairs towards her. "What the fuck do people wear to wineries?"

"I'm so flattered you think I know," Sadie said drily, leaning her hand against the door of her car. She looked faintly alarmed as she looked down at her neat but casual outfit. "Is this like, *going to a winery?*" she asked. "Or just dinner at a mate's place?"

"I don't know," Lara gritted out. She was nervous and she didn't like the feeling.

. . .

"It's just hard to understand what's happening here. You and Ollie Gabrielli want to fuck each other so bad that we're all going to family dinner?"

"I do *not* want to fuck Ollie Gabrielli," Lara hissed, as she reached the car, darting her eyes to where the kids were already in the backseat, happily engaged in more important conversations than whatever their mothers were talking about.

"Cool," said Sadie. "Your hair looks good, by the way."

"Fuck you."

They drove the winding track through the trees, Sadie slamming on the brakes for a wallaby, making everyone in the car jerk against their seatbelts.

"Mum!"

"Sorry."

"Are you nervous or something?" Lara tried to shift the focus from her own slightly tight chest.

"Actually," Sadie focussed out the windscreen at the road ahead, "I'm pumped. Great food, an entire family of extremely good-looking Italians. Watching you be weird. Best night out in years."

The sun touched the horizon by the time they reached the Gabrielli estate, the last rays glinting off the olive grove, drenching everything in dark gold.

"Is this where Aria lives?" piped up Tilly, belatedly invested in their evening as she peered out the car window.

"I don't know," she told her daughter. "It's where her grandparents live anyway."

She thought of Aria's mother, Natasha. Dinner with one of the school gate mums? What the hell was she thinking, agreeing to this?

They pulled up in front of a big wooden home. It was a sizeable Queenslander, but looked entirely modest, a gang of farm dogs scrabbling around to bellow at them, low porch lights already gleaming in the pink dusk. And standing on the bottom step watching them arrive - just as Sadie had predicted - stood their first extremely good-looking Italian of the evening. Ugh.

"Watch out," warned Ollie, as a small chocolate-coloured dachshund broke from the dog pack and flung himself like a small rocket toward them. "He's dangerous," she said drily, as the creature flung himself onto his back at Tilly's feet, short legs waving, tail like a rotor blade.

Her daughter squealed and she and Frankie practically collapsed into the dust right next to the car to play with him.

"Go on!" shouted a man's voice from the porch above them. "Give it up!"

The other dogs trotted off obediently, satisfied they'd completed their canine duties sufficiently. Lara looked up to see who the voice belonged to and saw an older man - balding, sun-baked and wiry - probably in his early seventies and yet still, squarely in the good-looking ball park, with his firm chest and loose white dress shirt. Jesus christ, what a gene pool.

He descended the steps while Sadie and Lara hovered awkwardly, Ollie next to them like some kind of bridge between the worlds, his expression unreadable.

"Welcome," he said, gripping Lara's hand between his two huge ones. He dropped a kiss on each of her cheeks like something she'd only ever seen in movies. If she'd been warned it was coming she'd have ducked out of reach, but now it had happened and she was watching Sadie receive the same treatment, she only felt oddly warm. Despite the space invasion it felt entirely fatherly.

"Dad," Ollie was watching, an odd expression on her face. Was *she* nervous? Lara couldn't get a read on her. "Lara and Sadie, you remember them from school. My dad, Giovanni."

· · ·

Lara's voice seemed to have deserted her. Meeting anyone's parents was out of the realm of any regular experience for her. A flash of the middle-aged couple who'd been her in-laws leapt into her mind. Their extreme awkwardness with her, their clear disapproval. The brief thaw when she'd birthed them a grandchild. Their grief-filled rage when Josh had died. They only lived on the road over to Silverbloom but neither she nor Tilly had heard from them since the week of the funeral.

She blinked and Giovanni was leading them all up the stairs saying something about wine already.

"You'll have to excuse him," came a woman's voice. Lara looked up to see Ollie's mother was pushing her way out the screen door. "He gets like this around beautiful women. All blah blah blah." She met first Sadie's and then Lara's eyes. "I'll get rid of him, don't worry."

Lara barely had a chance to smile before she got the same double cheek kiss treatment from the woman Ollie introduced as Francesca. She was entirely unpretentious - greying hair, wrinkles, a comfortably fitting floral frock - and quite adamantly beautiful. It was clear from which parent Ollie got her dark soulful eyes.

Inside the house was packed full of furniture, big couches, sideboards, fresh cut flowers, piles of books, comfortable clutter, framed family photos everywhere. Francesca Gabrielli kept up a comfortable patter as Lara paused in front of a photo of what was unmistakably a pre-teen Ollie, toothy smile too big for her face, late nineties hair, NSYNC t-shirt. She turned and smirked at the woman following behind her, sarcastically mouthing the word *cute*.

. . .

Ollie rolled her eyes, grabbing Lara's elbow and dragging her quickly past it, shooting her a dirty look before dropping her warm fingers from her skin. Lara realised Francesca was watching the interaction and she straightened her spine, wishing she could just remember to be nice for once in her life. She really didn't want this soft-eyed older woman to remember it was *nasty* Lara Bennett she'd let into her lovely home.

"Can I help with anything?" Lara looked toward the big open kitchen, oven going, pots boiling on the stove, a mouth-watering scent in the air. Ollie's older sister - Pia, she remembered her vaguely, a tall, excruciatingly pretty final year student when Lara was starting high school - was doing something complicated with pastry, a baby bump so large she could hardly reach the bench.

"Hi!" She gave them a distracted nod accompanied by a warm smile. "I'll come greet you properly when head chef here lets me go," she rolled her eyes toward her mother who was already bustling towards the food.

"Oh, you're a darling," Francesca called back to Lara, ignoring her eldest daughter. "I wouldn't dream of it. Stop mooching like a lost puppy, Viola, and go pour your guests some wine."

Ollie gave an identical eye roll to her sister's but led them out the living room door and into the open air. They stepped out onto a broad wooden deck filled with laughter and voices and Lara teetered for a second in the doorway, desperately wishing she could flee back to the safety of the warm kitchen.

Before them was a mammoth wooden table, already set for dinner, covered in bowls of salads and fresh bread, approximately a thousand wineglasses, and seated with several more good-looking humans. A small hoard of children ran by, her own included, with an ecstatic dachshund thundering at their heels. There was a sleepy-cheeked toddler snuggled against the chest of a woman Lara immediately realised was Natasha Gabrielli.

For a second, silence grew, as several sets of eyes just looked at them. Ollie made introductions. There was Matty, a bit of a legend amongst the community - especially the women - when she'd been in school, all thick football playing limbs and strong masculine jaw; Nico, more wiry, like his dad, lazily attractive stubble and liquid dark eyes; James Mackey, Pia's husband and the odd one out at the table with his light skin and decidedly ginger hair; Natasha, with her big grey eyes and wary expression.

Sadie and Lara nodded polite hellos. Suddenly, there was movement as Matty got to his feet, his grin wide and easy. The others followed his lead instantly and the two women found themselves in a swarm of handshakes and hugs and more damn cheek kisses. Lara didn't generally like being touched by strangers - in particular men - but she made herself tolerate it. Apparently the Gabriellis were a tactile bunch; she had to admit a part of her felt intensely warmed at the greeting.

Natasha was the last one to reach her. To her surprise the woman pulled her in for a hug too, light and tentative.

. . .

"Welcome," she said simply. When she pulled back she looked deeply uncertain and Lara realised she appeared slightly frightened of her, like she might bite her rather than just say hello. Usually this knowledge would give her a little quiver of power. Tonight, it just gave her a slight pang.

"Thank you," she said back softly, making sure to smile. Natasha smiled too, also seeming slightly surprised. Bloody hell, this town.

"Merlot?" offered Matty, bottle already in hand.

"Actually," interrupted Ollie, "Lara likes our chardonnay," she said, with a sly grin. Her hand reached over her brother's to pour from another bottle. "She's basically obsessed with it."

She handed the glass over to Lara who shook her head at the ridiculousness of Ollie Gabrielli pretending to know *anything* about her, even as she grudgingly accepted what she knew from the last bonfire night to be exceptionally good wine.

"Good to know." Matty gave his sister a sideways look.

"None for me," Sadie put her hand up to stop the offered bottle. "I'm sober driver."

. . .

"Are you sure?" Nico spoke up for the first time. "I mean, I can drop you all back if you want. I'll stop drinking right now."

"Um, I'm good." Sadie eyed him warily. He nodded and didn't push.

Ollie guided them both to chairs and took her own seat - not next to Lara, just as she'd promised, but opposite her - smirking a little across the table when Lara looked up.

"So," started Matty. God, what the hell were they going to talk about? "How's business?" he asked. Sadie and Lara exchanged glances. Sadie grew bush tucker plants for nurseries right across the Sunshine Coast but her business was as under the Ribbonwood radar as it was successful. Lara ran the most hated business in town.

"It's good," she said lightly, taking a sip of her wine. "Being the devil incarnate is really working out for me."

There was a brief silence. Then Matty snorted. Just as if they'd all been given permission, suddenly everyone fell into raucous laughter. Any lingering tension around the table melted into the darkening sky. Ollie caught her eye and smiled widely, giving her a small toast from across the table. Lara made herself look away as if she didn't remotely care.

Francesca pushed through the doors with a steaming platter in her hands, followed by her eldest daughter with another. Nico leapt to his feet.

. . .

"Sit down, Mama," he said. Ollie's head jerked up, clear befuddlement on her features. "Jimmy, christ, look at your wife, come on, help me serve up."

James looked suitably chastened though his wife sent him a look of solid amusement as he pulled out a chair for her. Lara wasn't sure what the deal was, as Matty and Ollie exchanged glances until the eldest Gabrielli looked over at Sadie and grinned broadly.

"You should come over more often," he said, "if it makes him get off his lazy arse."

"Shh!" Francesca hushed him. "You'll make the girl uncomfortable and then she'll leave!"

Sadie just laughed out loud, her dark eyes sparkling as her grin flashed. Everyone watched Nico as he returned, presenting the last platter and a pile of serving implements like he'd felled a deer for them all.

"What?" he asked, when he felt the eyes on him.

"Nothing," Matty said innocently. "We're all just enjoying the view of a man being whipped by a woman who hasn't even looked at him twice."

. . .

Nico went slightly pink, and by the look on his face as he opened his mouth to retort, was about to drop something truly vile when the screen door creaked again. He shot over to hold it open for his father, who was pushing a wheelchair. Inside it was the tiniest, frailest woman Lara had ever seen.

"Mama," Giovanni said, "Sadie and Lara. They're Ollie's friends from school," he introduced her, slowly wheeling her so she could see the guests. "Alessandra Gabrielli," he told them, "but you can call her Nonna."

Nonna nodded at them seriously as her son guided her to the table. Being introduced as school friends made Lara feel approximately eight years old. She found she quite liked it.

She imagined an alternate universe where the last two years of high school hadn't happened and her childhood had simply continued on, in a series of class parties, girl alliances and invites home. She wondered whether there was a world in which she, Sadie and Ollie could have been friends, instead of three separate teenage girls, all navigating the darker elements of life in Ribbonwood without each other. She swallowed the lump in her throat and pretended she couldn't feel the youngest Gabrielli's eyes burning against her skin.

Chapter Thirteen

Dinner had been - if anything - *under* advertised. Lara had never eaten such good food. The company was warm and easy, with chatter about the family business, about the kids and their school, interspersed with loads of teasing, the two guests absorbed with magnanimity. It felt like Lara was visiting a completely foreign land, one full of big families who loved each other well, like it was the easiest thing in the world.

"May I please have some bread?" Tilly piped up part-way through the meal.

"What beautiful manners," Giovanni said kindly as he passed her the bowl to pick from.

"That's from good mothering." Francesca met Lara's eyes

approvingly over the table. Damnit, that warmth hit hard. Her smile slipped out embarrassingly quickly at that one.

Sadie elbowed her own daughter.

"Say thank you would you?" She pretended to glare at Frankie who just giggled and stuck her tongue out. Sadie basked just as much in the laugh she got back as Lara had.

"Please, let me help," Lara insisted again, as the table was cleared. This time she ignored Francesca's refusal and helped anyway, ferrying empty plates to the sink, scraping off the leftovers, stacking the dishwasher.

"Advertising yourself as a future daughter-in-law are you?" whispered Sadie sardonically as they passed each other in the hall. Lara gave her a small hip check and a glare.

"Are *you?*" She looked pointedly at the fresh fruit platter her friend was holding. Sadie stuck her tongue out at her - looking momentarily identical to her ten year old daughter - and pointedly kept walking.

Francesca caved and put Lara to work whipping cream at the kitchen bench. Ollie cut strawberries next to her and the second her mother wasn't looking, let her eyes track deliberately over the apron Francesca had furiously insisted on, as if Lara's denim dress was couture to be protected.

. . .

"Cute," she mouthed, echoing Lara's tease from earlier. Lara made a point of turning her back to her, not missing a beat as she whipped. She wasn't about to let Ollie see her smile so damn easily. All that good wine going to her head, she told herself.

When dessert was wrapped and the table cleared once more, Nonna and the smallest children were tucked into bed while the older kids were popped inside in front of a Disney movie. The adults lazed back, some at the table, others along the deck, drinking and chatting. Lara watched as Nico slowly approached Sadie, taking the seat beside her Lara herself had been on her way towards. She watched her friend's face for a few seconds and then smirked to herself. She peeled away to lean against the deck bannister instead and gazed out over the dark winery beyond.

It was only a couple of moments, just as she'd known it would be, before she felt a presence beside her.

"Surviving okay?" asked Ollie, mimicking her posture and looking out at the pitch black view. "Tolerating my presence adequately?"

"I was until now," Lara smiled at her sweetly. She turned back to the winery and heard Ollie breathe out a small laugh from beside her. She didn't leave though, just let the quiet grow between them, the murmurs of conversation in the background, her family's laughter. "They're lovely," Lara said begrudgingly. "I have no idea why you turned out the way you did."

Ollie laughed again.

. . .

"Black sheep of the family," she said, her eyes sparkling as she turned to gaze at her.

"Clearly."

The silence grew again and Lara found she suddenly couldn't help but give her something.

"Chickens," she said.

Ollie's head jerked up.

"I'm sorry?"

"I don't have a dog, or a cat," Lara told her. "I have chickens."

"Oh," said Ollie. "I thought for sure you'd be a cat person. Goes with the whole witchy thing," she added, waving her finger vaguely around her, almost, but not quite, touching her skin.

"No," Lara denied. "I like a practical pet."

. . .

"Of course you do. Even you can't afford eggs at the prices you charge."

Lara burst into laughter. Ollie looked at her in askance.

"Well," she agreed, "that's true. My supplier is a real piece of work." Ollie looked confused by her clear amusement and she laughed again. "Free range, organic, local, ethical, boutique, Ribbonwood *heritage* eggs?" She couldn't stop her smirk. "They're from my own backyard. Most expensive part of the supply chain is the boxes they come in. I make a mint off those things from tourists."

Ollie stared at her, amusement - and something far warmer - glowing in her eyes.

"You're an evil genius," she said admiringly, her voice dropping low. "God, it's *so* sexy."

Lara looked back at her. The way Ollie was looking at her seemed to be giving her very little choice. At least, that was the only excuse she could give herself for why she couldn't seem to shift her gaze.

"I'm going to throw you a bone here," she said after a minute, looking down at the seemingly shrinking inches of deck rail between their arms. "Only one of those compliments actually means anything to me."

. . .

Ollie considered her.

"That makes sense," she said. "It's probably the first time in your entire life someone has ever told you you're sexy. It's thrown you." Lara huffed out a small laugh. Ollie tucked a lock of dark hair back behind her ear. Her fingers were painfully elegant, her nails neat and small. She gazed steadily at Lara. "Thanks for the head's up," she said softly. "I'll keep that in mind." Without looking away she shifted slightly, tilting her whole body towards Lara's. "I think you misheard me though. I said it was your smart scheming brain that I found sexy. Not...all *this*..." She slowly waved her finger again, at Lara's lips, her body, and screwed up her face. "Ugh," she tried.

Lara laughed. She'd been desired for her looks her whole damn life and it had never brought her anything that was truly good for her. She made herself look away, unsure why hearing the word *sexy* from Ollie Gabrielli's lips seemed to to be the exception that hit her low in her belly.

"Is my daughter taking good care of you?"

Ollie jumped back as her mother's voice broke the spell that was growing between them. Lara blinked too as the bubble burst, wondering exactly how Ollie had managed it. Francesca had a bottle in her hand and she looked pointedly at Lara's almost empty glass, forgotten on the rail beside her. Somehow though, Lara felt like her question insinuated a whole lot more.

. . .

"She's adequate." Lara smiled, absolutely not about to let Ollie's mother think there was anything going on, when there most definitely was not. Francesca laughed as she topped her up.

"We were just talking about Lara's chickens," Ollie tried quickly to defuse whatever her mother was about to say, and Francesca's eyes lit up.

"Oh! What kind do you have?"

Lara recognised the tone of a chicken fanatic and she found her smile stretching wide, watching Ollie start to wilt as her mother settled in for a long yarn about breeds and feeds, predator prevention and how to make a yolk truly golden.

"Have you tried colloidal silver for a sick chicken?" Francesca asked her a few minutes later and Ollie huffed with annoyance.

"Oh my god, mum," she sighed. "That's not science, I've told you."

"Oh, listen to this one." Francesca nudged Lara with her elbow. "Gets a medical degree, thinks she's a chicken doctor."

Lara laughed, enjoying joining forces with the woman who knew best of all how to get under Ollie's skin.

. . .

"You really do need some, " Francesca went on seriously. "It's a must for every chicken owner's medicine cabinet. Ollie," she instructed. "Go down and get some from the shed for her, it's on the back shelf. I make it myself," she told Lara, "so you know it's the good stuff."

"Mum, honestly-"

"Actually, take her with you." Her mother ignored Ollie's protest. "Show her the mealworm farm I've made for them too, she'll love that."

"I'm *sure* she would." Ollie looked so flabbergasted at the turn the evening had taken that Lara felt almost sorry for her.

"It sounds incredible," she told Ollie, her smile broad. "Please, lead the way."

Sadie broke from her conversation with Nico to give Lara a solid raised eyebrow as she and Ollie walked by, heading off the verandah into the dark together. Lara raised hers right back, looking sideways to where the middle Gabrielli brother was looking extremely chuffed with himself. She left her wineglass behind and stepped off onto the soft grass with Ollie who'd grabbed a torch from a porch shelf and was lighting the path ahead.

"God, I'm sorry about her," Ollie said, her voice strangely more intimate as they walked out into the dark of the night together. "She likes to take every chance she gets to make my life miserable."

. . .

"That's probably why I like her so much."

"We're not actually going to go look at weird chicken medicine and worms just so you know," Ollie announced.

Lara stopped still.

"Oh yes we are. What if she *asks?*" she hissed, horrified.

Ollie laughed.

"Are you serious right now?"

"*Yes.* She's hosting me! I'm not going to insult her potions."

Ollie actually giggled. She was shining the torch at their feet and Lara could barely make out her face.

"Wow. I didn't realise you were this... adorable," she teased her. Lara scoffed. "Come on then." She turned them down a row of vines. "This way. Jesus christ."

"Wait, where were you actually taking me?" Lara asked suspiciously.

.   .   .

"It's a winery," Ollie said. "There's about a thousand pretty places to take a girl to sit and stare at the stars."

"Nice try," Lara told her flatly. "Now take me to the mealworms."

Ollie laughed. She led the way past an extensive, neatly rowed vegetable patch and a small chook house locked up like Fort Knox for the night, until they reached a large potting shed. She was just reaching out to open the door when Lara grabbed her arm and pulled her back.

"Watch it," she said.

Ollie looked at her in surprise, but Lara didn't let go of her. She looked back at the shed and let out a shriek.

"Oh my *god!*"

"Calm down, it's just a python," Lara told her, but Ollie had stepped abruptly back right into her body. It was only a brief clash of warmth but Lara found herself surrounded by the scent of her citrus shampoo. She sucked in a breath. "Hey honey," she said, stepping around Ollie, refusing to be flustered, and addressing the snake instead. "Oh, you're a pretty one." The huge carpet python gleamed under the torch light, her long thick body stretching right out along the top of the shed then down the front to the door, the head swaying right next to the handle Ollie had been about to grab for. "No little chickens for you this evening, my friend." She watched the tongue flicker, the large dark eyes shining. "Or are you chasing possums tonight?"

"Oh my god, you really are a witch," Ollie practically squeaked out as she watched Lara admire the snake. "I think," she said a moment later, as the large reptile straight up refused to move, "that at least we hit on a valid reason not to go in the damn shed."

Lara laughed, but she let herself get led away. She blamed the wine and the still warmth of the evening for the fact she didn't even protest as Ollie walked them back through the vines again, up a grassy slope and through a small grove of trees to a long ridge above the property. Ollie switched off the torch and they sat side-by-side in the grass. As their eyes adjusted, Lara found herself smiling. The stars were astonishing. The stars were exactly the fucking same as the ones she saw in her own country backyard every night. The stars were still worth gazing at.

They were quiet. Aside from the rustle of small wild creatures in the trees behind them and the distant sounds of the dinner party continuing, all Lara could hear was their own breathing. Their bodies were close, both leaning back on their hands to gaze up at the sky, but to her surprise, Ollie wasn't making a single move to get closer to her. Finally, the suspense got to her.

"So is this the part where you're going to try to make out with me?"

Ollie grinned, turning her head to look at her.

. . .

"Is that you asking me to?"

Lara shot her a look back.

"You wish," she denied. "Though at this point you're pretty much the only member of your whole family who hasn't managed to kiss me tonight."

Ollie laughed.

"I mean honestly, who could blame them?"

"I'm just confused," Lara needled her. "Because ever since you got back to town you've been staring at me like you want to eat me alive, every chance you get. But now you've managed to manipulate things so that you've got me alone, full of wine, under the starlight and you're what... reconsidering?"

Ollie turned to face her.

"Oh, I want to kiss you," she announced firmly. An unreasonable spark of heat hit Lara's bloodstream, which made no sense whatsoever, since Ollie was only confirming what she'd already understood to be true. "Very much so. Tonight's not about that though."

. . .

"It's not?" For a second Lara wasn't sure she'd heard right.

"No."

"What the hell is tonight about, Ollie Gabrielli, if it's not about getting in my pants?" she demanded.

"Tonight's about amends," Ollie said softly, her gaze direct. "It's about not being a piece of shit, in your eyes. I won't be your hate fuck, Lara Bennett."

Lara was speechless.

The words hung in the air. She found herself laying back fully in the grass, her eyes on the stars, suddenly unsure if she was still winning here or not.

Ollie was *masterful*. She'd brought Lara there, right into her messy, chaotic, delightful family home. She'd introduced her to her gorgeous parents and her beloved dying grandmother, let her siblings mock her and her mother embarrass her, all so that Lara had no damn choice but to see her as a whole person. Not just a high school nemesis, not even just as a grown woman with a serious threat of hot sex in her big dark eyes. Instead, she'd made herself more. And even worse, she'd done the very thing that Lara secretly craved in her most hidden of hearts, and made her feel *wanted*. Not just desired - actually welcome - amongst a whole damn family at that.

. . .

For a minute Lara couldn't tell if she was slightly swept off her feet by such a move or actually just *pissed* at her. Ollie lived in Melbourne. What the fuck did she think she was trying to do? Lara almost jumped when Ollie chose that moment, to finally make her move.

Her hand found Lara's in the grass, threading her long slender fingers through hers with intense gentleness. When Lara didn't move an inch - for or against the contact - Ollie's thumb stroked achingly softly, a meandering path up and then down the inside of her palm. Lara, absolutely, one hundred percent, did not shiver. Ollie pulled her fingers away.

Lara bit out the words before she could stop them.

"I don't think you're a piece of shit, Ollie," she relented quietly.

Ollie exhaled a quick breath.

"That's the sweetest thing you've ever said to me," she told her. Lara found herself smiling up at the stars. She didn't dare look over at Ollie. They lay side-by-side until all she could hear was her own heart, beating loudly in her ears. "Come on," Ollie said a few moments later, stretching her back luxuriously and pulling herself up out of the grass. "I guess it's getting pretty late for the girls tonight, huh? School tomorrow and all."

. . .

Lara's head spun. Ollie reached down to grab her hand and tugged her to her feet.

"Really?" Lara said in absolute disbelief, tugging her fingers back, putting her hands on her hips. "You're chickening out *now?*"

Ollie's eyes were amused in the starlight.

"Oh believe me, that's not what's happening here," she said. "But I'm also not going to try to kiss you while we're half drunk and you're still using words like *manipulate* about the evening. I'm not that kind of arsehole."

Lara blinked.

Ollie had already flicked the torch back on and was several steps ahead down the slope before Lara had the wherewithal to catch up to her. They were silent all the way down the vineyard.

At almost the last row of vines, Ollie stopped so suddenly Lara nearly bumped into her. She turned off the torch again and Lara rested her hand on the solid wooden post at the end of the row, her eyes readjusting to the dark night again, light spilling off from the edges of the porch, closer now, illuminating their features.

"What?" she asked, as Ollie stepped in closer.

. . .

Ollie was less than a foot away - almost close enough to touch - her eyes serious.

"Lara," she said softly. "What happened with Robyn Lowe?"

It took a full five seconds for Lara's brain to comprehend the words. Then, she started to laugh.

"What did you hear?" she asked curiously. Of all the things she'd expected to happen with Ollie Gabrielli out here in the dark, this had not been anywhere on the list.

"I heard," Ollie's eyes held hers, "that you spread a fake rumour about her. That she was being unfaithful. But that actually she was sick in hospital at the time."

"It's all true," Lara said. "I did do that."

Ollie kept looking at her.

"Why?"

"Well," Lara said slowly, leaning back against the wooden post, "I'm a horrible, nasty bitch."

. . .

Ollie watched her face.

Then, she bit her lip. Her eyes were steady.

"I don't believe you."

"Well, you should," Lara shrugged. "I'm bad; everyone knows it. It's also why you want me," she pointed out. "And we both know that too." She let her head tilt back, just enough, exposing her throat. Her back was slightly arched, hips tilted towards Ollie and she watched the other woman track her eyes over her body and swallow. "It's so bad of you to want me so much," Lara whispered, delivering the killing blow.

Ollie looked at her for a long beat, her eyes drinking in their fill. And then she smiled. A big, warm, unstoppable smile.

"Lara Bennett," she said quietly. "I am going to figure you out. And you can't stop me with that shit."

With that, she tugged Lara by the hand and without letting go began to walk her up towards the house. Lara was so astonished that she let her for almost a full thirty seconds, before she remembered to snatch her hand back away and out of reach.

Chapter Fourteen

Monday dragged. To kill time, Ollie helped her brothers with pruning, her old trusty Akubra she'd uncovered from the back of her bedroom closet keeping the sun off her face.

"Look at you," laughed Nico as she arrived alongside them. "You can take the girl out of Queensland..."

"Highest rates of melanoma in the world," she shot back. "Had a skin check recently? You're going to look like a raisin by the time you're forty-five."

"Not all of us work indoors Miss Lily-white." He kicked a small spray of dirt at her legs.

. . .

Ollie looked down. Just a few weeks back home and she was thoroughly golden-brown. She was starting to look like she'd never left.

"So." Matty eyed her from the other side of a vine. "You and Lara Bennett."

"Anyone tell you that you gossip like an old woman?" she fobbed him off. She didn't want to talk about Lara. Well, that wasn't quite true. She wanted to talk day and night about Lara. But not while she kept floating just out of Ollie's reach, shrouded in rumour and protected by spiky defences. Ollie wasn't quite sure if she was planning a seduction or mounting an investigation at this point, but she definitely knew she was thinking way too much about Lara Bennett.

"You're the one inviting her home to family dinner and barely remembering to eat you were so busy staring at her," Matty raised his eyebrows at her. "First time I've ever seen you off your food."

Ollie stepped deliberately to the next vine.

"You're imagining things," she denied.

He lifted his head.

"You should stay away from her," he said seriously. "She's bad news."

. . .

142

"You don't even know her," she said, a spike of anger rising in her blood. "You're as bad as the rest of Ribbonwood."

"No I'm not." He let his pruning shares dangle at the end of his long arm. "I welcomed her into our home, didn't I? But it's one thing to watch you bond with an old school mate and another to watch you get tangled up in something you don't understand." He held up his hand as she scoffed. "You've been away from Ribbonwood a long bloody time," he warned. "Lara Bennett is dangerous."

Ollie's jaw dropped.

"Are you fucking *kidding* me?" She squared her shoulders ready to get into it.

"Sadie reckons she's alright," Nico piped up.

Ollie had never been so pleased to hear her middle brother's input in her life.

"Well, you would believe that," she said, raising her eyebrows, grateful at him for putting his head above the parapet, "since you fell into a little gooey puddle at her feet."

She ignored Matty's ongoing gaze for another three long seconds before he caved, the new low-hanging fruit far too tempting to ignore.

. . .

143

"Mate it was *tragic*." He turned on Nico. "Don't reckon you'll get another look in there."

"Will too," Nico said with a grin. "I'm taking her down the pub on Saturday."

"What?" Ollie clutched her hand to her hat. "Wow. She must have felt *really* sorry for you if she agreed to that."

They both continued to mock Nico who took it all with the pleased indifference of a man who at least had a date with the object of his affections. All Ollie really had to hold onto were a few hot-eyed glances and hints that Lara Bennett didn't really want her to leave her alone as much as she was pretending she did.

If Lara really didn't want anything to happen between them there was no way Ollie would push her. She could take no for an answer, no problem. But between the rebuffs that felt like come-ons and come-ons that felt like rebuffs her head was thoroughly turned. She just couldn't shake the idea that *something* - be it small town closet queerness, their own thorny history, or perhaps even everything she was starting to understand had happened to Lara - meant she couldn't drop her hard front and admit she was just as affected by Ollie as Ollie was by Lara. She'd felt it, she was sure, in the tingling in the air between them as they'd gazed up at the stars together, Lara's breathing speeding up in the night air beside her.

"Earth to Ollie." Matty's voice broke through.

. . .

She blinked. Both her brothers were eyeing her, one with amusement and one with concern.

"Jesus and you think *I've* got it bad." Nico raised his eyebrows. "You're a lost cause there, kid." He threw all brotherly attempts to protect her to the wind.

Ollie was starting to wonder if he maybe was right.

———

That afternoon she looked down at her phone screen, watching it ring. She gulped in a deep breath, her skin suddenly clammy.

"Hi Cherie," she finally made herself answer.

"Ollie," came the warm, patrician voice of the medical director of the Emergency Department at the kids' hospital. "How are you going?"

"Good," she said. "Yeah, really good." She began to pace the deck, the sun beating down on her shoulders. She felt agitated, the phone against her ear an almost physical threat. She fought the urge to throw it as far as she could, out towards the dam like a venomous snake.

"And how are you really going?" Cherie said gently. Ollie's shoulders dropped.

. . .

"I...I'm not sure?" she managed. It had been less than a month since Cherie had sat with her, side-by-side in the director's office, Ollie unable to stop crying and unable to fully explain why.

Sienna Lau. Aged four. Let go of her mother's hand and ran out into the street at just the wrong moment. The mother's scream when Ollie finally, finally stepped away from the ongoing resus and gently explained that they'd done everything they could. That it was time now, to stop.

It was by any measure, a terrible moment, and a terrible death. But not Ollie's first, nor her last. It was her fucking *job* after all and she'd coped before and she *could* cope and why couldn't she *cope*? Cherie was in her late sixties, tall and commanding, a fucking god in their field. Her eyes were infinitely understanding. *Honestly darling,* she'd said calmly, the voice of a woman who'd broken bad news to parents a hundred thousand times, *it would be more of a worry if you weren't crying right now, don't you think?*

But the thing was, Ollie didn't always cry. Rarely cried, in fact. You couldn't do this job day in, day out and fall to pieces every time you had a loss. There'd been a shift that happened inside Ollie at some point early on where she simply found solace in the fact that she was *damn* good at her job. If something happened to your child, she was the person you wanted to have there on those darkest of nights. It wasn't traumatising to see sick or injured children every day if you were the person *doing* something, using your well-honed skills to save a life or a limb. It was only traumatising if you were a bystander and Ollie was very much not a bystander. So she was, by any measure, always fine at the end of the day.

· · ·

146

Until she wasn't. And the thing that hit her, when Cherie gently sent her home, told her to take a couple of personal days and come back when she was ready, was the *shame*. Not shame that she hadn't been able to save a little girl's life - no, Ollie had known the futility within moments of laying eyes on the tiny body - but shame that she, *Dr Gabrielli, MBBS, FACEM, PEM* was, after all, just another member of the public after all. Not special. Just a human.

There'd been at least eight or nine other members of the team in there with her - nurses, doctors, orderlies - and she, the team leader, was the only one who had truly broken down. For fuck's sake, she was a consultant, the top of the top, the most trained you could bloody well be. There was always a kind of veiled machismo in critical care areas like E.D; everyone caught it. It was the badge of honour they'd all earned: *throw whatever you can at me, universe, I can handle anything.* Everyone had a bad day sometimes, everyone shed a tear from time to time, everyone needed a goddamned holiday, but Ollie... Ollie didn't seem to be coming back from it.

"Theoretically," Cherie said now, her voice low and calm, "you're due back at work in nine weeks." Ollie nodded. That was forever away. But also? It sounded impossible. Walking back into the E.D., seeing her colleagues again, having a child's life in her hands? Those same hands had started shaking at some point in this call and she didn't know when. "I'd love to see you back," Cherie continued, "because you're about near irreplaceable." There was a smile in her tone before she became serious. "But your wellbeing is my utmost priority."

"I appreciate that," Ollie managed. "I'll be back."

· · ·

147

There was quiet down the line for a long moment.

"I'm going to send you a name," Cherie announced. "She's Melbourne-based but she can do online appointments while you're away."

"Oh no," Ollie protested quickly. "Honestly, it's fine, I just need some time out. A reset."

"Mm," Cherie responded. "I think you're smarter than that, don't you?"

"Uh... no actually, apparently I'm not."

"Ollie." Suddenly Ollie could remember very well what it had been like to be one of Cherie's interns. "Put the fucking ego to the side and go and see the nice head doctor would you?"

Ollie spluttered out a small laugh.

"Ugh," she said. "Fine."

"Good girl," Cherie approved. "Now, how's your weather? I'd let you know that it's eleven degrees and raining right now but I want you to come back, so I won't."

. . .

Despite the pleasantries, Ollie's hands were still shaking when she hung up the phone.

Chapter Fifteen

Finally, Tuesday rolled around and it was time for the lunch date she'd been hanging out for. Ollie was thoroughly thrilled with the distraction as she stepped up onto the front door step of a sweet-looking weatherboard cottage on a quiet side street just off Ribbon-wood's main road and knocked.

"Come in," beamed Mrs Lowe. "Goodness, what a treat." She bustled down the hallway, gesturing Ollie out to her little back patio, surrounded in a lush tropical garden so dense it was like the rainforest had crowded in and sat down to behave. "Cup of tea?" she offered.

She watched her old teacher as she returned to the table with a tray holding a pot of Earl Grey, two tea cups, a milk jug and a plate of Tim Tams. She wondered exactly how old Mrs Lowe was. She could be anywhere between fifty-five and seventy with her long iron grey hair pulled back in a ponytail, softly worn skin and firm strong limbs.

Her eyes were as kind as they'd been in Ollie's memory and she wondered again how anyone could deliberately set out to hurt this woman.

"Thank you for having me," Ollie started and Mrs Lowe waved a hand shushing her.

"It's not every day you get to catch up with your most successful former student." She took her seat opposite Ollie. "Tell me about medicine," she said, her eyes warm.

Ollie sucked in a breath. Honestly, it was the last thing she wanted to talk about. But as she looked across the table at her old teacher, she found herself opening her mouth. Mrs Lowe listened attentively and without judgement, and somehow, Ollie's hands didn't shake.

"Viola, honey," she said, when Ollie had finished unburdening herself. "Can I ask you a question?" Ollie nodded. "Who's helping you, with all this?" Ollie blinked. She frowned down at the table. "I thought as much," Mrs Lowe said gently. "It's too much to carry on your own. You're allowed to ask for help, you know that right?"

Ollie nodded politely. Cherie and Mrs Lowe couldn't have been more different and yet somehow Ollie found herself ganged up on by silver-haired, steel-spined older women who were apparently in cahoots. *Ugh.* She knew that if a colleague had come to her with the same kind of issue, professional support would be exactly the first thing she would be suggesting. It was always so easy when it was someone else.

. . .

"Can I ask you something too?" she changed the subject, looking closely at the older woman across the table.

"Of course."

"Lara Bennett," she said simply.

Mrs Lowe narrowed her eyes, looking back at her. She looked wary all of a sudden.

"What about Lara Bennett?"

"I heard that she...hurt you," she said cautiously, not wanting to offend her by spelling out the details. "And I want to know if that's true."

"It's true she spread a rumour about me," Mrs Lowe said plainly and Ollie's heart sank. She could see from the retired teacher's eyes that there was real pain here. She still couldn't shake the feeling that there was more to the story. Lara had been so clear - *I'm bad* - she'd said, but she'd also been noticeably evasive. She'd tried to use her body to throw Ollie off the scent, something Ollie was sure was extremely effective nine times out of ten. But Ollie just couldn't bring herself to believe that the woman who'd brought everyone together around the bonfire to scheme for Eva Sinclair's protection would also act toward Mrs Lowe in bad faith.

. . .

"Robyn," she finally made herself say the name. "Lara... she's not what everyone says she is, is she? I just... I can't make myself believe that."

"Why are you asking me this?" Mrs Lowe was watching her closely.

Ollie swallowed.

"I've... I've been spending some time with her," she said delicately, unsure if the older woman would pick up the nuance of what she meant, or even if she wanted her to. "I actually think she's kind of amazing." Her voice came out soft. "Strong. Wily as hell. Kind." Her eyes met Robyn's. "Not in the bland surface kind of way. In the hard way, in actions, where it counts. But you mean a lot to me. You changed my whole life and I can't reconcile *this* about her."

Robyn looked at her for another beat. Ollie found herself going slightly pink under her frank gaze.

"Ah," she said.

"Yeah," Ollie agreed awkwardly.

"Well then." Mrs Lowe placed her teacup down on her saucer. She paused. And then she opened her mouth. "The truth is, Ollie, that

I'm a drunk."

"I'm sorry?" Ollie knew for sure she'd misheard her.

"A drunk," Mrs Lowe repeated. "It was ten years ago now," she sighed. "Things were... things were hard at home, in my marriage. I'd left my job. The drinking just crept up on me. A coping mechanism, you know?" Ollie nodded dumbly, her mind still whirling. "My husband told me he wanted a divorce. Surprisingly, it wasn't because of my drinking. That, of course, I'd tried damn hard to hide, but he also didn't take the time to really notice. Instead, he'd just gone and met someone else." She shook her head wryly, the stab of pain still clearly evident. "Our daughters were twelve and fourteen at the time. There was this terrible tension... some days he threatened me, saying he wanted full custody. Other times it was clear he wanted to skip out scot-free. He was half-in, half-out of our home, visiting his new girlfriend. I wasn't coping."

"I'm sorry," Ollie whispered.

"Lara found me passed out at the wheel of my car. It was right by the high school. Just before pick up," she said, shame and misery overtaking her features. "Lara was extremely pregnant at the time," she added, her eyes suddenly warming, "so to this day, I have no idea how she did it. But somehow she wrangled me from the driver's seat to the back and drove me and the girls safely home. David was away that week, thank god, and somehow she'd done it without letting anyone in town see the state I was in. What I'd almost done."

. . .

Ollie reached out across the table and grabbed her hand. Robyn blinked back tears.

"She stayed until I sobered up. Something about her... I just... told her everything." She shook her head in mild wonder. "She was so young, barely twenty-five. My ex-pupil. Honestly, it was absolutely inappropriate that I unburdened on her like that, but I was so desperate, not to mention an absolute mess. Perhaps because of what she'd been through herself or perhaps because she had that big old baby belly, I don't know, she just seemed so *mature*," she sighed. "Like she was far older than her years. She listened to everything I had to say, and then, just like that, she came up with a plan."

"A plan?" Ollie realised she was holding her breath.

"She arranged for my sister to drive down from Maleny to stay with the kids. Then she checked me into Silverbloom Hospital. They kept me in for a week for alcohol detox," she said, her voice cracking slightly as she remembered it. "I was so reliant on the booze at that point I couldn't withdraw at home without the risk of a seizure. Lara knew all about that. Her dad, you know."

Ollie blinked. She didn't know.

"I was so scared," Mrs Lowe whispered, "that David would find out. That he'd take the girls. It would be so easy for him now; I was clearly an unfit mother." She swallowed hard. "That's where Lara showed her true genius."

. . .

"The rumour."

"Yes." She began to smile. "It hit David where it hurt. It was one thing to think about taking everything from me and leaving me broken on the floor. That would have given him a real buzz," she said, a trace of bitterness flickering across her face. "But ultimately he was the one who wanted to be running away to his brand new life and now he was afraid I might get to do it first. From then on it was just a race for him to make sure he got out cleanly. In the end, he did every-thing by the book - didn't quibble about a fair financial split or child support - as long as he was the one who got to go live his best life. After all, he didn't want me running around town with a younger man while he stayed home with the kids."

"Oh my god," Ollie breathed, her head spinning. *Jesus christ, Lara.*

"You have to forgive me," Mrs Lowe told her. "It's a difficult story, and I don't tell it to just anyone. I'm sober now, of course," she added. "Plus, I'm a little protective of Lara."

"Of *Lara?*" Ollie stared at her flatly, something hot flaring in her chest. "All Lara gets out of you staying quiet is getting to be seen as the bad guy. Again."

Mrs Lowe nodded, slowly.

"That's true, on the one hand," she agreed. "But on the other, Lara plays a particular role in this town. If I went ruining all her secrets you have no idea of the things that would fall apart around here." She shook her head, wonderingly. Then she smiled. "Lara would probably have me buried in her back paddock within five minutes flat if I went public with the truth about her," she said with real warmth.

"What *is* the truth?" Ollie wanted to know.

Robyn Lowe shook her head. She fixed Ollie with a stare that suddenly made her recall being held back after class in year ten biology.

"You're a smart girl, Ollie Gabrielli," she said. "I think I've told you more than enough for you to work the rest out on your own, don't you?"

Ollie pushed back her chair.

"Thank you," she said, as she stood up. "I don't mean to be rude and rush away-"

"You should probably go." Robyn nodded approvingly. "There's somewhere you should be?"

"I... yeah. Yeah, there really is."

———

Ollie couldn't seem to move fast enough. She jumped into the farm ute parked outside, instantly stalling it, and cursing. She restarted the engine and it roared as she forced it into gear and got herself down the street to the corner. The heat of the day baked down on her as she jumped out onto the curb.

The general store was blessedly quiet when she all but burst in, her senses heightened as she skimmed for non-existent customers before she set her eyes on the shopkeeper who was arranging a mason jar of fresh cut flowers behind the counter in the golden afternoon light. Lara looked up in surprise as Ollie strode towards her, pushing back a lock of her hair with the back of her hand as she watched her approach. Her eyes widened as Ollie didn't slow for a second, lifting the old-fashioned hinged counter top and stepping through behind the register, her hands slipping around Lara's hips as soon she reached her and walking her firmly backwards until her back hit the wall.

Lara sucked in a surprised breath, her mouth dropping open.

"Ollie, what-"

"*Lara Bennett,*" she accused fiercely, the name coming out like she was swearing. She slipped one hand around the curve of Lara's delicate jaw, feeling the heat and softness of her skin, seeing the flare of her pupils dilating right up close. "How dare you be this way? Pretending to be what everyone says you are when inside you're *so* fucking beautiful?"

. . .

158

She took barely a second, watching her words land. Then she dipped in and kissed her and Lara Bennett, Ribbonwood's brazen queen bee, straight up *melted* in her arms. Ollie's brain went white, as Lara's mouth opened hungrily under her own, her curves pressing into her body like she just couldn't get close enough. If it wasn't for the wall at Lara's back they'd have hit the floor. Ollie's fingers slid into her warm hair, kissing her deeper and Lara gasped into her mouth, her own hands gripping almost painfully tightly to Ollie's hips.

The store's front door chimed and Ollie pulled back with difficulty, her breathing ragged, her eyes unable to let go of Lara's.

"We're *closed,*" Lara snapped, her gaze on Ollie's, managing to find a tone that could shatter glass despite the rapid rise and fall of her chest.

The footsteps down the aisle paused.

"It's one-thirty in the afternoon," came an aggrieved voice. "The sign on the door said open."

"It's my shop, I can close whenever I damn want," Lara huffed out as Myra Jenkins' affronted face came into view.

"It's okay." Ollie jumped into action. "Can I help you?" she stepped gallantly towards the counter, Ribbonwood General Store's most helpful new employee.

· · ·

Myra stared at her suspiciously, as did Lara.

"You don't work here," the elderly lady looked over to Lara, who was conspicuously flushed and breathing fast.

"No," Ollie agreed. "I was just asking Lara to explain why she's not stocking Gabrielli olive oil," she shot the actual shopkeeper a dirty sideways look.

"I see," Myra said snippily, "as well you might. I'm just here for some baking powder if you stock such a thing," she sniffed. "Normally I'd go to Woollies but the grandchildren are coming and I'm pressed for time."

"Certainly." Ollie lifted the counter flap and headed down the aisle, mouthing a wide-eyed *help me* over her shoulder at Lara. Lara, for once, actually helped her, pointing furiously over at the next aisle.

Between the two of them Myra had her purchase rung up and Ollie followed her politely to the door where she snapped the lock after her and flipped the sign to closed. Lara watched her do it, before Ollie strode back down the store towards her.

"You're losing me business-" Lara made a last ditch pretence at protesting and Ollie just laughed at her, already reaching for her and pulling her in close.

. . .

"Are you complaining?" she raised her eyebrows.

In response Lara tugged free of her grip, grabbed her wrist and led her straight through a back door. Inside was a store room, neat shelves of dry goods, dim filtered light from a small skylight, no handy couch or any damn soft surface in sight to Ollie's brief - desperate - perusal, so she pushed Lara against the small bench top, set with tea and coffee supplies, making the cups clatter.

She took one second to look at her again, Lara's eyes full of unmistakable hunger as her head tilted up invitingly and Ollie couldn't stop her satisfied grin.

"God, you really *do* want me," she observed, melding her hips up against Lara's, watching her mouth fall open at the contact.

Lara looked up at her, her bright blue eyes clear and blazing.

"Don't make me change my mind, Ollie," she warned, then reached up to the back of her neck to pull her mouth down against her own.

Ollie felt sure from the heat of her kiss there was very little chance of that happening, but she didn't taunt her further, hungrily exploring her hot mouth, her hands moulding over the delicious curve of her spine. Lara's own hands were bolder, sliding down over Ollie's ass, squeezing it hard, making Ollie smirk against her mouth - even as she burned with desire - at how extremely clearly Lara had been lusting after her.

. . .

Her thigh pressed just enough between Lara's, making her gasp at the contact. The kiss ratcheted in heat, Ollie groaning low in her throat as Lara blatantly ground her body against her thigh. Lara straight up whimpered against her mouth and then pulled back sharply, her hands gripping Ollie's hips.

"Are you okay?" Ollie quickly checked in.

"*No.*" Lara shook her head then let it fall back a little, gasping up at the ceiling. "*Fuck.*"

"What's wrong?" Ollie didn't let go of her, worry slicing in through her lust.

"I-" Lara paused, before she lifted her head and gazed at Ollie, a little dazed. "It's been a long, long time," she admitted softly. "I swear to god," she whispered, "if you keep doing that... you won't even have to take my clothes off."

Ollie felt her body clench at her frank words, not to mention the mere thought of shedding Lara of her clothes. Incredibly, she found that for once in her life she didn't want to tease Lara Bennett, not when she finally had her exactly where she wanted her. Not when she was looking so dizzily at Ollie, her cheeks flushed, her lips still parted and her breathing tremulous. Instead, she gently slipped her hand under Lara's left thigh and pulled it up until Lara had to wrap her leg around Ollie's hips to hold herself up.

. . .

"Really?" she asked quietly, letting her hand drift down between their bodies. Her fingers traced very softly over the seam of Lara's small denim shorts and Lara stopped breathing altogether. "If I just..." she ran her fingers slowly over her, again and again, her own breath ragged as she imagined the heat and wet she could almost feel through the fabric, "I'd make you lose it," she dipped her head around to brush her lips against Lara's ear, "all over little old *me?*" She couldn't help the small tease.

Lara struggled valiantly, but she couldn't do anything but moan as Ollie kept up the gentle stroking. She dipped in to kiss her again, both of them knowing Lara Bennett's defences were completely vanquished in this moment.

Just outside the roller door behind them, came the sound of a truck crunching its gears and a repetitive beep as it began to back up.

"*Damnit,*" Lara stuttered out a disbelieving breath.

"Leave it." Ollie kept stroking her, unable to take her eyes off her flushed face or the helpless hungry quiver of her hips.

"I can't-" Lara ground out, gripping Ollie's wrist and dragging her fingers away. Her foot slipped back down to the ground. "That's my weekly supplier. I could literally go broke if I don't answer that door."

. . .

"Worth it." Ollie bit her lip. Lara shot her a look and she grinned despite herself. "Then I'll come over tonight," she soothed the thoroughly riled looking woman before her, running her fingers through Lara's silky hair, shocked that this was a thing she could suddenly do.

"That's not how life as a single mother works." Lara looked at her flatly, a slight frown starting up, leaning back a little from Ollie's touch.

"Hm," said Ollie. "Well. This is a conundrum." She pressed a hot kiss against Lara's throat, feeling as well as hearing her shaky breath. "I guess if you want this to happen you *might* just have to figure out a way."

She pulled back to see Lara looking an extremely satisfying combination of entirely desperate and thoroughly irritated. She stroked her thumb over her ridiculously perfect cheekbone, smirked at her, and then, trying not show how intensely wobbly her legs were, she left, flipping the sign back to open on her way.

It was two nights later that Audrey rang her to tell her the news that Lara Bennett had called for another bonfire that Friday night. This time, Ollie was invited.

Chapter Sixteen

Chris Knight pushed back the stack of files on his desk and sighed. Honestly, this fucking place. Silverbloom was a backwater town, a poor cousin of the crowd-pleasers, Maleny and Montville; Jesus, even Kenilworth had the bloody cheese factory. What did Silverbloom have, except for fucking cows and trees? Ten years ago he'd been working down at Maroochydore, where he'd been able to take his lunch break gazing out at the waves on any one of a handful of the most beautiful beaches across the Sunshine Coast. He was already well on his way up the ladder when he'd asked for this transfer.

It was a mistake, he could see that now. He'd made it out of a misguided sense of duty and even sentimentality. He'd grown up in Ribbonwood, for better or for worse, and after his mother's death he couldn't bear seeing his father alone. All four of his siblings were scattered across the country, none staying for more than a few days after the funeral. Chris was the oldest son, a confirmed bachelor and the one closest to home; it had seemed like he was the one with smallest sacrifice to make, all things considered.

. . .

Only Chris's dad was a grumpy old bastard. The depression he'd plunged into after his wife's death never truly retreated and frankly he hadn't been all that cheerful to be around before. Oh, Chris tried, dragging him down the pub for a beer, dropping around to try to make him eat something other than another bloody meat pie, spending agonisingly miserable Christmases trying to cheer him up. By the time he realised the futility of this endeavour, Chris felt trapped here himself by his own growing lethargy. Every time he imagined moving back to the city to revive his stalled career aspirations, his confidence sputtered. Out here in the bush, he wondered if he was de-skilling. It wasn't like there wasn't work to be done, but the level of it was... well, it was monotonous.

"Sir?"

Oh for *fuck's* sake. Chris took a steadying breath.

"Yes?" he responded shortly.

"Ah, it's just, um... I've finished the report you asked for. On the burned out car out the back of Marblewood."

"Great. File it then. Close it off."

"The thing is, sir, I think it's... important."

. . .

Chris couldn't stop his sigh. He looked up. This fucking kid. Was this really the best the police academy could produce? His boots were shined, his trousers ironed, he looked the part. Except Chris was pretty sure the kid's mother had done the work for him. The face above his neat shirt collar looked a maximum of fourteen years old. And that was despite the outsized muscles the guy had clearly worked hard on. Jesus, Chris was getting bloody old, that was half the problem.

"Spit it out then, Constable Armstrong." He gave the kid what he hoped was an encouraging gaze. Joe constantly tripped over his metaphorical feet, so pumped to be a police officer that he overcomplicated everything. Send the boy on a welfare check and he'd race back with ideas about mafia hits. Tell him to respond to a broken window report and he'd posit a theory about a potential serial killer. It was exhausting.

"The thing is, the car's registered to a Dale Winchester," Armstrong said eagerly."He's a Ribbonwood local. His mother reported him missing back in March this year."

"Good work, Constable," Chris told him. "File it."

"But... it could be ...you know, a clue?"

"Armstrong," Chris said firmly. He couldn't let this guy get carried away again. "Dale Winchester is a scumbag. If there's trouble in Ribbonwood, he's behind it. Drugs, petty theft, fights, domestic violence... the guy is a real shit. It's a wonder he found anyone willing to file a missing person's report; you'd think even his own mother would be glad to be rid of him. He probably burned his own car on the way out of town."

"I read the file," Joe told him, unfazed by Chris's jaded assessment of the situation. "We didn't do much-"

"By we, do you mean me? *I* didn't do much?"

Joe swallowed, his face going pale at his misstep.

"No. You, er, were very thorough, sir. Interviewed the mother. Interviewed the girlfriend, a Chloe Perkins of Ribbonwood. They both said they were very worried about him. That this was out of character."

"Well," said Chris. "That's women, for you, isn't it? Apparently willing to believe the best of a man, even a scumbag like Dale. I can tell you, I met the guy any number of times and it's a bloody shock to me that he found anyone to love him, but here we are."

"The thing is," Joe wouldn't shut up. "There's some inconsistencies in the girlfriend's statement. Chloe said she was worried about him, agreed with his mother that it was out of character. She said he'd disappeared two weeks prior, out of nowhere, no warning; she didn't know he'd left, just woke up one morning and he was gone. Then, when you pressed her, she admitted that they'd fought. That he'd been violent towards her, then stormed out in the middle of the afternoon. *Then,* when you pressed her for details she said he'd never once been violent before, but there are plenty of reports on file of him abusing his ex-partner *and* the girlfriend before that, so what are the chances that he changed his stripes with Chloe Perkins?"

"Joe," Chris finally interrupted the increasingly excited diatribe. "What's your fucking point? We've got a missing scumbag and a burnt out car. Believe me when I tell you that Dale Winchester is more than capable of looking after his damn self."

"His girlfriend is changing her story about the circumstances of his disappearance," Joe said. "And his mother specifically mentioned how much he loved his car. There's something sketchy here, I can feel it."

Chris took a deep breath in. He tried to remember his doctor's warning about his blood pressure. He thought of his mother's sudden death from a stroke. He thought of all the other things that happened to men his age, men he'd grown up with. Ben Wallace, dead of a heart attack at forty-one. Davo Christie, suicide at forty-eight. The bush could be a hard place for blokes, hell, not even just the old ones. He thought of his old mate Josh Rees from the high school football team, dead at just thirty-six, fuelled by desperation and alcohol, wiped out on the road. Chris had seen far too many deaths like that. He looked again at Joe Armstrong, still filled with youthful naivety and misplaced drive.

"Alright, Constable." He just barely managed not to call him *kid.* Fuck, he really was getting old. "The case is yours. Make or break time," he said, just to rev him up a little more, make him feel important. "If there's a story here, I want you to dig it up. Not a rock unturned, you hear me? But kid-" oops, that one slipped out as he paused to temper just a little of the damage he could forsee if Joe Armstrong went in, guns blazing, "-keep it on the fucking down low, you hear me? Do it, but be quiet about it. No one should see you coming."

Chapter Seventeen

Oh god, this was stupid. Lara was not enjoying this. Every thirty seconds it seemed, her head would snap around to the break in the trees to see if another guest had arrived yet. And if that guest could possibly be a dark-haired, dark-eyed woman with a kiss that blazed through her like fire, then that would be...wonderful? Terrible? Lara could not make up her damn mind. Was this fluttering feeling in her chest because she couldn't wait for Ollie to arrive or because she was far too pent up to see her face right now?

"Have you got mosquito repellent on?" she stopped her daughter as she darted past the bonfire in the early evening light, dying for a distraction.

"Yes mum," Tilly huffed. "You asked me already."

.   .   .

"Excuse me for caring if you get eaten alive." She found herself smiling at her daughter's small, pointy, affronted face.

"You treat me like a child," Tilly complained.

Lara laughed.

"You are a child?" she reminded her daughter.

"Barely," claimed the ten-year-old.

"I'm sorry." She sat back in a deck chair, tugging her daughter along with her. "Did you start paying bills at some point or something?" Tilly giggled, snuggling back in her lap, barely fitting anymore. Lara felt a pang, even as she hugged her. "Get a job perhaps? Got some wrinkles starting I haven't noticed?"

"I could get a job," Tilly started to argue. Then she gasped. "Is Rocco here?"

Lara's head snapped up. Ollie was right there, long limbs bare in the dusk, her dark hair tumbling over her shoulders from under an Akubra - like she'd ever done a day's outdoor work in her life - and looking straight up edible despite it. The very first feeling that hit her chest at the sight of her was an almost shocking warmth. *Ollie.* She was right there.

. . .

"No," Ollie said apologetically. "I left him at home guarding the grapes."

"Did you bring Aria?" Tilly demanded as compensation.

"I'm afraid it's just me." Her eyes flicked to Lara's and held her gaze for a quick beat before smiling back at Tilly.

"Oh, man." Tilly's face dropped. She slipped off Lara's lap and ran back to Frankie. Ollie laughed.

"I'm sorry to be such a letdown." She watched Lara, the smugness on her face making it clear she was confident she was anything but. Lara pulled herself out of the chair, not wanting to stare up at her from such a disadvantage. Once up though, she wasn't sure what to do with her own limbs. She clutched at her still full wineglass.

"Nice hat," she said. "Did you buy it from a high street store in Melbourne?"

"Actually," Ollie said, raising her eyebrows, "it was a gift from my parents. For my seventeenth birthday," she informed her. "I couldn't have known that decades later these things would decorate boho hipsters from coast to coast."

"It suits the whole faux-country girl aesthetic you have happening," Lara told her.

. . .

"Oh, a compliment?" Ollie pretended to let her jaw drop. "That *must* have been a hot kiss."

Lara shot her a sharp look, trying not to look around to see if anyone was in earshot while equally, trying not to let herself blush at the memory of Ollie's fingers and exactly what they'd done to her. Ollie smirked at her perfectly knowingly.

"You didn't even come with wine?" Lara looked at Ollie's empty hands for distraction. She'd barely sipped from her own glass yet, having not trusted herself not to neck it in her inexplicable nervousness this evening.

"I'm not drinking tonight," Ollie said, her tone deliberate. "I find that given a situation like this-" she waved one hand at the space between their bodies, "I like to stay in control." Lara found herself swallowing at that, her body clenching noticeably at Ollie so calmly pointing out the elephant in the back paddock. Ollie stepped a little further into her personal space. "I also don't fuck drunk women," she let her voice drop low and soft, close to Lara's right ear. "So keep that in mind."

Lara looked her in the eye. She lifted her glass and took a solid mouthful of her wine, just to prove to Ollie that she couldn't care less. Ollie seemed to see right through her, laughing, her eyes just daring Lara to keep going. Lara walked away from her. She deliberately left her wineglass next to the BBQ when she went to check in with Eva, her fingers lingering on the stem, hyper aware of the eyes on her body as she did.

. . .

When everyone was finally in attendance, she called them all to business. There wasn't much to hear - a couple of updates, a couple of questions mounting, a few details that needed work - Eva a little teary as the women all checked in, little offers of help and expressions of care. Ollie only spoke when it was her turn to update them on her own part of the plan. Lara tried not to stare at her, but those dark eyes seemed to draw her in, even as she sat well away across the fire from her, the flickering light glowing on her skin.

Everyone seemed to want to chat that night, Chloe throwing log after log on the fire like she couldn't stand the thought of leaving its warm glow, and even though Lara knew very well the reasons the younger woman needed to linger - still needed the company of other women to help her through her week - she felt her impatience like an itch. Ollie was chatting across the fire from her with Audrey, looking for all the world like she was content to bond with her old soccer team- mate for hours but her eyes flickered to Lara's enough that she knew that she too, was very, very ready to get to be alone with her.

It had been three full days since they'd kissed, five nights since their moment in the vineyard, three long weeks since Ollie had first waltzed back into her store, beautiful, infuriating, her eyes holding both a threat and a promise. Lara had finally had about enough.

She grabbed Sadie's arm.

"You know that thing where you're going to take Tilly back to yours for a sleepover?" she started, a slight edge in her tone.

175

. . .

Sadie looked at her and a grin teased the corners of her mouth.

"You need me to do that now?" she asked. "*Right* now, so that you can shove Ollie Gabrielli down onto her knees and let her do what she's obviously been dying to do to you forever?"

Ollie chose that moment to cast her dark eyes on Lara again and she sucked in a breath at the heat of her gaze.

"Yes," she gritted out to Sadie, no longer caring about avoiding her friend's teasing, far too desperate for whatever would just get them all out of her house as fast as possible.

"Oh my god," said Sadie, her eyes going wide. "Seriously? I was never entirely sure if you were maybe into women, but holy fuck if anyone on this planet needs to get properly laid, it's you. She's going to eat you *alive.*" She looked thrilled. Then she caught the expression on her best friend's face. "Okay, okay, we're going," she pretended to cower. "Hey everyone!" she suddenly yelled. "It's late. Get the fuck out of here, our host needs her home back."

There were choruses of laughs and boos, and it seemed to take about nine hours for everyone to pack up, Esme dousing the fire while Sara covered the embers with dirt, everyone else collecting beer bottles and BBQ trays, picnic rugs and beanbags, the sounds of women's laughter echoing up the paddock as they all returned to Lara's house. Handbags were collected, rubbish put in bins, benches wiped, the toilet flushing repeatedly as they all drifted out, Lara eyeballing everyone to make sure there was a sober driver to every car that left, hugging her daughter goodbye and calling instructions after her.

Chloe hung back longer, looking for a maybe non-existent jacket, while Esme tapped her foot at the door ready to drive her home. Finally, Lara pulled the still slightly emaciated woman into a hug.

"Honey," she squeezed her. "Remember that you're safe now," she pulled back to try to look her in the eye. "Okay?"

Chloe's shoulders dropped, a tear spilling.

"Okay," she said tightly. Lara waited, until she finally met her gaze. "Okay," Chloe's voice strengthened.

"Call me if you need me."

"Thank you," Chloe whispered. Esme reached out a hand and gently tugged her out the door.

"Night ladies," she said.

When Lara looked over, Ollie was standing still in her kitchen, her stupid hat on the bench top beside her, her eyes on Lara and her gaze soft.

. . .

"Lara Bennett," she said, her voice low. She crossed the room and finally, *finally* touched her, a gentle hand tucking back Lara's hair, drifting to her shoulder, then both hands curving around her hips. "I'm not sure I even understand everything it is you do for the women in this town, but I do know a damn good person when I see one." Lara swallowed at the look in her eyes. Something made her sure Ollie knew what it meant to her, that word, *good*. "God, I just...admire you so much," Ollie said softly, and by her tone, Lara actually believed her.

"It's not your admiration I need right now," she murmured, almost dizzy with need now that Ollie was this close.

Ollie looked at her for a beat. Then she pushed her, firmly, to sit astride her own dining table, pressing between her legs, her hands resting on Lara's bare thighs, her fingertips just barely an inch beneath her dress. Lara's breath caught.

"Better?" Ollie asked quietly.

Lara nodded breathlessly and just like that, Ollie was kissing her.

The night was quiet. No customers, no trucks, no child, no neighbours. The moment was finally here, just Ollie Gabrielli and a whole dark night. Lara clutched her in tight like she might disappear, but Ollie just pressed in closer, the heat of her mouth, the firmness of her hands holding Lara's head to kiss her harder.

. . .

Lara's legs wrapped around Ollie's thighs, anchoring her there, her back starting to arch. Ollie's hands slid down the curve of her spine, a little low moan of approval as she held her.

"Fuck," Ollie breathed, pulling back slightly. "I don't know where to put my hands first... you make me feel like I've literally never touched a woman in my life."

"Do you need me to get you started?" Lara bit the corner of her own smile, somehow reassured by Ollie's clear fluster. She gripped the hem of Ollie's t-shirt and pulled it up over her head. Then she stared. "Oh *god*," she whispered.

She let her hands roam up the bare olive torso she'd just revealed. Ollie's skin was warm and achingly smooth and her breasts... Lara swallowed hard as she traced a finger wonderingly over the small firm curves disappearing into a black bra. She couldn't stop staring, pushing Ollie back just enough that she could kiss the tops of them, fumbling for an excruciating second before she successfully undid her bra and pulled it down her arms.

"Oh fuck," the words fell out her mouth like a prayer, her fingers trembling at the strength of her desire as she trailed them over Ollie's bare breasts, eyes full of wonder as she cupped them.

"I so called it," Ollie's voice was a soft tease. "You're extremely gay, Lara Bennett."

. . .

"Shut up," Lara slipped her mouth around Ollie's firm nipple, gratified to hear Ollie's tease sputter out in a sharp gasp.

"Mm." Ollie pressed her body closer into Lara's mouth and Lara just about lost it, one hand spread around Ollie's firm waist, the other cupping a soft breast, her mouth teasing a hardened nipple, her thighs splayed to let Ollie in. It was already complete overload and no one was even naked yet.

With that thought in mind, with effort, she pulled back. Ollie gasped as she looked down at Lara's parted lips and hungrily dipped to kiss her mouth, the hot slide of her tongue dragging a moan from Lara's throat. She slid off the table while her legs could still function and pulled Ollie down the hall to her bedroom.

Ollie didn't stop to pay attention to how absurdly neat it was, how perfectly made the fresh bedsheets were, all the tasks Lara had found herself anxiously completing earlier that day in anticipation of exactly this moment. Instead she pushed Lara down on the edge of the bed and straddled her lap.

"Had your fill yet?" she asked, quirking an eyebrow and pressing her shoulders back just a little, those *fucking* breasts at Lara's eye level. Lara squeezed her lashes closed for just a second, unsure how exactly she was going to survive this night between Ollie Gabrielli's smug face and killer body.

. . .

"That depends," she managed, her mouth already kissing across the top of Ollie's collarbones, "on whether you've figured out what you're doing yet."

Ollie laughed, low in her throat. She pulled off Lara and pushed her slowly back up the bed before pressing her down into her pillows.

"Oh," she said, her gaze tracking down Lara's body, "I'm fairly confident I'll work it out."

She wrapped her fingers around Lara's bare ankle, bending her leg at the knee and placing kisses up the inside of her thigh as Lara's dress slipped back to her hips. Lara whimpered. Ollie let her feel the wet heat of her mouth on her skin like a promise, slow and thorough. Lara began to ache. Ollie tugged the dress up, baring Lara's underwear, her stomach, her ribs, trailing her fingers and then her kiss over every-thing she'd uncovered, making Lara dizzier with every soft brush of burning skin.

Lara arched her spine to help Ollie drag her dress up and then over her head. The dress hit the floor and Ollie leaned down on one hand to stare at her body with awe.

"*Lara,*" she whispered. "God. You're so... fucking.... *smart,*" she bit her lip.

Lara laughed.

. . .

"You can say it," she told her, shockingly turned on by the sheer hunger in Ollie's eyes.

"Say what?" Ollie raised her eyebrows, feigning ignorance, even as she traced her fingers over the bra that was barely containing her, then trailed over her underwear, her gaze drinking her in. Lara rolled her eyes against her smile and Ollie snaked one hand between her shoulder blades, barely seeming to brush against her bra-clasp before it came undone. Lara's jaw dropped at the infuriating audacity of such a move.

"Oh please-" she started, but the words died as she saw Ollie's expression as she dragged Lara's best lace bra down her arms.

"*Lara,*" she whispered again, her voice almost choked. "*Lara...*"

And then she began to move. Oh god, Lara was not prepared for this, could never be prepared for the sensation of a half-clothed Ollie Gabrielli, sliding her silky smooth body against Lara's sensitive skin, a firm hip pressing between her thighs, hot mouth tracking down her throat, all over her large breasts and then her fiercely hard nipples. The wet of her tongue, the graze of her teeth. Gasping, drowning in sensation, Lara gripped tightly to Ollie's hips, fighting the desperately aroused haze in her brain as she unbuttoned Ollie's shorts, dragging them down, needing more of her - closer - needing everything.

Ollie's thigh pressed in again and now all Lara could do was cling to her, her hips already starting to writhe, her vision wavering at the edges as the sensations took over her, making her lose her breath.

. . .

"God." Ollie was watching her face closely. "Look at you," she breathed in raggedly, "you're *so* sensitive." She let her thigh drag against the soaked lace that had once passed as Lara's underwear, seeing her whimper, "you're close already aren't you? I've barely touched you and you're almost there," her voice was low, full of wonder.

"It's so *good*," Lara whispered shakily, shocked, needy, unable to stop the slow grind of her hips.

"I have to have you," Ollie begged, hooking her finger into the waist of Lara's underwear, dragging it down her hips. "Please let me have you-"

"*Please-*" Lara gasped back. "I'm not gonna be able to- *oh god-*" her voice stuttered out as Ollie's fingers stroked over her, the very second she had her bared.

Ollie swore. Lara was so wet it was tracking down her thighs.

"*So* sexy," Ollie ground out, slipping her fingers softly, around and around in the wet heat, watching intently as Lara struggled wildly for breath, her back arching in need, unable to control her body's response to the sensations Ollie was pulling from deep inside her. It has been so, so long since Lara had been touched like this. *Had* she ever been touched like this? Not even close.

. . .

"*I can't-*" Lara gasped, already drowning, "you're going to make me-"

"I've got you," Ollie didn't stop her perfect, swirling, knowing fingers, "oh you're right there, aren't you? *Fuck* - you're so pretty and on edge. *Look at you,*" she whispered, eyes full of hunger, "don't stop yourself honey," she argued firmly against Lara's emphatic struggle. "You know I'm just going to make you come all night."

"*Ollie-*" to Lara's deeply, entirely embarrassed shock, she found herself sliding unstoppably over the edge at that, coming helplessly, deliciously - immediately - from Ollie's confident, purposeful soft strokes. "Oh my *god,*" she ground out as her hips arched, deep waves of pleasure making her tremble as every muscle she owned contracted.

"Fuck," Ollie looked on the edge herself as she watched Lara's face crumple with her sharp desperate release. "You're the sexiest fucking thing I've ever seen. *God,* Lara," her voice was almost a whimper.

Lara clung to her, pulling her down to press her face into her shoulder, struggling to regain her breath, her body pulsating with pleasure.

"I can't believe you just *did* that to me-" she accused, faintly humiliated by how desperately her body had reacted to Ollie's touch.

. . .

"Mm," Ollie rolled them both slightly, running her fingers down Lara's naked spine. "Well, you did say it had been a while," she observed. "But I'm going to have to warn you: I'm *really* good in bed."

Lara burst out a small laugh, the aftershocks flaring into deep warmth, her limbs loose, something like joy blooming in her chest.

"I've never met someone so unbearably smug all the time." She tried hard to make her voice wry, but it was immensely difficult when Ollie was almost naked and pressed half on top of her.

"Give me a break," Ollie bit her lip, her eyes glowing. "I just made the hottest woman I've ever met orgasm in well under sixty seconds. This might well be the pinnacle of my life's existence," she said, her tone dreamy. "It'll probably be written on my tombstone: Made Lara Bennett come, hard."

"*Please* stop talking." Lara gave her shoulder a little push, trying not to laugh again, before pulling her down to kiss her. Ollie licked into her mouth, pulling Lara's thigh up high around her body.

"Now that we've taken the edge off," she flickered her eyes down Lara's still trembling body, "I want to take my time. Feel free to *try* not to come again just yet," she bit her lip, her eyes full of heat and confidence.

Lara had just enough time to gasp before Ollie began to take her apart all over again.

Chapter Eighteen

"Oh *god*," Lara squeaked out as Ollie traced her tongue luxuriously over her swollen wet arousal like she was going to fucking church. There were some rare moments in life that fell completely outside of the bounds of normality and into some other plane of time altogether, like floating right off this earth and into the divine. Somehow, finding herself not only let in through spiky Lara Bennett's defences, but right here, between her splayed thighs, tasting her dripping wetness while she slowly writhed against Ollie's lips, felt far beyond what anyone should be allowed to daydream about.

Watching Lara lose it for her had been heartstoppingly good, but now, Ollie found herself hoping that she'd be able to push her further. She couldn't help but want to make Lara truly hunger for her, to see her have to fight for her release. Lara was tart and sweet and the sounds she was making made Ollie want to stay there forever. She swirled her tongue slowly, easing back in pressure, then licked her firmly, experimenting, feeling out what made Lara cry out and what let her catch her breath. And then, she simply didn't stop.

. . .

Her hand slipped up to join her desperate enjoyment of Lara's beautiful body, reaching up high to grasp the hard point of her soft full breast, listening to the moan that choked out of her as she let her fingers catch, grasp and squeeze, pinching slightly harder as Lara got slightly frantic.

Then, she let her fingers slip down into the wet heat, pulling back her mouth just enough to ask.

"Can I fuck you?" she asked, teasing Lara's hot soaked entrance with her fingertips.

"*Mmhmm,*" was all Lara managed to gasp, pressing her thighs a little wider in hungry invitation and Ollie nearly died right there of anticipation.

"You want it?" she bit her lip, enjoying the frustrated buck of Lara's hips.

"*Yes,*" the tone of her voice was as close to begging as she was pretty sure Lara would ever get. Ollie smiled. She slipped her fingers slowly inside, where Lara was burning like a wet inferno.

"*Fuck.*" She dragged her fingers back and then pushed them in firmly. Lara bucked her hips ravenously, her muscles clenching around Ollie's fingers, a moan escaping her throat. "God," Ollie gasped. "Lara, this fucking *pussy*. So sexy," she swore, fucking her slowly with her fingers.

"Please," Lara gritted out. "Your mouth-"

Ollie was pretty sure she was having an out of body experience, fingers deep inside Lara Bennett while Lara begged for her to lick her. She curled her fingers firmly and contracted hard at the cry Lara let out as her tongue slipped over her, swirling and teasing and revelling in her taste.

"Oh god," Lara was not going to be able to hold on much longer, Ollie could feel it. She smiled against Lara's pussy and eased back to tease her some more. *"Ollie!"* Lara was not having it, her hands grabbing the back of her head, fingers slipping around her jaw, pulling her in greedily. Ollie moaned in deep enjoyment. From Lara pretending not to even know her to desperately riding her mouth was too wonderful.

She pulled right back away from Lara's body, fingers sliding out, listening to her cry out in agitation.

"Be good," she warned her, enjoying the desperation in her face a little too much. Lara was too far gone to do anything but whimper helplessly. Ollie pressed Lara's thighs as far open as they'd go, moaning a little at the sight. She bit her lip and watched her own fingers push slowly inside, sitting back and watching Lara's whole body writhe in pleasure and need.

· · ·

Then she leaned in again to taste her, knowing exactly now what moves to make to bring Lara all the way to the brink. Finding the pressure that set Lara off, bucking her hips with frantic need, she didn't let go of her pace. The moan that hit her ears sounded wrenched from deep within Lara's chest. Ollie pressed and rubbed her fingers inside her tight walls until she heard Lara's breath suck in sharply and stop, and that's where she stayed.

Ollie lost track of time, focussed so deeply on her work, on the sensory overload that was Lara Bennett that it felt like both joy and loss when suddenly Lara was clenching and spasming hard around her fingers. Her back arched ferociously, her hips flexing to get more of Ollie's tongue on her, crying out at top volume. Ollie's mouth was suddenly lapping an intense amount of moisture, Lara's wetness slipping down her forearm. She licked Lara through it all, not letting up until Lara wrenched her hips back, her hand pushing at Ollie's forehead to make her stop.

"*Lara,*" the name fell from Ollie's mouth in her ecstatic shock, her lips just about spilling other words, pet names, the intimacy of the moment catching her short. "Oh my god." She sat up between Lara's trembling thighs, holding up her hand and looking at the pornographic sight of Lara's wetness dripping down all the way to her elbow. "You can *squirt?*" she breathed.

Lara's hand shot out and grabbed her firmly by the back of the neck, pulling her down on top of her flushed shivering body. She didn't stop trembling, Ollie holding her tight, letting her recover. Lara did not seem to be recovering.

· · ·

"What did you just *do* to me?" she whispered shakily, shifting her legs and gasping at the sheer amount of wetness between her thighs.

"Lara." Ollie pulled back to stare at her flushed, beautiful, extremely startled face. "If you thought I was smug before... I think I just made you *ejaculate*," she breathed in absolute wonder.

"Oh my god," Lara managed, her thighs still trembling, her breath coming in gasps. "Please tell me that's not true. You're already *so* unbearable."

Ollie laughed, tugging her up and slightly away from the absolute mess they'd just made of Lara's sheets.

"I swear to god I thought that was a myth up until about two minutes ago."

"Me too," Lara looked wide-eyed, raw and vulnerable.

Ollie cupped her face and kissed her.

"How am I going to survive you?" she murmured. "You're so hot I might die."

Lara managed a small laugh even as she shivered.

. . .

"You're not the one *squirting*," she bit her lip, shock still on her face. "Over Ollie Gabrielli of all people," she tried for a dig but her eyes were too filled with awe for it to land.

Ollie laughed out loud and in barely a second Lara was kissing her hungrily. She could feel Lara's smile against her mouth and she pulled her in harder, unable to get anywhere near enough of her, even with Lara's bare skin flush against her own and her taste on her tongue.

"I'm going to have to change my tombstone epigraph," Ollie started.

"Don't say it-" Lara tried to wrestle her into a kiss to stop the words but Ollie lifted her head just out of reach.

"Here lies Viola Gabrielli," she intoned seriously. "Once made Lara Bennett ejaculate. Officially deceased, 2024."

"I'm sorry," Lara was the one to dodge her smug kiss this time, "you only managed it *once?*"

Ollie sobered quickly.

"You're very sweet and innocent," she said darkly, "if you think you want to make dares like that with me."

. . .

They kissed for a long time. Ollie went into the kitchen and brought them in two glasses of water.

"After all," she teased Lara, "you're probably dehydrated after all that."

Lara rolled her eyes, but gulped the water gratefully.

"How long *has* it been?" Ollie asked her curiously. "Not since... not like, since your husband died, right?" Lara shot her a look from the pillow next to her. Ollie remembered belatedly that not everyone talked about death as frankly as physicians did. "Shit, sorry," she apologised. "Is that not okay to talk about?"

"It's not that," Lara said. "I just can't tell what it means that you think I might not have had sex in literally eight years. Considering this whole town seems to think I'm fucking every other woman's husband that walks by me."

Ollie slipped to lie back down in the bed, her eyes on Lara.

"I don't think either one of those things. I'm asking you, because I'm curious about you. But you can also tell me to fuck off. I'm nosy but I'm very resilient."

Lara watched her for a beat. Then she put her glass aside and also slipped back down in the bed. She rolled on her side and faced Ollie.

. . .

"It's been three years," she said. "I didn't touch anyone's husband, but I did let Nate Kerr fuck me in the back of the mechanic's shop once," she revealed, her eyes glowing slightly. "*Some* of the rumours are true."

Ollie bit her lip.

"Why does that turn me on so much?" she asked wonderingly, her fingers slowly stroking down Lara's bare arm as the image hit her mind, the intensely feminine Lara Bennett, getting thoroughly fucked surrounded in car parts and the scent of engine oil.

"Well," Lara said, "you're a sex freak, obviously."

Ollie grinned.

"Mm." She chose not to argue with that one, tonight. "Anyone else?"

"Hot labourer that was working for Sadie," Lara told her. "The year before that. He was just passing through Ribbonwood. Jacked muscles," she said and watched Ollie swallow. "Very pretty and quite dumb," she added, a smile teasing her lips. "Just how I like them. How many degrees do you have again?"

. . .

"It's just the one," Ollie said quickly. "And they let pretty much anyone into med school these days." Lara smirked at her. Ollie kissed her thoroughly. "So you wouldn't quite describe yourself as gay?" she asked as she pulled back, tracing her finger along Lara's collarbones.

"I don't know," said Lara softly. "I guess it depends how you measure it. I like men's bodies but even then I think I'm probably 70/30 in favour of women," she revealed. "And I can't imagine ever falling in love with a man." Her eyes flicked quickly to Ollie and away again. "Actual encounters aren't the only measure," she pointed out evenly. "I've been aware of women my whole life."

Ollie stroked her thumb down her cheek to the soft corner of her mouth, slightly mesmerised by hearing *Lara Bennett* talk about her feelings about lust and love. Then she stopped.

"Wait," she said. Lara waited, a knowing look in her eye. "Three and four years ago," she said, pointing at Lara. "Two hot and sweaty, semi-anonymous encounters with men. A few years before that, marriage. Anyone else in between?"

Lara smiled. She sat up, letting the sheets fall off their bodies, Ollie drinking in the sight of her nudity all over again. Then she reached over and slipped her fingers into the waistband of Ollie's underwear and slowly dragged it down her legs. Ollie swallowed, hard, as she watched Lara lean over her.

"To answer your actual question," she said, gazing down at her. "Yes. This is my first time with a woman right now."

. . .

"Lara," she breathed out. "Holy shit." Lara pressed up Ollie's knees and sat herself neatly between them. "You don't have to do anything you don't feel comfortable with-" Ollie started.

"I didn't tell you that because I'm nervous," Lara interrupted her, meeting her eyes with a glint of heat. "I told you that because you strike me as exactly the kind of smug, competitive jerk who's about to come twice as hard, just from knowing that you're the woman who got to have me first."

With that she settled in and took Ollie in her mouth. Ollie's eyes rolled back in her head in shocked desire as Lara licked her with immense sweetness. *Oh god,* she absolutely was that jerk. Flashes of the evening flooded back to her. Lara Bennett, shakily running her fingers over Ollie's breasts, her eyes wide with desire. Lara Bennett coming in three seconds flat from Ollie's soft strokes. Lara Bennett *squirting* the first time a woman went down on her. Lara Bennett, right now, her tongue buried in pussy for the first time. Ollie moaned at the sensation, Lara's mouth both hungry and delicate.

Lara drew back a little and Ollie looked down. Between her thighs, Lara lifted her eyes to meet Ollie's, her tongue slipping in to lick her as she did. Ollie gasped and she saw the satisfied smirk in Lara's eyes as she held her gaze and swirled her tongue. Ollie moaned with quickly building desperation as she watched Lara eat her out, Lara watching her right back, little hums and moans of pleasure escaping her throat as she worked. It was by far the hottest sight Ollie had ever seen in her life. Was it performative? Sure. Lara knew how damn hot she was. But as she watched Lara's eyes, burning into her with desire,

Ruby Landers

a little intermittent frown of concentration as she tugged Ollie unstoppably closer to the edge she knew Lara was absolutely getting off on getting her off.

"Oh fuck, Lara," she groaned. "Oh god yes *please*," she begged her as Lara hit a desperately good pattern, wet heat, hungry licks, little moans, blazing blue eyes. Ollie felt herself get dragged under, waves of heat rippling out through her body with every stroke of Lara's tongue. She pressed helplessly up against that pretty mouth, her head falling back as pleasure wracked her, her cry coming out like an almost sob of delight. "Oh honey," she gasped out as the spasms began to slow, "so *good*," she dragged Lara up to kiss her, tasting herself on Lara's kiss and moaning all over again. "How are you *this* good?"

"I take it back," Lara pressed her slightly slick face against Ollie's neck, both of them breathing hard, "definitely 90/10."

Ollie smiled broadly up at the ceiling, her arms encircling her old nemesis as her breathing slowly settled. The thought made her smile even wider as her post-orgasm goofiness set in.

"Can you imagine," she said softly, "if we'd known this was going to happen back when we were seventeen?"

Lara stilled. She didn't say anything, her face not moving from Ollie's neck. Ollie stroked her hair back and a second later she felt a different kind of moisture, a couple of hot tears slipping silently down onto her chest. She shifted quickly to pull Lara in and hold her tighter.

"I'm sorry," Ollie tried to backtrack. She'd hit some kind of high school era nerve and she wished she'd kept her damn mouth shut.

"No," Lara whispered. "I just wish I'd known it back then too. I was just imagining," she said, "if you had been my first. Instead of *him*."

Ollie heard the stab of anger and pain in her voice as she said the words. She kept holding Lara tight, then dropped a kiss into her hair. She wanted to bring Lara back, to banish the memories that were still clearly hurting her in the here and now.

"Just think," she murmured gently. "How cute would we have been?"

She felt a small smile against her throat. Lara's rigidity loosened a little.

"So cute," she said softly. "Your stupid little soccer outfit," she remembered.

"You'd have been into it," Ollie argued. "Sitting on the sidelines, waiting for me to score."

. . .

"Oh, so you could score *after* the game?" Lara leaned back, raising her eyebrows. Ollie grinned. "I'm not sure you remember how the 2000's worked. That sounds like a teen Netflix show from like, this year."

"That's true," Ollie kept stroking her spine. "Our version would have been a super closeted, confusing, extremely annoyed make-out session right after you'd said something mean to me in public and I couldn't take it anymore."

"Hm. Sniping at each other despite how much we want to make out. It's lucky we've grown and matured so much since high school."

Ollie laughed out loud as Lara arrived back on safe ground.

"Oh, she has *insight* now," she teased, pulling her in to kiss her.

"In my defence," Lara cocked her head, "you're also extremely annoying."

"The problem with this line of argument is that forever after I'm going to win it with just one word," she said. "*Squirting.*"

Lara's mouth dropped open. She shoved her down onto her back, pressing Ollie down with her body like they were about to wrestle. Then she bent her head and kissed her, hard.

. . .

"Mm," Ollie bit her lip, looking up at her. "That'll teach me."

Lara kissed her again and Ollie pressed her thigh up between Lara's, making her gasp. Lara's fingernails dug into her skin and desperation dragged them under all over again.

Chapter Nineteen

The flip side of having been given a whole night off to indulge herself was that by Saturday night, Lara's home was filled with the shrieks of two slightly overwrought pre-teen girls, who were now on their second consecutive night of sleepovers. Sadie was out with a Gabrielli sibling of her own and Lara was extremely sleep deprived.

"Girls!" She finally intervened when what had started out as karaoke in front of the TV had devolved into a straight up screaming competition. "Let's start to unwind can we? Come on, pick a movie, I'll make some popcorn."

Once they were settled, Lara slipped out into the still warmth of the night, making sure she was fully covered against the threat of mosquitoes. She took a glass of well-earned wine and sat on the deck with her back to the wall of her house and finally, just breathed.

. . .

Ollie had left that morning. Lara hadn't been experienced in the etiquette of one night stands with hot, female, ex-classmates, in your own home. She wondered if she should have done something cute, like made her pancakes. Ollie had seemed more than content with the coffee she'd brought her, then helped herself to a bowl of cereal - *for energy*, her eyes had glinted - before pulling Lara back down in the sheets with her until Lara could no longer remember her own name. Ollie had kissed her goodbye at the front door, Lara wearing nothing but a pair of underwear and a dazed smile, Ollie groaning as she let her hands roam, before finally slipping out the door.

It was only after she'd left, Lara drifting hazily through her morning, showering and changing the sheets they'd comprehensively ruined together, slowly trying to rebuild herself into someone's mother and not a wanton sexpot, that Lara realised all the things they'd left unsaid.

Was this a one time thing? She suspected strongly that it wasn't, not with how comprehensively Ollie had pursued her, nor with the heat of her goodbye kiss. She felt sure that neither one of them wanted to let it go after just one night. So, what then? Like... a fling? Lara thought of a whole series of nights like the one she'd just had and found she could absolutely get behind that idea. Ollie Gabrielli, hers for a couple of months, stolen moments with those elegant and extremely skilled fingers, her hot mouth and long lovely body, her warm arms.

She grinned up at the stars as she imagined herself and Sadie striking a regular babysitting deal with each other in order to accommodate their newfound Gabrielli requirements. She found herself hoping Sadie's date was going extremely well, though she was equally sure no one on this entire planet was having sex as hot as what had happened in her own bedroom last night.

She let herself do what she'd been longing to do all day, which was take a quiet moment and let her mind drift over the highlights, her teeth sinking into her lower lip. She thought of Ollie losing herself against her mouth, of Ollie's hands gripping intimately to Lara's ass while Lara rode her face, of the long tease she'd put Ollie through, trying to maintain a conversation while Lara slowly stroked her with her fingers, head propped up on her hand watching Ollie struggle not to lose it, her chest flushing, her lips parting, her breath getting short before she dissolved into shaky pleasure right before her eyes.

Lara was thirty-five years old when she learned for the first time that sex could feel like this. For all the slurs that had been cast at her - *slut, whore, home wrecker, husband-stealer, man-eater* - she felt deeply inexperienced when it came to shared pleasure. Oh, she'd had a couple of extremely hot moments in her life, all about being intensely coveted and briefly possessed, but she'd never had a whole night of someone dedicated to making her *feel* things.

There were so many things she'd missed. Lara squeezed her eyes closed, her mind spooling back through the years.

There'd been a lot of sex with Josh; sex she'd been too young to contextualise or control. Then, years of perfunctory, barely even performative sex, sex that was a duty as his wife, without much of a pretence at caring if she enjoyed it, and only just barely an option that Lara could say yes or no to, as long as she didn't say no too often. Her whole marriage had been in a grey area when it came to what was a choice and what was something she had to tolerate. For a time she'd been wracked with guilt by the very first feeling that had hit her when the policeman had knocked on her door, early on the morning her husband hadn't come home: *Oh god... I'm free.*

Her body was free, her days were free, her life was her own, all of it for the first time since her second-to-last year of *high school*. And with that, belatedly, came a huge wave of anger she'd suppressed all those years. That *motherfucker*. What had it been, about her, that had made him pick her, of all the girls in Ribbonwood? A seventeen-year-old, just a baby. Then, came the grief, for the girl she'd been, for the daughter she had, for the life that felt both only just beginning and already wasted.

From there came a long and terrible anxiety. She would never, *ever*, let someone control her like that again. She felt, fully for the first time, her own vulnerability, and in response she built up her defences. *Never* again. Lara's life would be her own.

She spent her days wrapped up in the gentle joys and frustrations of parenting a pre-schooler, delighting in Tilly's bright face and chubby limbs, the sweetness of their days together now unbroken by what had been unrelenting sulks and dark moods to carefully manage when her husband was alive. She tried to untangle the mess Josh had left - debt, mismanaged business, his collection of "vintage" sports cars he'd been "working on" that cluttered the property - and fumed as she tried to figure out how the hell they were going to survive. When the insurance money arrived one day, seemingly out of nowhere, she'd found herself sobbing, completely taken aback that somehow, somewhere in it all, Josh had thought to take care of her and their child.

. . .

And then she'd grieved him.

It was all extremely complicated. So no, in Lara's life, both during and after her marriage, there hadn't been a lot of time for pleasure. No awkward goofy teenage fooling around, no mid-twenties spent flirting in bars, no dating app hook-ups, flings or short-term relationships. She was far too wary of finding herself in another unequal power dynamic to entertain the men who pursued her and too shy, quite frankly, to pursue any women that caught her eye. Besides, there was the reputation out there to contend with: Lara Bennett, the seductive sexpot, who could suck a man's soul right through his dick.

It came in handy at times. She'd used it to lure a bad husband or two, to help out a woman who needed an out. She'd come to pick them easily, the other women in Ribbonwood who held a repressed rage and fear in their eyes that she instantly recognised. It didn't take long to push through the barriers that had initially pit them against Lara. When you scratched the surface there was too damn much they had in common.

The first time she'd done it, she'd caught sight of a heavy distinctive bruise around Jen Hungerford's wrist as she'd gingerly put down the child she was holding at the Ribbonwood kindergarten. There was a sleeping baby strapped to her chest and her eyes looked just about dead. She'd been too raw to resist the fact it was Lara Bennett, town harlot, that was offering her an ear and within minutes of walking down the street and sitting in the park together she was spilling her pain everywhere, like it was too big to finally contain in her own body.

. . .

The rest came easily. A staged seduction down at the Ribbonwood pub, Lara almost spilling out of her little dress, her giggle helpless, five foot three of pure walking temptation. The public showdown with the innocent wife who walked in, more than forty witnesses to the upstanding Tony Hungerford's uncharacteristic indiscretion. No one but Lara knew that the kids were already in the car along with everything Jen could pack from the house. No one but Lara knew that Tony had threatened her that if she left him, no one would ever believe her. He was the principal at Ribbonwood High. She was just the wife no one really knew or cared about. After all, she had no friends; Tony had made sure of that.

That night there was no one in the pub who wouldn't believe her. The refined Mr Hungerford had to be held back by almost three men while he raged at her, purple in the face, fists clenched, filthy words spat from his furious, humiliated mouth.

Jen was in Perth now, sole custody, remarried to someone kind. Tony had left town too, his teaching registration suspended after he finally had a single conviction against his name from all those years of violence. The incident had lingered on in Ribbonwood lore: Lara Bennett, the woman at the centre of a scandal.

That was how she and Sadie had finally become friends. She'd been at the pub too that night, the only person to see how meticulously the pieces had been put in place.

. . .

"So. You're a whore," she'd greeted Lara cheerfully at the bar after Jen had escaped and the police had escorted Tony to the station for glassing Chris Wiseman in the face during the fracas. There were drops of blood splattered on the bodice of Lara's dress and Sadie grinned at her broadly. "Can I buy you a beer?"

Audrey Coleman had sought her out not long after that. Her husband came from money and made her sign a prenup, grossly restricting what she'd be entitled to despite the career she'd given up, the four children she'd borne him. *There was this one clause though...* And so began a pattern. Lara had a new reputation in Ribbonwood, only amongst a few of the women: the ones on the fringes and the ones who might need a friend. Eventually, she'd brought them all together. Bonfire night. The night to remind them that none of them had to be alone. A night to make plans.

So there she was. Small town widow, single mama, shopkeeper, some form of social-worker-cum-vigilante-for-women - though Lara was starting to think she liked Ollie's take of *witch* even better - with a best friend and a community of sorts. More or less content with her life and her freedom. And then Ollie Gabrielli walked in and reminded her of everything else she was missing: heat, pleasure, want; how it felt to lose every shred of her tightly wound control while held safely in someone else's arms.

She'd gazed at Ollie lying beside her in her bed, finally exhausted. Ollie had drifted to sleep, still facing her, her long hair in a gleaming tangle down her shoulders, her lips kiss-swollen, bare to the waist above the sheets. Lara felt something crack open inside her.

. . .

"You're so fucking beautiful," she whispered as she gazed at the sleeping woman in the low light, unable to hold the words in any longer. Ollie cracked open her eyes and smiled. Lara sucked in a breath. "I thought you were asleep!" she hissed. She turned away and snapped off the lamp, letting the darkness hide the heat of her cheeks.

"I basically was," Ollie said, her voice sleepy but irritatingly amused. "I'd definitely wake up for *that* though." She gathered Lara in close and found her mouth in the dark, kissing her all over again. She wrapped her whole damn body around her, Lara's face resting on her upper chest. She inhaled the scent of Ollie's warm skin, silently revelling in the feel of the firm arms around her. It felt impossibly luxurious.

Ollie drifted back to sleep and Lara only hoped she wouldn't remember it in the morning, the tender slip-up falling from her lips in the intensity of the moment, dazed by how it felt to be held like this. *I was today years old,* Lara closed her eyes in wonder, *before I learned about this.*

Chapter Twenty

"So what's it like being back home?" Audrey asked her as the two of them strolled side-by-side up Silverbloom's main street.

Ollie found herself smiling as she realised the place felt bustling to her after Ribbonwood's sedate pace. The population of Silverbloom was something like four thousand people. Melbourne's was over five million. She'd barely been home more than a month and already she was turning back into a country girl.

"I mean," she corrected them both, "*Melbourne* is home. But it's actually really nice being back?"

Silverbloom was an extraordinarily pretty, if increasingly touristy town just up the range from Ribbonwood. There was a long wide main road, showered in purple petals from the rows of blooming Jacaranda trees shading either side of the street. Ollie looked at the shops they were passing by: independent luxury clothing brands next to a Mitre 10 hardware store that had been there her whole life, a place that seemed to only sell fancy candles, followed by a fish and chip shop and a boutique selling everything you could think of made from alpaca wool. There were all the hallmarks of a rapidly gentrifying country town.

A local busked for spare change with a beat-up guitar and a surprisingly moving cracked voice, clearly hoping for some kind of trickle down from the well-heeled tourists who crowded the streets, even on a Monday. Ollie wondered grimly if his home had been turned into an AirBnB yet as she tucked twenty bucks into his guitar case.

She'd met Audrey for brunch at a cafe that wouldn't have seemed too out of place in central Melbourne. Exposed brick walls, hipster service staff, bloody good coffee. There were a hell of a lot more tans up here though.

Audrey was one of the only school friends she'd stayed in any kind of touch with over the years. Back at Ribbonwood High the two of them had been an unstoppable duo on the soccer field, Audrey the relentless midfielder who could always boot the ball to Ollie no matter how far up the field she was. She'd set Ollie up for probably eighty percent of the goals she'd scored, the two of them colliding in sweaty boisterous celebrations as Ribbonwood won again and again and again.

It was kind of hilarious now, looking at the refined woman across from her. Auds was Chinese Australian, hair sleek, make-up meticulous, her clothes neat and feminine. She'd been a high achiever too, just pipped at the post by Ollie's competitive streak, something she'd tolerated with slight shock as Ollie suddenly cruised past her test scores at the age of fifteen. Since Ribbonwood wasn't exactly bustling with diversity, Ollie - a *wog* - had actually understood a fraction of what Audrey had experienced when her doctor parents decided on a tree-change when their only daughter was in Year Eight. The two of them were the *ethnic kids*, bonding over the experience of having their lunch box contents ridiculed daily by girls named Jessica and Sarah.

In recent years they'd almost lost track of each other altogether. It was a couple of christmases ago that Ollie had met up with her finally for a drink, Audrey hiring a babysitter for the occasion and getting flushed and teary after a single glass of wine as she deplored the sacrifice of her career for a guy whose idea of a work ethic was to have an impressive title gifted to him at his dad's company then spend all his time schmoozing younger women in the industry.

Now though, Audrey commuted three days a week into Brisbane, using the settlement from her divorce to cover a nanny. She looked incredibly content.

"Honestly, fuck men," she'd said over her eggs florentine that morning, before she met Ollie's eyes and started to laugh. "Well. I guess I'm preaching to the choir in this instance," she acknowledged.

"Only if you'd said *don't* fuck men." Ollie grinned back. A quick indecent flash of Lara Bennett naked and arching beneath her made her grin impossibly wider.

. . .

When she and Audrey hugged their goodbyes, Ollie accepted an invitation to come have dinner with her family the following week. God, it actually was nice to be here for long enough to rebuild a friendship, she reflected.

It wasn't that she didn't have friends in Melbourne. She had extremely close workmates, two old flatmates she saw regularly, an ex-girlfriend from yonks ago that had somehow become a solidly good mate. It's just that since she'd been home - no, not *home,* Ribbonwood - she'd found herself leaving their text messages on read. She'd missed a call from Sasha and two from Chelsea. She'd call them back soon, she promised herself. Life in Ribbonwood was just *busy.*

Her family could be so all consuming and she wanted to spend as much time as she could with Nonna, although the elderly lady was starting to sleep more and more during the day. Her nieces and nephews were ridiculously delightful. She wanted to soak up hours of conversation with her sister before her life got sideswiped by another small infant. And then, there was Lara.

She bit her lip as she walked. It had been barely two days since she'd dragged herself out of Lara's bed and she already wanted to be back there more than she could handle. There was a mouth-shaped bruise on her shoulder that made her smile every time she got undressed, remembering Lara straight up biting her at one point as she came desperately all over Ollie's fingers.

. . .

Ollie was a massive idiot who hadn't even thought to leave her phone number as she'd stumbled out the next day, drunk on spectacular sex and Lara Bennett's breathtaking body. She'd thought about it and overthought about it, trying not to crowd the woman or show quite how extremely her head was turned by her, before she'd decided she'd go and see her at the store tomorrow. Not too early on, she reminded herself, mentally counting the hours. Maybe early afternoon? She wondered if lunch breaks were a thing Lara took and if she could entice her back into that little store room, even for half a stolen hour for the taste of her kiss. God, she really was way too keen. Maybe she should wait until Wednesday instead?

She walked on, heading towards the farm ute she'd parked up at the top of the street when she felt the eyes on her. There under a broad sun umbrella at a table outside one of the cafes, sat Lara herself, alongside Tilly. Lara watched her approach, the faintest flush on her cheeks. Immediately, like an absolute dork, Ollie couldn't fight her wide smile.

"Hey," she said as she reached them. Lara wore a little white and navy striped t-shirt under a black pinafore smock with a touch of red lipstick that together made her look simultaneously like a slightly hip urban MILF and an impossibly young student. It was ridiculous to think she was thirty-five. Oh shit, her daughter was there; Ollie really had to stop staring at the woman. "Are you wagging school?" she asked Tilly instead.

Tilly giggled. Lara was watching Ollie back too, a look in her eyes Ollie wasn't sure she could interpret correctly. She sat, experimentally, on the edge of the picnic bench on Tilly's side and saw to her relief, Lara failing to bite back a smile. She swung her legs under the table fully and smiled back.

"It's a teacher's only day," Tilly informed her. "Mum took me shopping for new art supplies," she announced excitedly, pointing to the big brown paper bag already pulled open on the table next to her. Lara had a large half-drunk coffee and there was an empty plate of cake crumbs between them. Oh fuck she was pretty. *Stop staring Ollie.* Do *not* think about the sex.

"You're an artist?" she asked Tilly instead. Tilly's eyes got bright.

"Uh huh," she said. "I won an art competition at school. We had to paint our favourite place on earth. I was going to paint the beach but that seemed too boring, so I painted our chicken coop instead."

"Ah," Ollie grinned. "Another crazy chicken lady."

"I love them!" Tilly beamed. "They're so cute and fluffy. I know every breed there is," she boasted. "Mum pretends they're hers but they're actually mine."

"You know you say that," Lara spoke up for the first time, "and yet suddenly they're mine when it comes to cleaning out the coop."

"You're the grown up," Tilly explained with a shrug. "I just get the fun stuff. Like cuddling them."

. . .

Ollie started laughing as Lara lifted her eyes skywards, her hands around her cup.

"You've got her there," Ollie told Tilly. "Sounds about right."

"You can have Stella," Tilly said to her mother with a tone of great generosity. "She's the head chicken," she explained to Ollie. "She's really small, but she's super feisty and the boss of all the other chickens anyway."

"She sounds like the perfect chicken for you," Ollie told Lara. "Think of all you have in common."

Lara eyeballed her and Tilly giggled.

"Can I please have a macaron?" she asked, suddenly shifting track. "They've got the blue ones in again." Her eyes got huge as she stared over her mother's shoulder into the shop.

"We literally just ate vanilla slice because you said it was the only thing you'd ever wanted in your whole life," Lara told her. "Your teeth could fall out from the amount of sugar we just ate."

"I mean," Ollie interjected, "macarons are *really* little when you think about it."

. . .

Lara shot her a look of disbelief and Ollie smiled at her guilelessly. Tilly bounced a little on the seat beside her, her eyes beseeching.

"Is this because *you* want a macaron?" Lara raised her eyebrows.

"I mean not a blue one," Ollie denied. "I'm not a savage."

Tilly laughed.

"You really do have a sweet tooth," Lara shook her head at her.

Ollie bit her lip and looked at her for a beat.

"I really do."

Lara flushed extremely pink.

"*One*," she turned to her daughter to warn her, and quickly left the table to head inside the cafe.

Tilly and Ollie grinned at each other.

. . .

"I think my mum likes you," Tilly said curiously.

Ollie's eyebrows hit her hairline.

"What makes you say that?" she asked cautiously.

"She saw you coming up the street and said *oh shit*," Tilly told her. "Then she put her lipstick on."

Ollie fought extremely hard not to smile.

"Well," she said, "I am very likeable."

"Do you like chickens?" Tilly asked her, her small sharp features making her look like a little fairy tale elf.

"Is this a trick question?" Ollie asked her.

"It's an important one."

"I mean, maybe I just haven't met the *right* chickens," Ollie told her. "It's possible I could start to like them."

. . .

"I'll introduce you," Tilly decided. "Maybe we should just start with Moonbright," she mused. "She's an Orpington and very gentle."

Lara returned with a plate with three macarons on them. Tilly squeaked and grabbed the blue one.

"Thanks mum!" She bit into it, making an exaggerated happy face.

Ollie reached over to the plate and Lara quickly swiped the hot pink one from beneath her fingers.

"Uh uh," she told her, leaving her what looked like salted caramel.

"See?" Ollie told her, watching her intently as her neat white teeth sank down into the pink sugar. "You're grateful now, aren't you?" Lara pretended to ignore her. Neither of them looked away. "Just imagine," she said to Lara, "if your whole day had gone by without this."

Lara lowered her lashes. Her smile turned Ollie into liquid.

"Nice ride," Lara teased her a few minutes later as they stopped on the way up the street beside her vehicle.

"You keep thinking I'm not a country girl," Ollie rolled her eyes, looking at the beat up farm ute. "But it doesn't get more country than this."

Tilly drifted away to stare into the window of a shop filled with gleaming glass trinkets. Lara watched her for just a second, then turned abruptly to look at Ollie.

"Was the other night just a-"

"No," Ollie interjected. "Not for me. Can we do that again soon? Please?"

Lara smirked at her. She looked a little relieved.

"Wow. You're so cool, Ollie," she told her. "Honestly, anyone would think-"

"That I'm dying to fuck you again?" she whispered. Lara narrowed her eyes, but she also flushed just enough to ruin the effect. "You're crazy if you think I don't want more of that."

"I mean it was hard to tell," Lara pointed out. "After all, you just left. No follow-up plans, no conversation, I don't even have your phone number."

. . .

"In my defence, you were wearing very little at the time and my brain may have not been at its optimal level of function," Ollie told her. "Give me your phone."

Lara handed it to her.

"Uh, you need to unlock it."

Lara huffed and grabbed it back. When she handed it to Ollie again, Ollie added herself. She typed for a second and they both heard a small ping as Ollie's phone chimed from her back pocket. Lara cocked her head.

"Did you just text yourself?"

"Oh look at that!" Ollie pulled out her phone. She looked down at the message. "Lara Bennett," she frowned, tapping her chin. "Whoever she is she sounds *extremely* keen."

Lara grabbed for her own phone but Tilly arrived back at her side.

"Can we get a sun catcher?" she asked.

"What?" Lara looked down. "*No.*"

. . .

"They're really very little," Ollie started.

"Oh my god you have *no* control," Lara shot back.

Ollie just smirked at her.

"See you around, you two," she said.

"I'll tell Moonbright you're coming!" Tilly said chirpily and her mother gave her a sideways look.

Ollie watched them both in her rearview mirror as she drove away. She could not, for the life of her, stop smiling.

Chapter Twenty-One

Tilly had run into her room with her new art supplies before Lara got a second to look at her phone. She choked on her own saliva when she saw what she'd allegedly texted Ollie right there in the street.

> I want to come in your mouth again

"Oh my *god*," she said out loud in her kitchen. She gazed up at her ceiling feeling a combination of outraged, amused and extremely turned on, a feeling that she was increasingly starting to associate with Ollie Gabrielli.

> You are other level, Ollie Gabrielli

She sent an real text this time, entirely unable not to scold her.

Ollie must have been waiting, because she texted back immediately.

> Obviously. Since you're already begging me for my mouth.

Lara put her phone down. There was no way she was going to give Ollie the satisfaction. Seconds later, her phone pinged again.

> I want it too though. You riding my mouth

Lara swallowed. She stared as the little dots came up again.

> You bent over in your store room, getting fucked hard by my fingers

Her breath got short and her skin flared hot. Ollie was still typing.

> You begging me for it, unable to stop yourself

Lara gripped the edge of the bench, her teeth sinking into her bottom lip. This was stupid, this was just text messages, this was *oh fuck another message.*

> Knowing how wet you get for me

> Try not to touch yourself until I get to. I want to see you on the edge again. Desperate. So pretty.

Lara was typing on shaking fingers before she could think twice.

> Tomorrow. At the store.12pm.

Infuriatingly, Ollie didn't text her back.

———

Lara felt it like a Pavlovian response when the bell at the door to her shop chimed at precisely 11:59 the next day. Time seemed to slow as she heard Ollie click the lock and saw her hand reaching up to flip the sign to closed - those lovely elegant fingers in sharp focus - before she arrived at the front counter, her eyes dark and her lips parted.

"Reporting for service, ma'am," she said, with utmost seriousness.

. . .

Lara responded with a roll of her eyes, hoping to cover for the fact that she already knew how wet she was from the sheer anticipation alone. Three years she'd gone without sex and yet three *days* without this had been too long. Ollie didn't hesitate for even a second, lifting the counter top and stepping through to grab Lara's wrist and pull her urgently into the store room behind her. Lara tried, as hard as she fucking could, not to literally swoon.

When Ollie turned to look at her, her eyes were blazing. Without waiting for a second to kiss her hello, she tugged Lara's t-shirt right up to her collarbones and shoved down the cup of her bra, her hot mouth encasing her nipple.

Lara gasped in absolute shock. Ollie walked her backward until Lara's back hit a shelf, anchoring her there with her body. Her hand slipped down the back of Lara's skirt to grip tightly to her ass as she licked and bit her nipple and Lara groaned, her knees turning instantly to jelly.

"*Ollie,*" she gasped, her fingers slipping under Ollie's shirt to scratch at her skin, not one chance of disguising how badly she wanted this.

Ollie's hand slipped boldly down the back of her underwear, squeezing her bare cheek, teasing down the cleft of her ass and making her shiver. She slipped down even further, learning immediately exactly how wet Lara was for her. Ollie took a sharp breath against her breast at the discovery.

. . .

"You need it, huh?" she sounded far too victorious for Lara's liking. Lara opened her mouth to snap back but she had *nothing*.

Ollie pulled her hand back and sunk to her knees, jerking Lara's skirt up around her hips and tugging underwear down her thighs. She paused to look up at Lara's face and to Lara's agitation *smirked* at what she saw there before she pressed right in to taste her.

"Oh-" Lara cried out. Ollie had been in the store for less than a minute and she was already exquisitely working Lara up with her tongue. Lara, to her intense surprise, found that Ollie had intuited quite correctly that she didn't need the foreplay, that the foreplay had happened already with Ollie's dirty texts, her leaving Lara hanging as if she *might* just not come in today, with the sheer urgency of her need to touch her.

Ollie used her whole mouth - lips, tongue, chin - so hungry for her that Lara's legs trembled. She wasn't rough - just the opposite - every movement thorough but precise, swirling the way she'd learned so quickly made Lara crumble. Lara's hips began to buck reflexively and Ollie used her hands to pin her tightly, not letting her move. She cried out in frustration and Ollie took over full control, swirling her higher, then higher, then impossibly higher as the sensations began to build. Lara could smell her own arousal, sex in the air, Ollie moaning as she licked her, not a fraction harder, keeping her at a desperate precipice, Lara agonised by the heat of it. She wasn't coping, she *couldn't* take this, she-

. . .

"*Oh god-*" Lara spasmed, then spasmed again, the thought hitting her that Ollie hadn't put her fingers inside her, that the orgasm purely from Ollie's mouth was so different, that it was earth-shatteringly good, that she'd *never* come from this before her, but- "*oh god, Ollie!*" Lara felt herself contract then shatter into a million tiny pieces before she melted right off the face of the earth, her mouth wide open like she'd never catch her breath again.

"Mm," Ollie leaned back on her heels and wiped her mouth with the back of her hand. "Good girl," she said her eyes dark and Lara heard herself whimper. Ollie got back on her feet, leaned in and kissed her, her mouth soft and tender and Lara was *not* okay.

"Oh my god." Lara shoved at Ollie's hip, even as she grabbed her in closer, her voice slightly dazed even to her own ears. "What the fuck, Ollie?"

"We don't have much time," Ollie bit her lip. "Can I make out with you while you recover?"

Lara's mouth fell open but she was already nodding. Yes. Yes please. Ollie kissed her for a long sweet minute, before her tongue slipped hotly in her mouth, tasting like pussy, her fingers becoming firm on Lara's jaw, possessing her easily.

Lara reached for Ollie's fly and quickly unbuttoned her, Ollie's shorts slipping down her legs, tugging her underwear after it. Ollie pulled back and in a quick motion had stepped out of everything, bare footed, long smooth legs. She looked at Lara's face then tugged her own shirt over her head and undid her bra.

Lara stared at her, a moan escaping. Ollie was entirely naked, right there in her store room in the middle of the damn day. Suddenly, needing to feel everything, she stripped off her t-shirt and stepped out of her shoes, Ollie tugging Lara's skirt down urgently as Lara practically ripped off her own bra.

"Oh *this* is good," Ollie pulled her in, burning hot skin against burning hot skin. She was so silky and soft Lara shivered, the two of them pressing in against each other, Ollie already starting to writhe. Then an incredibly wicked grin hit her face and she stepped back, spinning Lara and pushing her down firmly against the little kitchen bench, her torso and breasts against the cold stainless steel, her gasp short and hard. "Okay, honey?" Ollie paused briefly to check. Lara nodded, wanting all of it, whatever Ollie had for her, already hungering like she'd never hungered before. "Good, cos I *really* need to fuck you now."

Ollie tugged her hips back and pushed her fingers in from behind, Lara crying out in desperate heat at the sensation. Ollie paused.

"*More,*" Lara choked out.

Ollie made a sound like an almost hiss, then Lara found herself thoroughly filled with Ollie's fingers, fucking her firmly, one hand grasping around her breast, squeezing, catching her nipple roughly between her thumb and first finger and making her cry out in pained pleasure.

. . .

"You okay with this?" Ollie checked in one more time and Lara contracted around her fingers. This sweetness combined with roughness was going to blow her damn mind.

"*Yes.*" Her voice was almost a whine, unrecognisable to herself. Ollie took a half step sideways, her thighs straddling Lara's. Then Lara felt her press up against the curve of her ass cheek and start to grind. A moan of white hot hunger escaped her as she felt Ollie's heat and wetness against her ass, Ollie's hips rolling to chase her own pleasure as she fucked Lara with her fingers. Lara used one hand to just barely manage to hold herself up while her other snaked around behind them to grab at the back of Ollie's thigh, pressing her ass back against her. "*Fuck me,*" she demanded. Ollie gasped, her hips flexing harder.

Lara could barely breathe from all the sensation: Ollie's hot smooth body, the heat of Ollie's desire as she ground up against her, her long lovely fingers thrusting, the firm grip on her nipple. She was dying of heat and frustration in equal measures, nothing touching her clit, every other part of her stimulated to an inch of her life. She writhed and bucked, wriggled and moaned, wildly turned on, frantically tortured. She could hear Ollie's breath getting harder, suddenly extremely grateful for her years of athleticism as Ollie thrust her fingers into her and rode her at the same time. God those fingers, oh *fuck,* her nipple. The pain was sharp and delicious and Ollie wasn't letting up.

"*Please.*" She finally couldn't take it anymore. "Touch me."

. . .

Ollie's fingers seemed to press deeper inside her, hitting new sensations and she cried out.

"No," Ollie said.

Lara's eyes flew open.

"But... I need it-"

"I know," Ollie said simply. And with that she kept going, fingers buried inside her, sharp pressure on her nipple, hungry thrusts against her ass. Refusing to give Lara what she needed, keeping her so close to perfect pleasure, but not resolving the torment.

"*Ollie,*" she gasped. She was not coping, she needed this-

"I like you too much like this," Ollie ground out. "You're so hot when you don't get what you want. I can feel how much you need it," she panted. "You're *dripping* wet."

Lara could do nothing but moan. She'd never felt desperation like this. She let go of Ollie's thigh, determined to relieve the pressure herself but Ollie pushed her in harder against the bench stopping her hand from reaching its destination. The edge of the bench was hard against her torso, her hips trapped between Ollie and the firm surface.

· · ·

"I don't think so," Ollie stopped her. "I think you might just have to do it without any touch at all."

"I *can't*-" Lara was so pent up she was almost sobbing. "Please-"

"I know..." Ollie's voice got low and sympathetic even as she ground herself harder against her ass. "You can't come, can you honey? It's making you so wild."

"Do you want me to beg?" she managed, not one care left for her own dignity, her body burning like a fire.

"Oh, I'd love to hear you beg," Ollie said, her voice tight, "it won't help you though. You're just going to have to get through this aren't you, baby?"

Something in Lara snapped. Ollie's clear arousal at edging Lara within an inch of her life, the easy dominance, the rough treatment, the softness of Ollie's little endearments - *honey, baby* - accompanied by an even sharper squeeze on her nipple and suddenly her whole body clenched on the fingers wedged deep inside her, intense pleasure rippling out from her nipple to her clit as sure as if she'd been touched there. Lara came *apart*, her cry almost panicked with the shock of the release as she felt Ollie's hips jerk furiously against her, heard Ollie's cry join hers, both of them crumpling into each other with the intensity of the shared orgasm.

. . .

Lara went limp, her head falling on her arm against the bench, gasping as Ollie dragged her fingers out. She could hear Ollie breath roughly behind her. Then, Ollie pulled her up, gathered her into her arms and held her against her body, dropping a soft kiss against her shoulder.

"Are you okay?" her voice was gentle.

Lara was momentarily lost for words.

"You're a... *terrible* person," she managed, even as her hands came up to encircle Ollie's waist. Ollie pulled back to search her eyes. Whatever she saw in them made her smile.

"Made you come pretty hard though," she pointed out. Lara couldn't argue with that. Ollie's face got serious. "There's this dynamic here," she pointed between them, "that I can't help but find seriously hot." Lara watched her face. She couldn't argue with that either. "But I never want to push you somewhere you don't want to go."

Lara felt her knees get weak all over again.

"I wanted that," she assured her. "I mean, it was *torture*," she amended. "But I liked it."

Ollie looked relieved.

· · ·

"I just don't want you to think you have to be up for anything," she said cautiously. "Hot girl pressure to take whatever's dished out. Because believe me, I'll be thrilled just to get to touch you in any way at all."

Lara bit her lip.

"God," she said. "How are you so nasty and so sweet at the same time?" She shook her head. She said it like she was teasing, like the word *sweet* was a taunt, but she really meant it. Men had tried getting a little rough with her before, but not one of them had made her feel safe enough to enjoy it. She gazed at Ollie, her voice dropping low. "If there's one thing you should know about me it's that I don't take *anything* I don't want to take. Not anymore."

"Okay," Ollie slipped a lock of Lara's hair softly behind her ear. Lara felt the touch all the way through her. "Good."

"Do you want a safe word?"

Ollie's eyes went wide. She chewed her bottom lip.

"Are you saying you might want to get a little *more* dirty with me?" she clarified quietly.

Lara couldn't help her smile at the hopefulness Ollie was trying very hard to hide.

. . .

"I'm saying," she leaned up to kiss her mouth, "that I'm into you." She swallowed. Oh god, that was slightly more truthful than she'd intended. "I'm into this," she amended. "I'm kind of struggling to think of anything I might not enjoy taking from you if you want to dish it out."

"Lara," Ollie's voice was low. "If you're trying to make me come right now without even touching me-" Lara felt a small laugh fall out her mouth at Ollie's seriousness. "I'm just saying it's working."

"So a safe word." Lara watched Ollie's dark eyes flare. "Probably should be something really unsexy. Something you know I'd never say in the heat of the moment." She pretended to think. "Soccer," she said decisively.

Ollie's jaw dropped.

"Oh," she said darkly, "I'm going to find a way to make you take that back. It's just been so long since you've seen me getting hot and sweaty and winning all the time that you've forgotten how good it is."

Lara leaned back.

"Hot and sweaty and winning all the time. Isn't that *exactly* what I just witnessed?"

Chapter Twenty-Two

Ollie was on cloud damn nine. Higher than that; cloud nine hundred. On Friday, Lara had invited her over, her daughter away on a sleepover. She'd pulled Ollie instantly through the door to kiss her hotly, the two of them tumbling through the living room as frantic as teenagers. They'd barely even made it to the bedroom before they'd crossed the line from fooling around to something far hotter, Lara gasping into her mouth as Ollie's hand slipped up beneath her dress. The night had passed in a heady blaze, the heat ratcheting between them now they were learning each other's desires and *oh my god* were they ever complementary.

"You're actually evil," Lara gasped out, her whole body flushed and trembling after Ollie had withheld her orgasm from her so long she'd become nothing short of frantic.

Ollie laughed even as she dripped with desire from how hot Lara had looked as she'd finally, utterly lost control.

. . .

"I told you I could make you come like that again," she beamed triumphantly. "Oh god," her thighs slipped and slid between Lara's as she straddled her, "oh my *god-*"

"You like saying no to me far too much," Lara's breath was still short as she pulled her down on top of her, Ollie starting a slow grind of her hips against her intensely slippery thigh, even as Lara listed off her complaints. "You like to deny me," Ollie kissed her throat, "push me too far-"

"Mmhm," Ollie started to see sparks, "god yes."

"Make me beg," Lara let her voice get soft, gazing up at her as Ollie ground faster, "fuck me without letting me come. Drive me crazy, work me up-"

"Can't help it, looks so good on you-" she gasped.

"You like watching me hunger for it," Lara whispered, fingers slipping between them, giving Ollie something to grind upon, "knowing you could give it to me any time you wanted, but you just want to push a little longer, make me wetter, make me lose my fucking mind-"

Ollie squeezed her eyes closed, not remotely coping with the first time Lara was the one to dirty talk.

. . .

"You're just so pretty when you're desperate-" she ground out. "Oh *fuck-*" she threw back her head, hips thrusting and Lara watched her intently, teeth sinking into her lower lip as Ollie came sharply, back arching, shuddering in pleasure, unsure whose wetness was whose anymore.

"I'm not the only one who's hot when they lose control," Lara murmured against Ollie's earlobe. "I like to watch you lose it over me."

She pulled Ollie down to kiss her as she writhed with aftershocks. Honestly, this much Lara Bennett should come with a warning; how was she supposed to cope when Lara looked at her that way?

The sun was almost up before anyone had gotten a wink of sleep.

They'd eaten pancakes in the kitchen late in the morning, Ollie tugging off Lara's singlet to drip maple syrup over her bare nipples, Lara shrieking and struggling and laughing, and then losing her breath, then her underwear. Ollie thought of the spiky defensive woman she'd seen the first time she'd met Lara as an adult and wanted to *die* with how she looked, bare skinned and glowing, her cheeks flushed with laughter.

"You're something else," Ollie pulled her into her lap where they'd tumbled onto the kitchen floor. She kissed her and kissed her. "What am I going to do with you, Lara Bennett?"

. . .

Cloud nine thousand and nine.

———

On Sunday, just before midday, Ollie sat out in the shade of the deck umbrella with a coffee, sun blazing overhead, Nico beside her, his feet up on the deck rail.

"How's things with Lara?" he asked her, a solid smirk in his voice.

"None of your business," she tried not to smile. "How's things with Sadie?"

Nico was silent for a long moment.

"Mate," he finally said, "she's fucking incredible."

Ollie turned her head and looked at him. Nico was looking away over the grapes but there was a slightly dazed grin on his face. She couldn't remember him looking like that ever before.

"Is she just?"

"She's coming to family dinner again tonight," he told her. "Thought you might want to know, just in case you want to embarrass yourself a second time making eyes at her best friend all night."

Ollie breathed in at that. It had been one thing to invite Lara over before they'd ever hooked up. It was a whole other thing to bring her to family dinner now *something* was happening between them. She was pretty sure Lara would think so too.

She could imagine Nico with his wide goofy grin, holding hands with Sadie at the table, clearly intent on letting everyone know they were a *thing*. She felt a flash of jealousy. She and Lara had a time limit hanging over them. She was trying to avoid thinking about it but the idea Nico might be settling into something real while Lara was only ever going to be hers until Summer... the thought stuck like a barb in her throat.

And yet, despite it all, Ollie found she wanted her there anyway. She wanted the sweetness of Lara being all cute and uncharacteristically polite for her parents, Tilly jumping up and down to see Rocco, Lara with a glass of wine in her hand looking beautiful and relaxed. If they were only going to be together for a little while, shouldn't they get to enjoy every moment that they could?

She wandered indoors.

"Hey mama," Ollie said as she found her already doing early meal prep for dinner.

. . .

"Hi darling." Her mother looked up. "Ah good, can you dice the pumpkin for me?"

Ollie got to work.

"You know how I asked you to give Lara a chance the other week?" she started. Her mother lifted her head.

"I'm not afraid to say I was wrong, Viola," she said firmly. "This town is full of terrible gossip and everything Pia said about what happened was true. That Lara Bennett, she's an absolute darling - such an angel - and her little girl-" her mother clutched her chest "-just beautiful."

Ollie smiled. She'd been hearing various repetitions of this for a fortnight.

"I mean an angel might be pushing it," she said, trying not to smirk, "but I like her. A lot."

"Well, I figured the sleepovers at her house made that quite clear." Her mother narrowed her eyes.

Ollie quickly dropped her gaze to the cutting board. Even now she was thirty-five years old her mother's view on her children having extramarital sex was not exactly glowing.

. . .

"It's just...tricky," she tried to explain it, "with the fact that, you know...come December, I'm going back to Melbourne."

"Are you sure, Ollie?" Her mother stopped dicing, putting her knife down to turn and examine her face.

Ollie was startled. She'd lived in Melbourne almost longer than she'd lived in Ribbonwood now. It wasn't even a *discussion*. Melbourne held her entire adult life, her friendships, her career, her deeply loved little townhouse, her...job. Ollie swallowed, a slight tremor returning to her fingers. She felt a little winded. Ribbonwood had always been a place she'd fled from; never once had it felt like a place she might want to escape *to*. Ollie made a mental note to get around to calling the damn therapist Cherie had referred her to, ASAP.

"Yes, Ma, of course I'm sure. Jesus."

"Hmm," was her mother's only comment. Ollie shook her head, knowing better than to give the woman an inch in this conversation. Quickly, she got them both back to the matter at hand before this thing could spiral any place Ollie did not want to go.

"Would it be okay if I invited Lara to dinner again tonight?" she asked, avoiding her mother's overt stare.

"Because you like her, even though you're going to drop her like a hot potato in a couple of months?" her mother clarified.

. . .

240

"No!" She was flabbergasted. "It's mutual, mum, she knows the deal." While they hadn't discussed it in depth, Lara had said as much, when she'd invited Ollie over on Friday. *It's not because I can't wait to see you or anything like that,* her text had read, *I just figure I should use you for everything I can get until you leave again.* Ollie had seen through the snark and known Lara absolutely couldn't wait to see her. At the same time it had been good to know their understanding was matched.

"Well," her mother said with a small frown, "I can't begin to understand what you think you're doing, but Lara Bennett is welcome here anytime. Besides, I've got that new nesting material with the flower petals in it and I want to know if she's tried it."

"No mealworms." She pointed at her mother.

"Ollie, they're-"

"Absolutely not!"

She'd finished dicing the pumpkin and walked away to text Lara.

> If this is too weird just say so...but come to Sunday dinner again tonight? Sadie will be here. And I want to fill you up with wine and make out with you this time.

Lara texted back a full hour later. Ollie wasn't sure whether to read into that.

> What does your mother say?

Ollie smiled. Lara and her damn mother.

> That I'm a deep disappointment to her as a daughter since I'm still going back to Melbourne in December but she very much likes your extremely pretty face and wants to talk your ear off about chickens.

There was another pause. Ten minutes went by before the response came through.

> As long as you don't try to sit next me or anything, Ollie Gabrielli.

Ollie's mouth twitched into a smile. She tried not to think too hard about just how much she couldn't wait to see Lara again.

Chapter Twenty-Three

Ollie and Nico seemed to be in some kind of a competition to out-casual each other as they both just happened to be lounging near the front of the deck as the sun began to sink. No one's ears were pricked for the sound of car tyres in the drive, so no one jumped to their feet when the dogs started to bark.

"That's probably them," Nico stretched.

"Probably," Ollie shrugged.

"Better stop dad bothering them I s'pose." Somehow he was already moving.

"Guess so." She was already on his heels.

· · ·

Nico wore an actual shirt with a collar for once and he smelled like fresh-scented surprisingly tasteful man spray instead of his usual sweat and sunshine. Ollie would have loved to have mocked him, except for how she too had washed her hair and applied her favourite scented moisturiser.

"Get away!" Their dad was already shooing the dogs off as the car doors opened.

"*Rocco!*" Frankie tumbled out to throw herself at the enthusiastic dachshund, Tilly practically landing on top of them.

Lara slid from the passenger door. God, for a relatively small woman she really managed to have an incredible pair of legs on her. She had that look on her face again, slightly and uncharacteristically shy, as she cast her eyes quickly from Ollie to Ollie's dad. Ollie watched as he greeted her warmly again. She barely registered Nico steal a kiss from Sadie while their dad's back was turned, though she did manage to catch Sadie swot him and hiss *get off me* with a smile.

"Hey." Ollie pulled Lara in next, Lara sucking in a slight breath as she smoothed over the awkwardness by repeating the same greeting, kissing both of her cheeks. Lara flicked her eyes up to her, knowing full well the gesture came with a lot less innocence.

"Hi," Lara said back. God it was hard not to actually kiss her.

. . .

She'd been right; Nico absolutely tried to hold Sadie's hand as they all trooped up the steps. She shook him off though and Ollie's mum forwent the formal greeting to hug her tightly, before she did the same to Lara. Ollie's date looked both startled and relieved at the extra warm treatment, a faint pink to her cheeks.

"Can I help?" Lara once again offered, looking towards the kitchen.

"No," Ollie and her mother spoke in unison and Lara smiled, letting Ollie take her by the hand and tow her out the door to pour her a glass of wine.

Matty caught her eye as they arrived out on the verandah and Ollie held her breath just slightly, his words still ringing fresh in her mind. *You should stay away from her. Lara Bennett is dangerous.* He'd given Ollie a short meaningful stare when she'd told him, very casually, that Lara was coming for dinner again tonight. She shouldn't have worried though; Matty took his hosting duties seriously. Anyone who hadn't been out at the grapevines with the three of them would have had no idea at his reservations as he grinned and kissed Lara's cheeks, immediately followed by his wife who smiled and squeezed both her arms like an old friend.

They all sat around the table, Nico slinging his arm around the back of Sadie's chair. She shot him an *I can't believe you* look, but her eyes were shining. Ollie sat next to Lara, her fingers squeezing her knee under the table. Lara quickly prised her fingers off and Ollie grinned to herself.

. . .

"Sadie." Matty fixed her with an earnest stare. "I gotta say, I mean - I just need to put this on the record now so in future when you start complaining about him at family dinners years down the line you can't say no one warned you: you're too good for him."

Nico flushed and Sadie laughed. Everyone around the table grinned at them. It was quite clear this was Matty's version of a stamp of approval.

"I told her that too," Nico leaned back smugly in his chair, ready to take it.

"I mean, to be clear, so did I," Sadie said wryly but as everyone laughed she let Nico finally take her hand and this time didn't let it go.

Ollie found Lara's knee again, making her fingers soft - just a tease - and Lara gripped them gently before pushing them firmly away. Neither one of them wanted the scrutiny Nico and Sadie were under, considering the basic facts of their arrangement. Sex... then an end date.

Dinner was served and everyone ate heartily. Everyone except Nonna, who only picked listlessly at it. Ollie tried not to focus on it; it was all part of the process. She'd taken her grandmother to her most recent palliative care appointment where they'd upped her pain medications. Nonna was comfortable. She was part of family dinner. It was all they could hope for. She felt Lara squeeze her knee gently under the table and realised her worried gaze must have been obvious. Her eyes flicked sideways to Lara and found herself catching her breath. Goddamnit, she was so beautiful, Ollie also experienced it as pain. Lara ignored her stare but her hand didn't leave her knee this time.

By the time dinner was over and dessert demolished, Nonna tucked up in her bed, and the kids indoors, excitedly bouncing on the couches, Ollie was determined to steal a moment with Lara. She'd been glowing with prettiness all evening, holding her own amongst the family's teasing and chatter, speaking with apparent passion to Ollie's mother across the corner of the table about the merits of blue and green-egg laying chickens and Ollie was *dying*.

She thought of Lara's solid talent for sass, her sharp edges and steely defences. She thought of Lara's power as she secretly ran rings around this town, of her holding court and busting bad men's kneecaps at bonfire night, of her wry warmth as a mother. And she thought of her naked, panting, shivering out her release with those blue eyes hungrily fixed on Ollie's face.

Fuck. Ollie sucked in a breath. Was she in over her head here?

At first Lara had been a sexy challenge; then she'd been a puzzle to unlock. Once Ollie had figured out the key, Lara had been a deep dive into desperately delicious pleasure. But Lara Bennett at family dinner made her chest ache as well as her teeth. Perhaps this hadn't exactly been her best idea.

· · ·

It would be okay, she told herself. After all, they both knew what this was. For a second she thought of discussing some clearer - firmer - parameters with Lara. It's what she'd want to do if she was in a casual situation with anyone else. But Ollie couldn't bring herself to want to pull this back, make it *just sex* and cut out all the sweetness. Not only did she like seeing all the different facets of Lara, but she also would never do it to *her*.

Lara Bennett had been treated like sex was all she was good for, for her whole damn life. Lara Bennett deserved family dinner and laughter on the kitchen floor and coffees out with her daughter and Ollie could *handle* this. She could deal with the happy kind of sadness that would be a short-term romance. She imagined kissing Lara goodbye longingly at the airport, both of them changed for the better, Lara maybe even whispering sultrily into her ear, *see you at Christmas,* before she sauntered away at the airport gate. It was doable.

"Want to come for a walk with me?" Ollie murmured as everyone started to drift into separate conversations. Lara met her eyes.

"Okay," she agreed, a small flicker of desire clear in her gaze.

They both got to their feet.

"Lara!" Frankie suddenly appeared. Her eyes were wide.

"What's wrong?"

. . .

"Can you come? Tilly won't come out of the bathroom."

Lara shot Ollie a look. She followed Frankie into the house and Ollie hesitated. This seemed like a mum thing. Lara was gone for what felt like a long time. When she reappeared she was pale.

"Is everything okay?" Ollie asked, worry spiking through her.

Lara pulled her aside.

"Tilly just got her period," she said, her voice stiff.

"Oh," Ollie was relieved. "Is she okay?" She looked a little more closely at Lara. "Are *you* okay?"

Lara looked at her distractedly. She looked straight up sick.

"Ollie. She's ten years old."

"That's okay," Ollie told her. "It's very much within the range of normal."

. . .

"She's just a baby." Lara looked like she was cracking. "She's way too young. She's not ready for this... she's a *child*."

Suddenly, Ollie got it.

"She's still a child," she reassured her. "This doesn't change that, not at all. Listen, I'm going to drive you both home, okay?"

Lara looked quickly over to where Sadie and Nico were sitting, in a bubble together, laughing as she shoved him in the ribs. She nodded.

Ollie made excuses for them.

"Lara's got a headache," she told her family. She saw Sadie clock Lara's pale face and frown before she got up and followed her back into the house. When they all emerged at the front door together Ollie could hear a soft murmur of voices, Lara's arm wrapped around Tilly, Sadie's arm wrapped around Lara. Tilly looked faintly startled but not obviously distressed.

Ollie started up the old farm ute, Sadie and Frankie standing by to wave goodbye. She waited until Tilly was strapped in the back seat, Lara rigid in the passenger seat beside her, then she started down the long drive, headlights picking out thousands of moths in the dark.

"Did you tell her?" Tilly asked uncomfortably from the back as the ute bumped out the gate.

.   .   .

"Yeah, honey," her mother said. "It's not something to be ashamed of."

Ollie could hear the extreme discomfort belying Lara's calm words and she knew Tilly could too.

"I'm probably going to get mine in the next day or two," she told Tilly lightly. "I know because suddenly I want to eat all the chocolate in the world."

Tilly looked up in the rearview mirror.

"Why do you want to eat chocolate?" She sounded confused.

"Honestly, I have no idea. Hormones probably," she told her. "It's a whole thing. You start to get used to it after a while and then, you just *eat all the chocolate.*"

Tilly laughed. Then she was silent.

"You okay, honey?" Lara managed.

"No one else has their period yet," she said shortly. "I thought that was a thing that happened when you were a teenager."

. . .

Lara tensed up even further in the seat beside her. She was silent. Ollie opened her mouth.

"No," she said, "the average age is twelve. But any time from nine is completely normal."

"How do you know this stuff?" Tilly sounded suspicious.

"Oh, I'm a kids' doctor," she told her. Lara glanced at her in surprise. They'd really never talked about her work.

"*Oh.*" Tilly sounded surprisingly reassured by this. "So you would like... know."

"Sure do. You're one thousand per cent normal," Ollie reiterated. "And I'll bet you're not the only one in your class either. People just get weird talking about this stuff which is super silly, because most of the girls and women you know will *all* get periods for about half of their lives."

"It's gross," Tilly said flatly.

"It's not honey," Lara told her, her voice so calm she sounded almost automated. "It's totally fine."

. . .

"Oh *you* think it's gross?" Ollie tapped the brakes as they hit the bend she knew the roos hung out at. "Kid, you have no idea! You live in the golden age of period pants. When your mum and I were young we had to have these weird creepy pads jammed down our knickers. It was like walking around with a whole pillow under your bum."

Tilly laughed.

"What are period pants?"

Ollie looked at her watch.

"Want to take a quick trip to Woollies?" she asked. "Bet you didn't think you'd get to go buy a whole bunch of treats tonight since your mum's going to be all soft and easy while she's freaking out."

Lara glared at her but the smallest of smiles finally slipped out.

"You *are* freaking out," Tilly said, her voice both teasing and wildly unsure.

"Sorry sweetheart," Lara said, her voice somewhere approaching normal. "It's a me thing, not a you thing. You know how I get when I think you're getting all big. You're still my *baby*." She made her voice soft and a little sing-songy.

"*Ugh*," Tilly groaned. "You're so embarrassing."

. . .

Lara actually smiled at that.

Ollie grabbed a trolley and they sped through Silverbloom Woolworths together, just before it closed. They grabbed a bunch of small-sized period pants, Ollie making a point of throwing them at Tilly and making her laugh. She remembered the hushed, embarrassing experience of buying tampons for the first time with her mum and was determined that in 2024, that should not be a thing. Then the three of them hit the sweets aisle.

"Can I have *everything* I want mum?" Tilly slyly - and immediately - ruined it for herself, but by the time they hit the register there was still a solid stash of junk food on the conveyor belt.

"I'm sorry, aren't you a doctor?" Lara raised her eyebrows. "Shouldn't you be encouraging healthier choices or something?"

Ollie smirked at her.

"Everything in moderation," she intoned. And then she shrugged. "Mental health is important too." She nodded towards the Caramilk Kit-Kat Tilly had coveted. "I'll write a prescription for that tonight if it makes you feel better."

It was just over a half an hour's drive back to Lara's and on the way home no one seemed too fussed to talk much more about periods while Tilly munched on her sugary snack contentedly. When they arrived at the house, Ollie walked up to the front door with them. She hesitated, honestly just wanting to sneak a quick goodnight kiss, not wanting to outstay her welcome on a big mother-daughter night, but Lara held the door open for her as if it was a given she was coming in.

"Movie and a sugar coma?" she invited. "After all you're responsible for most of this." She lifted the grocery bag in her hand.

They vegged out together, Tilly between them on the couch. She had a hot water bottle and some ibuprofen, and between the chocolate and the Disney channel seemed all the way back to cheerful.

"Alright honey," Lara snapped off the TV as the movie ended, "bedtime. Go brush your teeth before they all fall out."

Tilly rolled her eyes but mooched off to the bathroom.

"I can head off now," Ollie said to Lara as she went to follow Tilly down the hall, "if you want."

Lara looked at her for a beat.

"I don't want," she said softly. "But if you need to-"

"I'll be here," Ollie cut her off.

. . .

Lara nodded.

When she returned about half an hour later, Ollie had raided her kitchen and found an extremely respectable bottle of Japanese whisky and poured them both a drink.

Lara looked at her coffee table and snorted a small laugh before she sank down next to Ollie on the couch.

"I looked that bad, huh?"

"You looked like you'd earned an actual drink." Ollie handed her the glass.

Lara accepted it gratefully and sipped it, neat. Ollie's attraction to her went up another eight notches.

"I fucked that up," Lara said quietly, frowning into the distance.

"No, you didn't."

"Only because you saved the day." Lara turned to look at her. "I made it scary for her, with my reaction, I know I did."

. . .

"She looks absolutely fine," Ollie told her. "You just needed a minute."

Lara shook her head. They sipped in silence for a few moments, and when Ollie turned to look at her she saw tears streaking down her face.

She wrapped her arm around Lara's shoulder and pulled her into her chest.

"God," said Lara ruefully. "This is super sexy."

Ollie kissed her hair and ignored the attempt at an apology.

"So," she said softly, "this is triggering as fuck, huh?"

Lara pressed her face into her shoulder and Ollie held her harder.

"Turns out," Lara managed, as she tried not to weep, "yes."

"What's getting you the most?" She tucked Lara's hair back from her damp face.

"Is it my fault?" Lara whispered. "Like did I do something wrong? Her diet or something?"

. . .

"No," Ollie said firmly. "I wasn't making up those numbers. Girls have been getting periods earlier and earlier for decades. There's nothing you should have done differently. And," she pointed out, "there's nothing wrong with hitting puberty, it's a normal part of life."

"But at *ten*," Lara raised her head. "I want her to be a child for as long as she can."

"Lara," Ollie said as clearly as possible. "She is. She will be. I know what you're afraid of," she whispered, "and what happened to you was *not* okay. But honey, Tilly's got *you*. She's got the fiercest, most powerful, man-destroying, scary-ass *witch* of Ribbonwood as her mama. She's going to be just fine."

Lara cried hard then and Ollie confiscated the dangerously tilting glass of whisky from her hand and didn't let her go.

When she calmed down Lara stalked away to go blow her nose and when she returned her expression was all the way back to rueful.

"I might not be exactly experienced at this stuff but I'm pretty sure having a trauma meltdown all over you isn't quite in the realm of hot hook-up territory," she said wryly, sitting down a full foot from Ollie and picking up the remains of her whisky.

. . .

"Oh, you really *haven't* met many lesbians." Ollie raised her eyebrows and smiled. "This is how we do foreplay."

Lara laughed. Even after a good cry she looked ridiculously appealing.

Ollie reached out and tugged her hand into her lap, intertwining their fingers. Slowly Lara lost her standoffish edge and let herself rest against Ollie's body as they sipped.

"Thank you, for your help tonight, by the way," she said. "Who knew having a stray paediatrician around would come in handy?"

"Paeds FACEM," she said automatically. Lara looked at her quizzically. Ollie blinked and shook her head. God, what a nerd. "I'm not a paediatrician, that's a different kind of thing. I'm an emergency doctor who specialises in kids."

Lara studied her.

"I can't tell if that's hot or terrifying," she said, slowly.

"The second one," Ollie sighed. "It's why I'm taking three months of leave."

. . .

Lara nestled in a little closer to her, her hand curving around her thigh.

"I just want you to know that I'm entirely confident you'd manage to make a trauma meltdown look sexy, if you want to have one too," she offered.

Ollie laughed.

"I'll save that for if you want to spice things up sometime," she declined. She put the rest of her glass on the table. "That's enough for me, I've still got to drive tonight," she remembered.

Lara stilled.

"Stay," she murmured.

Ollie looked at her. She knew, with one hundred percent certainty, that with Tilly here and the night Lara had had that they were not going to be having sex tonight. Absolutely nothing about this felt like a casual hook up anymore.

"Okay," she said.

Chapter Twenty-Four

Lara was not having a good week. Crystal Berry had marched into her store at barely nine a.m. on Tuesday morning, shouting at her, convinced she was the reason her husband had stayed out late on Saturday night and had recently changed the passcode on his phone. Lara had made it abundantly clear that she wouldn't touch Crystal's egotistical, chauvinist, *boring* husband with a barge pole and now Crystal was mad about that too.

"You've *always* thought you were too good for everyone around here!" Crystal had thumped her hand on the shop counter.

Lara had let her eyes get as steely and hard as they ever did.

"Which one is it, Crystal? Are you mad because you think I fucked your husband or you're mad because I never would? Make up your damn mind!"

. . .

There'd been an accident blocking traffic coming up the hill and apparently her delivery driver had decided that made the whole trip not worth it and wouldn't reschedule for two days, which left her completely out of fresh fruit and dairy. Meanwhile her chooks were off the lay - Lara suspected something was bothering them, either a competitive brush turkey or a lurking carpet python - so she'd had to put in an egg order as well.

Tilly had quickly moved past the cute, snuggly bonding stage of getting her period and straight into the cranky, annoyed and put out by absolutely everything about her mother stage. It was a constant pitched battle to get her to put her clothes on for school, pick up after herself, or do her homework and Lara was *exhausted* by it.

"Why do we have to eat *this?*" Tilly stared at her plate with dismay after Lara had forced herself to cook something nutritious and flavourful after a very long day. "I don't feel like it. Can't I just have chips?"

Can't you just be grateful? Lara cried internally. Can't you see how hard I work for you? How well I provide as a single parent? Do you want to know what kind of food I had to eat at your age? How desperately I longed for a mother who'd cook a lovingly prepared meal for me?

"No sweetheart," she said instead. "This is what's for dinner. You don't have to love it but if you're hungry that's what's on offer."

. . .

Surprisingly, this wasn't the end of the argument.

She didn't want to be the mother who used guilt to motivate her child. She didn't want her daughter to ever have to understand that Lara was already trying to figure out how to cook at Tilly's age, just so someone in her household would make a hot meal once in a while. It went in cycles. Sometimes her dad got off the booze, remembered he had a child and the house would be clean, the clothes laundered, the meals perfunctory but edible. And then he'd fall off the wagon.

She'd forgiven her dad a long time ago. He'd done the best he could with what he'd had, but what he'd had wasn't much. It was hard not to forgive him when she visited him every Monday lunchtime, to see him at only sixty-seven, doddery and frail beyond his years. He had all his meals taken care of in the Silverbloom nursing home now, his brain so pickled by the years of booze that no one had ever tried to dry him out. Instead he had glasses of box wine measured out by the care staff over the day. It kept him mellow and happy enough. He always had an improbable story to tell her, about his week or about her childhood, most of which was almost certainly made up to try to cover for the fact he couldn't remember anything much of anything at all.

The home had called her twice this week, once to tell her he'd had a fall and given himself a black eye, and once to remind her about a bill she'd forgotten to pay. That was unlike her; Lara was hyper-organised about her life admin, having learned the hard way from her husband what happened when you buried your head in the sand. Of course, she'd been more than a little distracted lately.

· · ·

Which was the other thing. Was she fucking this up with Ollie? Because *for crying out loud, Lara, have even a little bit of chill.* First, the sex was so goddamn hot that Lara had not a single chance of hiding how absolutely swept off her feet she was, practically drowning in a puddle of orgasms every time Ollie looked at her, longing for more, drifting through her days thinking of those devastatingly beautiful fingers, Ollie's smug mouth and burning hot gaze. It was like she just couldn't bring herself to say no, couldn't stop herself from inviting Ollie over, couldn't even turn down confusing invitations like dinner with her family because she just wanted *more*.

Then she went a whole step further - a hundred miles further - way outside her comfort zone and found herself letting Ollie into her daughter's life - letting her damn guard down, *crying* on her - and then worst of all, inviting Ollie into her bed for no gain to Ollie except to hold a clothed, raw, emotional woman all night long. What had she been thinking? *Nothing*, Lara had been thinking *nothing*, just letting herself get sideswiped by the feeling of pure safety and comfort that she gained from Ollie's warm arms and soft voice.

It wasn't until she'd woken up the next day in a fluster, raced her daughter off to school and came home to find Ollie still damn asleep that the vulnerability hangover had truly kicked in. She'd slipped out of her clothes and into the sheets, Ollie waking up fast when her hands discovered bare skin, Lara being thoroughly sure to more than make it up to her.

"Oh fuck, *Lara*-" Ollie had been startled but adamantly not complaining when Lara went down on her a second time in short succession. Or, at least, at first she wasn't. "Oh... god, *mmmm*, not that I'm complaining, but - *ah!* - is this, are you - *oh my god* - is this because we didn't have sex last night?"

Lara ignored her; her mouth was busy after all, and oh fuck she enjoyed this, the hungry jerk of Ollie's hips, her taste, her helpless gasp. Ollie though, had other ideas.

"*Lara,*" she pushed her head back. "Come here a second."

"I'm extremely happy where I am." Lara raised her eyebrows, propping her chin up on her hand. "Are you not going to let me have what I want?" She let her voice go sultry, biting her lip and Ollie groaned.

"You don't owe me anything," she managed, her eyes not leaving Lara's. "There's no making up to do here, you know that right?"

Lara huffed. It was annoying as hell how accurately Ollie kept reading her.

"Are you finished?" She licked her lip slowly. "Because I really want you on my tongue right now."

Ollie drew in a sharp breath.

"*Come here,*" she said firmly and Lara sighed.

. . .

She moved up Ollie's body and then frowned as Ollie pushed her up and grabbed her hips to turn her. She squeaked slightly, as Ollie tugged her thighs back until they were either side of Ollie's head.

"Okay," Ollie said lightly. "You can lick me now, if you want." She tugged Lara down and set to work, giving her a whole new view of Ollie's competitive side.

So, okay, Lara had all up recovered things pretty well from her vulnerability slip-up, but it haunted her, despite Ollie's longing goodbye kiss at the door later that morning. Because *she didn't do this.* She was self-reliant, she was an excellent mama, she handled her own damn emotions, dealt with her own fucking trauma, held *herself* together in her bed on a bad night. She'd had some kind of a moment - a lapse - seemingly driven mad by Ollie's frustrating *goodness.* Ollie's care, her easy competence with Tilly where Lara had fallen down, her unfazed but warm response to Lara's tears would have been a lot for anyone to resist. Lara would adamantly not mess up like that again.

Maybe she should lay off on the Gabrielli family dinners.

They didn't see each other all week. Lara's life was busy - and honestly a mess this week - and Ollie had a day in Brisbane catching up with an old friend from med school, then her grandmother had a couple of alert days and she wanted to stick around home during the daylight hours.

. . .

They texted, Ollie's messages reassuringly full of heat and hungry threats, Lara's all denials and teasing. It felt far more comfortable all of a sudden, to revert back to Ollie in pursuit and Lara just a step out of reach.

> No convenient sleepovers for Tilly this week?

> Sorry. Single mothers are such a bummer to sleep with

The truth was that Sadie had offered and Lara had made herself say no. She needed a minute just to gather herself. Besides, better to be unavailable than to be... clingy. Lara winced at herself. God, how embarrassing.

> That's true. I sleep with so many of them. It's a nightmare trying to find babysitters this week.

> Hard life you lead

Lara refused to take the bait, though the thought hit her exactly how many mothers - single or not - had probably gotten weak-kneed and starry-eyed over Dr. Gabrielli swooping in competently to save their child. She thought of Ollie, sweeping her giggling daughter through Woolworths, her eyes sparkling, making everything normal and right. God help her, Lara would definitely be that single mother.

> Lara. I'm pretty sure you don't know this, but you're fucking beautiful. If it turns out you're not free for the next six months just text me the minute you are and I will jump on a plane in a heartbeat

Ugh. The feeling that hit was deeply bittersweet. For once, Lara actually cared that someone thought she was beautiful. It felt different now, Ollie kissing the silver stretch marks on her abdomen and the fine lines around her eyes, that look on her face when she said the word that made it adamantly clear she meant far more than just the way Lara looked. And then... the plane reminder.

Lara had to get her shit together. She did not want to blink and miss this.

Chapter Twenty-Five

She hadn't heard from Ollie all day on Saturday. Lara was finding far too many moments to frown at her phone, increasingly cranky at cockblocking her damn *self*. Friday was usually their night. For the last handful of Saturdays she'd been on an absolute sex high, mornings in bed with Ollie, drowning in pleasure, before opening the store for a few hours of peak business in the afternoon.

Instead, Sadie had just shrugged and dropped Frankie off to her place on Friday evening, telling Lara there was a good gig on in Silverbloom that she wanted to take Nico to. When she'd arrived back to pick up both girls in time for Lara to open the shop the next morning, Sadie was the one clearly on a sex high.

"You're a disgrace," Lara informed her when she burst in Lara's front door, twenty minutes later than she'd promised, bed hair, shirt inside out, beaming.

. . .

"Oh, don't start with me." Sadie had just grinned at her. "I have plenty of ammo on you. Didn't I literally catch you singing along to Taylor Swift at top volume when I dropped the girls back to you last Saturday?"

"No," Lara refuted succinctly. "I don't even know her." She turned away and called down the hall. "Girls! Time to go!"

"Lars," Sadie suddenly sobered. "What's the deal? Why are you avoiding hanging out with Ollie? You seemed so... glowing. I liked it."

"I'm not avoiding her," Lara lied. Sadie stared her down. "Fine," she huffed. "Maybe a little."

"Why?" Sadie looked genuinely curious. "The sex is hot, she makes you laugh and you look so close to whatever I assume your version of happy looks like that I'm worried you're going to lose your reputation around town as a lethal fucking witch any second now." She hovered, her expression intensifying as she examined Lara. "What's got you running? Is it because she's leaving?"

"I'm not running." Lara turned back to the hall again. "Girls, come on!"

"Getting too good?" Sadie's eyes turned into dark laser beams. "Getting too close? Getting too vulnerable? Like it too much?"

. . .

"Tilly Rees and Frankie O'Malley, I said *now!*"

The two girls finally came thundering up the hall, the two of them lugging a truly outlandish amount of crap they'd deemed necessary, despite the fact Lara was only going in to work for five hours. Lara helped hustle them all out the door. Sadie did not seem to share her urgency, yelling out she needed the bathroom and then fluffing around for what seemed like ten minutes while Lara squinted up into the sunshine, trying not to lose her temper. When Sadie finally emerged, she waited until the last possible second before she pierced Lara with a solid stare.

"Don't sabotage this because you're scared," she warned her, slamming her car door closed before Lara could retort.

That had rung in her ears all afternoon, Lara ruining half a box of avocados by jamming them too forcefully into their tray. She wasn't *sabotaging*. And she certainly wasn't scared. Of someone hot and beautiful and kind and leaving? Lara wasn't afraid of being alone. She preferred it. This was a little blip in the scheme of her life, a short moment she'd somehow stumbled into where someone could turn her on like crazy while somehow making her feel actually seen. That possibly in future she and Ollie could *maybe* decide to see each other when Ollie popped home once or twice a year was a bonus. Actually, that was a perfect arrangement when you thought about.

It's just... why wasn't Ollie texting her? It had been well over twenty-four hours. Oh for fuck's sake. Lara put down her phone and refused to be the one to chase if Ollie wasn't chasing her. That was *not* her role in this. If Ollie was playing hard to get or being cool then she had no *idea* who she was dealing with. Lara had made cool and untouchable look good for the better part of the past decade.

Just before she flipped the door sign to closed, her phone pinged. She grabbed her phone so fast she was embarrassed for herself, but it was just Sadie changing plans on her. The kids were driving her nuts so she'd gotten them outdoors, up to the lookout for a picnic. Could Lara please bring some fancy cheese and snacks because she only had pizza shapes in the house.

Lara drove the long winding road to what should have been a tourist attraction, except that the signpost had either fallen down or been sabotaged by locals who wanted one damn pretty place just to themselves. The lookout was perched halfway up the range and was ostensibly a carpark with a view out over Ribbonwood and the valley below. If you squeezed through the gap in the trees there was a small roo track that led you to a little grassy clearing where you could watch the sunset over the rainforest.

When she entered the carpark her gut clenched. Sadie's station wagon was nowhere to be seen. Instead a distinctively crumbling old farm ute sat in the far corner.

Lara didn't know whether to laugh or cry - or worse - collapse into a puddle of gooey relief. So instead she got mad. Striding through the little winding track to be confronted with a blazing pink sunset, a picnic rug set with wine and an extremely attractive woman waiting for her, she threw up her hands.

. . .

"What the *fuck,* Ollie?"

Ollie jerked her head up from where she'd been lazily reclining, watching the view.

"What's wrong?"

"I don't like surprises!" Lara felt ambushed. "And I don't like being tricked! Especially when I just wanted a little bit of space!"

"What are you talking about?" Ollie scrunched up her elegant brow. "You asked me to meet you here!"

"No, I didn't!"

Ollie loosened her jaw, her head cocked to one side.

"You texted me literally this morning?"

Lara's mouth stopped halfway through her next retort. Her teeth clenched together.

"Give me your phone," she said shortly.

· · ·

Ollie squinted at her like Lara might be losing her damn mind but she handed over the device, opening it to the message thread.

I want to see you, Lara had allegedly said at eleven-forty-five this morning. *Meet me at the lookout at 5:15 and bring wine.*

Oh I'm in, Ollie had responded within two minutes flat.

Don't message me for the rest of the day, Lara had - quite rudely - responded. *I'm busy. Save it for when I see you.*

Ollie had - quite classily, she reflected - taken her at her word and refused to even respond.

Lara started shaking her head. Those messages were conspicuously absent from her own phone.

"Sadie," she said tightly. "She set us up."

"Oh fuck." Ollie's forehead furrowed, some of the light disappearing from her eyes. "Wait, so you didn't want to see me? Why is Sadie making you see me?"

"I..." Lara didn't know where to turn first, her chest tight, her face burning. She was pissed off and exposed, and this was *not* what she thought she'd be dealing with this evening and- and- *wait.* She forced herself to step on the brake and take a breath. She fully took in the sight of Ollie, sitting bolt upright now, those dark eyes full of concern and confusion.

Without another second to reconsider, she let her body cumple, dropping down into Ollie's lap to straddle her thighs and meet her gaze. Oh god, she appreciated the way those eyes stayed locked to hers, as if to Ollie understanding Lara was everything, and not the tits she'd basically just shoved in her face. And then there were Ollie's hands, already holding her securely. Lara leaned in and kissed her breathless.

"So... do you want me to take my wine and go?" Ollie's voice was soft but a little wry as she drew back and gazed at her.

Lara rolled her eyes but her smile slipped out anyway.

"Give me one sec," she said.

She extricated herself from Ollie and headed back up the path to the car park. She rang Sadie to tell her if she ever, *ever* pulled something like that again, and to check in with Tilly. Then she grabbed the bag of fancy snacks Sadie had annoyingly decided she needed and headed back down the track.

"Wait-" Ollie held her hand up dramatically as Lara reappeared, as if to ward off disaster. "Which one am I getting this time, a telling off or making out?"

. . .

Lara shook her head. This was all kind of a clusterfuck. The sunset at least, was perfect.

"Cheese," she told her, lifting up the brown paper bag with the Ribbonwood General Store logo on the side. "And a whole pile of other crap you tourists like."

"Don't even try with me, Lara Bennett. I've seen the hipster whisky you drink."

Lara set out the picnic she'd made for them - or for someone, anyway - and Ollie watched her do it. She poured a glass of wine, but held it back from her fingers just as Lara reached for it.

"Speak," Ollie denied her, holding her wine hostage.

Lara glared at her. Their fingers tangled together around the stem of the glass until Ollie relented and let her have it. She didn't stop looking at Lara though.

"Sorry," Lara sighed eventually. "It's been a shitty week."

"One you want to talk about?"

. . .

"Not really." She took a sip of the wine.

"Okay then."

Lara looked at the blaze of pink-gold and deep lavender above, the valley sea-green in the light.

"I just thought I should take a minute," she admitted, on unfamiliar ground now. "This is kind of... intense for me. I haven't done anything like this before."

Ollie was quiet, letting her talk. When Lara didn't go on, she nodded and shifted her gaze to the sunset too.

"You can take all the minutes you need." Her voice was calm. "I get it. It's kind of intense for me too."

"Do you need some space?" Lara quickly offered, a perverse sinking feeling in her chest. "Because it's fine if you do." *After all, I'm a lot.*

Ollie didn't reply straight away and when Lara finally managed to drag her eyes from the horizon and look at her, she seemed to be struggling with herself, until finally a slightly exasperated smile broke through.

· · ·

"I don't," she said. "I don't need space. I'm fine with you taking space," she clarified. "But honestly, if it were all up to me right now I'd have more of you. So much more." She swallowed and a blaze of heat and warmth hit Lara squarely in the chest. "I know that's not fair, I mean... I'm the one leaving in six weeks. I'm fine with you setting the pace you're comfortable with. I just can't seem to stop wanting more of you." Her last words came out whisper soft.

Lara let her lashes drop. She'd really thought it was more like eight weeks.

"You're not the only one," she confessed.

"Lara, I know. Half of this damn town wants you." Ollie shook her head, doing her level best to break the moment.

"Hilarious," Lara said with her best attempt at a reproachful glare. She slipped her fingers into Ollie's. She knew she was being given an out. She didn't have to say one single further thing that exposed her; she could simply pull Ollie into a kiss and maybe move things to the point where she slipped her fingers inside Ollie's pants and made her see stars. Or, they could just picnic and tease each other and every-thing would feel - mostly - smoothed over. "You're a lot," she said instead.

"*You* are," Ollie accused, raising her eyebrows.

.   .   .

"No," Lara said. "You are. You think you can just swan into town, be so gorgeous it's actually revolting, throw me into bed where you're just... I don't know, averagely good-" Ollie snorted and Lara couldn't stop her own smile. "Fine, throw me into bed and drive me completely crazy. Make me crave you, make me desperate." She bit her lip, embarrassed at the words spilling from her now. "And you're just... fucking *sweet* to me and to my kid and we're at Sunday night dinner with your family and movie nights at home with my daughter and-"

"It's too much. I'm being too much," Ollie bit out.

Lara stared at her.

"*No.* You're so..." she struggled for the word. "Good. You're so *good.* You're good to me and it feels so good and I am not handling it well."

"Ah."

"I don't let people in my bed," Lara told her.

Tiny twin sunsets reflecting in the dark of Ollie's eyes.

"But you let me."

"Yeah."

. . .

Ollie contemplated that for a while.

"Do you need us to slow this down, or... stop? Switch things up? Put some boundaries in or something? I don't want to hurt you here-"

"*No*," Lara told her, her tone coming out slightly more fiercely than she'd intended. She didn't want slow. She didn't want to stop. She had her own damn boundaries she could assert any time she wanted, *was* asserting right now in fact. "I'm not being hurt," she denied. "I just needed a minute," she said, faintly exasperated. *Jesus Christ, Sadie.*

"I can handle that," Ollie said matter of factly. "Have a glass of wine with me so we don't waste this ridiculous sunset and then go have your minute. I'll still be here. I mean, not *here*, specifically - I'm pretty sure it's going to rain tonight - but I'll be wherever you want me to be when you're done."

"Oh for fuck's sake-" Lara groaned and climbed all the way back into Ollie's lap. This time Ollie didn't stop the quick flicker of her eyes over Lara's body and Lara found she definitely didn't hate that either. "I've had it," she told her. "I've had my minute. Can we get back to making out now?"

They could.

. . .

It was a long time before the wine or the cheese got any attention, but Lara already felt drunk just on kissing. Ollie's hands didn't even drift anywhere that wasn't entirely G rated and Lara still felt like she was coming out of her skin. *Making out like teenagers* was the phrase that hit her mind and she couldn't stop smiling against Ollie's lips.

Eventually they picnicked, the sunset fading into night. Lara slowly caught her up on her shitty week and Ollie told her about Brisbane and life at the winery while Lara struggled not to stare as she spoke. Why exactly did she have to be *that* beautiful? It was so fucking distracting.

The mosquitos arrived and comprehensively ruined the moment. As they hit the parking lot and Lara put the remains of the picnic into the back of her car, Ollie paused and drifted closer.

"So, with this whole Sadie setting us up deal." She traced her fingers over Lara's hipbone when she turned back around. "Does that involve any further babysitting?"

Lara smirked at the clear intent in Ollie's eyes.

"You want to know if Tilly is having a sleepover and if you get to have one too?"

"I really do."

. . .

"Meet me at mine?"

"Lara." Ollie grabbed her hand, pulling her back as she turned to go. "I'm going to tell you something."

"Okay?"

"Last week, on Sunday night, when I stayed over?"

"Mmhm." Lara grimaced. She didn't need to be reminded.

"I fucking loved it," Ollie said. "You looked so cute in your jammies." She smirked and Lara's jaw dropped. She shoved Ollie back slightly. Ollie pulled her back in, her face growing slightly more serious. "I liked getting to hold you." Her voice was low and direct. "I liked that you let me. I liked that you wanted it. I liked every second of it. I kind of figured," she said as Lara frowned at her, trying extremely hard not to show how annoyingly moved she was by this and by Ollie's infuriating perceptiveness, "that being that our... situation is what it is, maybe you should hear that."

"You're extremely corny," Lara told her, even though she could feel how damn flushed she was. "Honestly Ollie, why are you like this?" She tugged her down to kiss her again, against the lump in her throat. She felt Ollie's smirk against her lips and knew she wasn't hiding anything from her convincingly. "If you play your cards right," Lara pulled back and fixed her with a look, "I might not take my clothes off tonight either."

. . .

"Is that a challenge?" Ollie ran her finger slowly between Lara's breasts down to the the button on her shorts where they stayed, just toying gently. "Because you know how I get when you start getting cocky like that."

Lara did know. Suddenly getting home felt extremely urgent.

Chapter Twenty-Six

Ollie had been in Lara's house on a number of occasions now, but she still found it as fascinating as she had the first time Audrey had driven up and parked on the grass that bonfire night. *Lara Bennett's home.* She hadn't been inside the walls until Lara had been the one to invite her in and she was extra glad of that now.

Lara didn't let a lot of people in. Not to her bed or to her life and here Ollie was in both. She felt every inch of that privilege as she followed Lara in through her front door on a Saturday evening.

The house was so damn *pretty*. From the paint accents on the Victorian detailing on the exterior, to the smooth lines, polished floorboards, delicate art on the walls and the enamel jug full of fresh flowers that always seemed to sit on her dining table, changing every week. It was the girliest house Ollie had ever walked into; even down to the dusky pink of Lara's bed sheets. Ollie was intensely curious about every single deliberate thing about it.

· · ·

Lara had first shared this house with her husband but it seemed scrubbed of him now. Ollie figured that was intentional. Ollie herself owned a small terrace house in Brunswick that had been built in 1896. It was filled with generations of history, absolutely none of it hers. Lara's house was a map of her experiences and Ollie longed for the key.

Lara was in her kitchen now, pulling out ingredients, getting ready to make them dinner and Ollie caught her breath yet again at the sight of her. The sheer, over-the-top attractiveness of her. The complexity of knowing, but not knowing her for so long. If she tried really hard, she could probably conjure up a memory of Lara aged nine. For crying out loud they would have been in kindergarten together. Her high school memories of Lara Bennett had moments that were still vivid, but they were followed by not even a glimpse of her for over a decade and a half. Zero contact. So much history missed and yet somehow, the main events of Lara's life had reached her ears anyway.

That she knew what the back of Lara's head looked like as she bent over her exam papers at fifteen, that she knew without having to be told that Lara had cooked in this same kitchen for Josh fucking Rees for years, that she would have sat right here in this living room, hearing for the first time that he was gone... all these moments rushed over Ollie in a wave. It was like looking at forty different versions of the same person, but all from the wrong end of a telescope.

"What are you thinking about?" Lara looked up and caught her expression.

. . .

Ollie blinked.

"That I'm going to make you dinner," she told her. "Sit the fuck down."

In the end Lara leaned back against the kitchen bench while Ollie cooked, making snarky comments and getting her smart mouth kissed. She poured them both a small splash of wine, Ollie trying to bite back a grin at the size of the pour; Lara had yet to try to test her on her threat she wouldn't have sex with her if she was intoxicated. She'd meant it and the rule was sticking. Especially the kind of sex they were having, and especially with Lara's history.

"Is it weird-" she found herself blurting as she sautéed vegetables "-still living here?"

"In Ribbonwood?" Lara asked, her fingers toying with a sprig of fresh thyme. "Always. It's home though, I guess."

"Well yeah," Ollie agreed. "I meant this house though, specifically."

"Oh." Lara's head came up. She watched Ollie for a beat. "You mean with the ghosts?"

"I guess?"

. . .

Lara took a sip of her wine.

"I remodelled it," she said after a moment. "As far as possible. New kitchen, new bathroom, new paint. Moved that wall-" she pointed. "Put in the fireplace. Stripped the floors. It's kind of unrecognisable."

"Right." Ollie felt weirdly relieved by this. "Makes sense."

"The night after he died I started sleeping in the spare room," Lara said. "You must have noticed I don't sleep in the master bedroom."

Ollie blinked. She'd not thought a lot about Lara's bedroom aside from the fact that it had romantic lighting, soft sheets and Lara Bennett in it. But now that she did she realised it was right off the living room and not especially large.

"The master bedroom is the guest room now," Lara went on. "Sadie sleeps in it more than anyone. Tilly's still in what was her old nursery, but honestly she ended up just sleeping in the bed with me until she was about seven anyway." She gazed skywards before her eyes flicked to Ollie's again.

Ollie felt a clench in her abdomen at that look. She was starting to recognise it. Lara didn't let people in her bed. Or in her head. And here she was, sharing intensely intimate details of her life with Ollie. The look said, *is this too much?*

. . .

She let the spoon drop into the sauce and took three steps to tug Lara's chin up and kiss her.

"It's beautiful," she said. "You did a beautiful job. Of all of it," she told her, hoping Lara knew she wasn't just talking about decorating.

"Thank you." The fact that Lara turned away to study her wineglass, slightly too late to hide the fact that her eyes had misted, showed that she did.

Ollie kept feeling gut-punched with wonder. Sharp-tongued, standoffish, sassy, flirty Lara Bennett was secretly incredibly sensitive. For one wild second Ollie allowed herself to imagine what it would be like if a future between them was possible. She knew without even a second's hesitation that she'd be all in, giving whatever she had to figure out this woman. The thought was dizzying.

She focussed hard on the sauce, while Lara stared into her wine.

———

"That," Ollie bit her lip, catching her breath and gazing down at Lara where she had her pinned, "was almost disappointingly easy. I mean, disappointing except for the fact that you're now entirely naked." She let her eyes wander where they wanted, which was damn well everywhere.

. . .

Lara was breathing hard, her eyes sparkling, despite her struggle to lift her wrists off the bed.

"You don't play fair," she complained after trying to push against Ollie's grip got her nowhere. She tried to use her hips to throw Ollie off. Ollie only pressed her own hips down, making Lara gasp, her movements turning more to a slow grind up against her. Ollie smirked down at her.

"Getting impatient are we?"

Lara rolled her eyes.

"I'm fine," she tried, making her body still. "Whatever."

Ollie laughed and without letting go of her wrists began to kiss her throat hotly, Lara moaning in response and arching her back. Well *that* was never a fair move when you had the body Lara Bennett did. Ollie was up for the challenge though. She shifted her weight and the angle but managed to keep Lara firmly pinned while she teased and licked her breasts and nipples, listening to her cries get desperate.

Lara's hips were grinding up against hers again when Ollie started to grind back. She leaned in and murmured in Lara's ear.

"You know, this reminds me-" she let go of Lara's wrists, but was up and off her body entirely before Lara could reach her.

. . .

"No-" Lara choked out, looking faintly anguished and Ollie smirked. She paused, leaning back in to press her lips against Lara's earlobe and murmur exactly where her mind had just gone. She drew back to watch the heat rise up Lara's neck.

"Yeah?"

"Mmhm," Lara managed. She bit her lip, her eyes hungry. "Yeah."

Ollie left the room, finding her bag. It took her a few minutes but when she walked back in - also naked now, except for one critical detail - Lara who was reclining back on her elbows sat bolt upright in the bed. "Oh *lord.*" She stared. She looked slightly lost for words.

"Yeah?" Ollie raised her eyebrows, wanting to be sure.

"*Yes,*" Lara confirmed adamantly. She took a sharp breath. "Ollie Gabrielli, you sure as hell better have bought some lube wherever you bought *that* monstrosity."

Ollie laughed and ducked back to grab the other recent purchase she'd almost forgotten in her eagerness to test out how Lara felt about the concept of strap-ons.

"You're right," she agreed as she stood watching Lara, quickly slicking the strap until it gleamed. "How's that?" She couldn't stop her small grin at the expression on Lara's face as she watched Ollie's hand moving.

Lara hadn't taken her eyes off her and Ollie could see her breathing getting rapid. She looked aroused as hell and Ollie couldn't wait to watch her take it, the same way she drove Lara insane with her fingers: fast and dirty.

Then she hesitated. *You must have noticed I don't sleep in the master bedroom.* Ollie hadn't noticed. She was going to start noticing.

"Come here," she said. Lara bit her lip. She came up off the bed and Ollie sat on the side of it, hips all the way back, feet on the floor for steadiness. She crooked her finger at Lara who eyed her, then smirked in understanding. She came and stood straddling Ollie's thighs, looking down with anticipation at the adamantly not small erection she was sporting. Ollie pressed Lara back slightly before she tugged her down, so she was in Ollie's lap but with the strap-on trapped between them.

"Ollie-" Lara's voice came out strained.

Ollie smiled. She loved how Lara got when she wasn't getting what she wanted. It was clear what she wanted right now.

"Are you cool with this?" She checked in anyway.

. . .

"I'm not cool with *this*-" Lara squirmed in her lap, eyes narrowed. "But yes, I want this. Now, please." She tried to shift up and Ollie held her firm.

"You know I like to push you a little."

"Yes please-" Lara was perhaps a little too far gone for this conversation to land.

"Anything I should know?" Ollie persisted anyway. "Anything you know right now is a no?"

Lara lifted her chin to meet Ollie's eyes.

"Are you being sweet again?" she asked, her tone slightly exasperated, but her eyes incredibly soft.

Ollie shook her head.

"No," she denied. "I just want to know your likes and dislikes before I fuck you hard and fast."

Lara's head fell back in clear want. When she raised it again she fixed Ollie with a look.

. . .

"I'm not going to suck that thing," she told her, "and don't go thinking you want to try to stick it *anywhere* else." She raised her eyebrows for emphasis.

"Right," Ollie said, trying not to smile. "Just fingers there," she said with utmost seriousness. More than once recently Lara had come incredibly hard when Ollie had teased her back there. Lara glared at her, her cheeks flushing slightly. Ollie kept her face innocent. "And maybe my tongue."

"Oh my *god,* Ollie," Lara shook her head. "You're out of control." Then she smirked. "If you think you can fuck me with that thing and tongue my ass at the same time then you can be my guest."

Ollie nearly fell backwards laughing.

"You know I can just unstrap this right?" she pointed out. "Be careful what you offer me Lara Bennett because I will take you *on.*"

"That's not what I meant!"

"Lara," Ollie managed to stop laughing. Lara's hair was out, tumbling down over her shoulders, bright gold in the lamplight. Ollie twisted a lock of it around her fingers. "You can say no to anything," she reminded her.

. . .

Lara leaned in and kissed her, long and slow.

"Did you hear me say no?" she said when she finally drew back, her eyes sparkling.

"Lara Bennett." Ollie shook her head slowly. "You have no idea what's coming for you."

"Then enough *talk*," Lara stood up. She shifted forward so that the head of the strap was right where she wanted it.

"Use your safe word." Ollie smirked up at her.

"You're cute," Lara bit out. Then she sank slowly all the way down until she was sitting in Ollie's lap again. Ollie could have come just watching her, Lara's lips parting in a slow gasp, her eyes scrunching closed in concentration, the hazy look in her eyes when she opened them on Ollie's face. "Oh yes please," she whispered in hungry anticipation. And then she began to move.

Later, Ollie did push her down, on her hands and knees, fucking her hard and fast, Lara's back bowing in pleasure, Ollie's hands gripping her waist, their bodies slapping together. When Lara's orgasm hit her, it was loud, incredibly hot and immensely satisfying.

But as she lay awake that night, listening to the rain on the roof, Lara asleep in her arms, it was the first round that kept replaying in her mind. Not just how Lara looked as she writhed in her lap, but the way they couldn't stop looking at each other. The expression in Lara's eyes as Ollie gazed back, Lara's shaky gasps against her mouth when she kissed her, as her soft moans turned staccato, turned to stuttering breath, turned to her coming undone, right there in her lap. The intense intimacy of having a front row view to Lara's undoing, of being the first thing she saw when she opened her eyes again, that gaze full of *something*.

Ollie knew she would never forget it.

Chapter Twenty-Seven

Lara walked into the beer garden of the Ribbonwood pub at lunchtime the following Thursday. She didn't often close the store completely for her lunch break, usually choosing to eat where she could still hear the door chime. But there were perks to owning your own business and one of them was deciding that when the weather was gorgeous and balmy and a friend wanted to catch up, a pub lunch was a solid choice.

Eva Sinclair had, to her surprise, started to become just that: a friend. Lara was pretty close with a lot of the women who came to bonfire night in a half-way sort of way. She knew incredibly personal details about them, and they knew the basic facts of her life too. There was a gratitude towards her for the help she'd been willing to offer and then a camaraderie built from the ongoing bonfire nights. They'd laughed together and drank together, but the occasional crying or venting came from the women she'd helped, never from Lara's end. Lara thought of it as almost a professional boundary. She had to hold it together so that they could let go. If they thought of her as strong then they could be strong too.

Eva though, had snuck in under Lara's radar. She didn't know what it was about her, but for all Eva had been through she felt like an increasingly solid presence. She was stocky with a rigidly upright posture and a sly sense of humour that snuck out more frequently now that she wasn't living in pure survival mode. Lara liked her. Somehow, the lines were blurring because Lara found she could fight through her own shyness and actually talk to her.

"I heard a new rumour about you," Eva told her now, turning her beer glass around in her hands.

Lara raised her eyebrows, her chip hand pausing on the way to her mouth.

"If it was from Crystal Berry," she started, "I can confirm that I did not fuck her husband but I *did* tell her he was about as tempting as a bundle of dry sticks."

Eva cackled. Then she quickly turned her head, finding Spencer was still miraculously snoozing through it all in his pram.

"Not that one," she said. "Amber O'Brien said she drove past the lookout the other night and saw you making out with Ollie Gabrielli in the carpark."

. . .

Lara blinked.

"Actually," she said, "we were having sex, right up against a 2015 Ford Fiesta. She must have missed the finer details."

Eva laughed again.

"I'm not going to lie: I'm pretty sure I believe that rumour. There were vibes," she pointed a finger at Lara, "at bonfire night."

Lara hesitated. She'd never come out to anyone that wasn't Sadie. Or, she supposed, Ollie.

"Can you blame me?" Her smile slipped out, making the decision for her. "She's hot."

Eva looked both appropriately scandalised and straight up smug, clutching her hand to her chest.

"I knew it! That *we hated each other in high school* thing... then all of a sudden you're making eyes at each other over the bonfire."

"I wasn't *making eyes*," Lara denied.

. . .

"Yeah, sure. So you're a thing?"

"Yes and no," Lara said. "We're seeing each other, but she lives in Melbourne, so it's not going anywhere."

"Lara," Eva widened her eyes. "Move to *Melbourne*."

Lara laughed. Despite everything, Eva still had an over-inflated sense of romanticism.

"Not a chance." She shook her head, firmly relieving Eva of the notion. "I hate cities. Ribbonwood sucks but it's still my little corner of the world. I know who I am here and who my daughter goes to school with. My mind would be lost in minutes being surrounded in all that concrete. I'm not going to move interstate to be miserable with someone I-" she hesitated, "am having *incredibly* hot sex with."

Eva smiled conspiratorially, but she wasn't dissuaded from the romance novel track it was heading down.

"Would she stay?"

"No," Lara said immediately. "Here? Fuck no. It just...is what it is. A good time, not a long time."

· · ·

"Hmm," Eva looked at her. "So this whole glow you've got going on is just sex huh?"

Lara thought of Ollie almost fucking her through the mattress on Saturday night, making Lara limp and boneless with pleasure. She thought of *you looked so cute in your jammies* and Ollie cooking her dinner and *you did a beautiful job of your whole fucking life Lara* and Ollie's dark eyes and heated kiss and hands curled around her hips, *you can say no to anything.*

"Yep," she said. "Just sex."

"Righto," said Eva. She sipped her beer. "Want to hear my latest?"

"I so do."

Eva told her Dan's most recent bullshit and Lara felt her blood get hot. So far their plan had worked as far as getting a little regular chunk of money in Eva's bank account, enough to keep the lights on and stop them going hungry, but now Dan was getting nasty.

"Honey," Lara told her. "He's not going to get away with this. I swear to god, we're going to find a way to make him pay."

"That sounds so mafia," Eva managed, scrunching up her eyes to stop the tears from escaping.

. . .

"He'll sleep with the fishes," Lara promised her darkly.

Eva snorted slightly.

"I believe you," she said. "After all, Chloe Perkins being safe to walk this planet is on you. If you can get rid of a threat like Dale, then Dan is just small fry."

"Honestly?" Lara frowned. "I hope I never have to go to that kind of extent ever again. It was messy. But I promise you, Dan won't even know what hit him."

"You right, mate?"

Lara looked up to see Eva was addressing a vaguely familiar young man, absurdly large muscles bursting from his running gear, sitting over at the next table, his eyes as wide as saucers as he stared directly at them.

"Ah, yeah- yep," he stammered, his face going red. He looked down at his half-eaten burger and cleared his throat. "Sorry, just... daydreaming."

Eva gave him a hard stare for a couple more seconds. Then she rolled her eyes at Lara.

. . .

"Joe Armstrong," she shook her head, her voice low. "My babysitter dated his brother. He seems to have taken a fancy to you." She looked over to check that Joe wasn't staring any more. "Honestly, is it like this every time you leave the house?" Lara snorted and shook her head. Eva took a solid mouthful of her beer. "Have you considered a potato sack? Maybe two?"

———

Lara had enjoyed a pleasant walk back in the sunshine to her store. She'd crossed paths with Kimberley Evans, the girl who'd once been her best friend, ages eight through sixteen. She'd ditched Lara like she was literal poison in Year Eleven. Kimberley had approached Lara exactly once since then, two years ago. She'd heard, like, Lara did favours for women who needed them? She wanted Lara to humiliate her husband who she'd discovered was trying on her clothes when no one was home. Lara had distinctly refused and Kimberley's ex was now living a much happier life in Sydney. To say it was satisfying when Kimberley glared at her on the way up the footpath, like Lara was gum on her shoe, was to understate the pleasures of small town life.

Just as she went to unlock the front door and flip the sign back to open, her phone pinged with a message. She saw Ollie's name flash up and instantly smiled. And then, she frowned. She left the sign on closed.

When her car bumped up the gravel drive through the olive grove and stopped in front of the house the dogs didn't erupt out to greet her, though she could hear their barking contained somewhere. On the front porch stood a very attractive young woman with flaming red hair cascading down her spine. She and Ollie stood close, in an involved conversation.

Lara got out of the car and Ollie looked up. The expression on her face went intensely soft and Lara swallowed. She hung back, leaning against her car, watching the conversation play out. The redhead gave her a polite - slightly uncertain - smile as she passed Lara on her way to her own car. Lara made her way to the porch steps.

"Who was that?" she asked immediately, trying to hide her intense irritation at the way the woman had touched her hair as she looked up at Ollie.

"The palliative care nurse," Ollie told her, reaching out to pull her in close.

"She's hot," Lara observed, narrowing her eyes at Ollie.

"Yeah," said Ollie. "We were just about to fuck actually but then you got here."

Lara snorted out a small laugh and shoved Ollie's hip. Ollie slipped her hands into her hair and kissed her until Lara felt a little shaky.

"Am I getting in the way, being here?" she asked, her voice coming out way too soft for her own liking.

· · ·

"I'm so fucking glad to see you," Ollie told her. "Just this little stolen moment out here?" She drifted her hands down Lara's sides, stroking her hips. "Means the world."

"Want to go for a walk?" Lara offered. She hadn't been sure what to expect when Ollie had texted her that her grandmother was dying, really dying now, not in the slow way she'd been before. She thought of the tiny frail lady in the wheelchair, of Ollie's gaze full of worry and love as she watched her pick at her dinner. She reached out and took Ollie's hand.

She didn't let go as they passed the vegetable garden, the hen house, the dam, the vines, the trees. She felt conflicted. Was this okay, that she was here, holding Ollie's hand like some kind of girlfriend? Was it the right thing for either one of them? Ollie had been so good at being present for her. Now she wanted to do the same for Ollie. And god, if Lara had learned anything new recently it was how damn good it felt for someone else to catch you when you were falling, if only for a moment. And so she held her hand anyway.

They reached the crest of the hill and sat down side-by-side to look over the valley in the afternoon sunlight. Ollie's eyelids were swollen. It was clear she'd been crying but right now she looked calm, almost peaceful. She slipped an arm around Lara's shoulders and Lara leaned in against her body. Goddamnit, this was nice. She hoped the warmth felt that way for Ollie too and by her small sigh it seemed that it did.

"It's so cute that you were jealous of literally my grandmother's nurse," Ollie said out of nowhere and Lara's head jerked up.

. . .

"Oh I *was not-*"

"You looked like you were going to walk up and knee her in the guts," Ollie grinned.

"That is pure invention on your part," Lara told her. "We all know I'm world famous in Ribbonwood basically just for my resting bitch face." Ollie looked entirely unrepentant as Lara kept trying. "I was checking her out actually," she added, doubling down.

"Really?" Ollie cocked her head. "Hey quick question. How do you feel about threesomes?"

"Ollie, I swear to *god* if you touch that woman-"

Ollie burst into laughter.

"I knew it." She squeezed Lara's shoulders and Lara rolled her eyes.

"I'm not jealous," she tried one more time to deny it. "I'm just entitled enough to tell you that since I only have you for another like, six weeks, that you do not have time to be sleeping with anybody else, even pretty redheads, are we clear?"

. . .

"Oh, you're entitled to me," Ollie bit her lip. "I'm in full agreement on that." Lara couldn't take the sight of those neat white teeth sinking into that full lower lip another second so she kissed her. When Ollie drew back, her smile was soft. "Also, it's not quite five weeks, just so you know. So you better keep some room in your schedule for me, Lara Bennett." She paused. "You know. Sometime after my grandmother dies."

Then she cried.

As Lara held onto her, a weird feeling grew in her chest. This was... this was *nice*. Lara had hugged plenty of crying women, it kind of came with the whole secret witch business thing, but this was something else altogether. To know that the woman who'd given her such comfort and care could also experience it from Lara? It made her feel like she was... good. Not good deeds good. Not helpful or practical or smart with a sneaky plan. Just deep down good, for Ollie Gabrielli to find solace in *her,* Lara Bennett of all people.

When Ollie straightened up, she pulled back, checked her pockets and coming up empty straight up tugged up her t-shirt to wipe her face. Lara watched, slightly gobsmacked. It should have been off-putting watching a grown woman wipe her nose on her shirt. It was perhaps a solidly concerning sign that the extended flash of athletic torso was enough to make her want to pull Ollie urgently down in the grass with her, despite every reason that would be absolutely the wrong move right now.

When Ollie met her eyes, she caught the look on Lara's face and her mouth quirked sharply.

. . .

"Told you," she said. "Foreplay."

Chapter Twenty-Eight

Nonna died on Tuesday morning. The sun was beaming through her bedroom window onto the hospital bed they'd hired, Portia curled up at her feet purring like she had for a thousand mornings before, the whole family surrounding her, holding her hands, stroking her hair, telling stories. They all sat for a long time after her last breath, talking to her like there was still so much more they had left to say.

Afterwards Ollie found herself on the porch steps with just her siblings, like everyone's grief was equally real but theirs was specific to them. They hadn't lost their last parent like their dad just had, nor a very elderly great-grandmother like the youngest Gabrielli kids. Nonna had moved in with them to help when Matty had been only three years old. There was no family memory they held that didn't include her in the mix.

"Do you remember that possum she used to feed? I swear to god he got so fat the delivery guy thought we had a rottweiler."

. . .

"Do you remember that time she caught Nico googling pictures of boobs? I'm not sure his balls ever descended again after that."

"Remember Nonna and those bloody ducks she was so obsessed with?"

"Remember that time-"

At some point in the afternoon Matty wordlessly started pouring them all wine and the three of them - minus Pia who grimaced as she couldn't partake - got quietly very drunk, laughing and crying and telling more stories. Ollie found herself calling Lara, holding herself strictly, carefully contained, so nothing she didn't want spilling out of her mouth could escape *in vino veritas*. She didn't remember the exact words Lara said back, just the incredible sweetness that lingered after she hung up the phone.

"You've got it bad," Pia informed her when she drifted back to join them.

"Mate," Nico said, "you're in real trouble, just look at you."

Ollie just shook her head at them all and threw back a solid swig of wine.

. . .

Neighbours started to arrive, bringing casseroles and lasagnes, hugs and kind words. Eventually their dad came to join them, Matty slinging an arm around him, their mother doing what she always did and staying busy through her grief. When Ollie went to check on her she found her doing an intense amount of meal prep as if ready to cater the whole funeral party herself. Ollie hugged her and slowly sobered up as she tried to make herself helpful, absolutely in the way but at least sure her mother wasn't alone.

Time moved weirdly after that. The first night seemed horribly long, then the next days skipped, until all of a sudden she was making it through Nonna's funeral, her father somehow delivering the full eulogy, Ollie and Pia gripping hands in the front row as they wept. As they filed out behind the coffin she spied Lara sitting next to Sadie somewhere near the back, her eyes filled with sadness as she sought out Ollie's as she passed.

The wake was both private and overwhelming; just Gabriellis but oh god there were a lot of them. Up from Brisbane, from Toowoomba, from Adelaide. The next week slid by with extended family, food, stories, wine, more food, more family. It was dizzying and it never seemed to end. Aunts and uncles she saw twice a decade, cousins she'd run around causing havoc with as kids, tiny second cousins she'd never yet met. Kids shrieking and running underfoot, wine bottles open everywhere, endless meals, laughter and tears, hot-blooded opinions and everyone wanting to hug her and hear every minute of her last ten years in detail. Chaos, exactly the way Gabriellis did it best.

A week after the funeral, Ollie cracked.

. . .

I miss you she typed and then quickly deleted. *I miss your pretty face* she sent before she could rethink it. It was some version of the truth after all.

When Ollie pulled up at Lara's house that evening it was Lara waiting on the porch steps for her for a change. Ollie couldn't fight her smile if she tried. Outside of the funeral glimpse it had been almost two weeks since she'd gotten to see her.

"Holy shit, you're a sight for sore eyes," Ollie greeted her. Lara's hair was held back in what Ollie understood to be an artfully arranged messy ponytail, wisps of gold escaping around her face, short denim skirt, t-shirt that hit all the right spots. "How are you this beautiful?" she sank down on the step next to her and pulled her immediately over into her lap to kiss her thoroughly. Lara spluttered out a small gasp of a laugh and kissed her back.

"How are you?" she asked, her voice low.

· · ·

"So much better now," Ollie kissed her again. "It's such a relief to see someone I'm not related to."

"I mean I hope you don't greet your relatives like this." Lara glanced down at her bare thighs wrapped around Ollie's hips.

"I probably would if they looked like you," Ollie told her.

"That's fucked up," Lara observed, her smile slipping out sideways.

"Mmhmm." Ollie kissed her again. She tugged at Lara's t-shirt and pulled it up over her head. Lara looked at her in disbelief. Ollie noticed she was wearing that bra again, the one she'd worn the first night they'd spent together. "What?" she said, trailing her fingers along soft skin, "it's not like you have any neighbours."

They made out heatedly, Ollie feeling desperate and slightly shaky, like the time apart had made it new all over again.

"Missed me huh?" Lara observed, slightly wide-eyed at the greeting.

"You have no idea."

"I thought I was inviting you over for a cup of tea and gentle conversation," she told her, eyebrows raised, her smile almost a smirk. God she liked Lara's mouth.

. . .

"Can we do that part after I take you to bed? Holy shit-" She attempted to cover Lara's breasts with her hands. "I didn't even ask if Tilly was here."

Lara burst out laughing.

"You're safe," she told her. Ollie grabbed her hand and tugged her into the house.

Everything got so hazy after that that she felt drunk. Hot skin, blue eyes, arched back, nipples hard and slick from Ollie's mouth. The taste of her, Lara's breath getting shaky, the sound of her cry as her whole body contracted around Ollie's fingers. Lara's hands on her skin, her gaze growing intensely focussed as she stroked Ollie with her fingers, pleasure wracking her as Lara watched her come completely apart with rapt attention as if there'd be an exam on the subject later.

Ollie was raw, cracked open, everything heightened, all of life suddenly in its clear and rightful context.

"*Lara,*" she murmured into her skin as they both lay gasping. "We only have three weeks. Can we... can we just fuck whatever the rules are supposed to be in this situation and just... have everything? Just for now?"

. . .

Lara clung tight to her.

"I don't know what that means," she told her. "But I think I'm in."

Ollie pulled her back down into her arms and kissed her, nothing but heartache and deep wistful want filling her veins.

Lara closed the shop for three days - Tilly having a best friends mini-break with Frankie - and Ollie took her camping. They didn't have to go far from Ribbonwood for a perfect spot: a semi-wild campground out the back of someone's bush block, no tourists sharing it mid-week, nothing but trees and the riverbank, stars for days and a campfire every night.

The first half of the trip was all lazy day hikes, making love in the afternoons, squealing and splashing in the icy cold stream in lieu of a shower, Lara laughing at Ollie's attempts to cook literally anything in the campfire embers, coming to the rescue with pre-made snacks and endlessly decadent store treats that Ollie now understood were entirely Lara's secret champagne tastes.

"I don't understand how a wide-eyed country girl got to be such a hipster foodie jerk," Ollie teased her.

Lara rolled her eyes.

"You understand we have the internet here too, right?"

. . .

By day two they were barely even wearing clothes anymore, the weather so balmy, the location so private, their desire only heightened it seemed, by the impending end of it all.

"God," Lara groaned from inside their tent as she collapsed into a sweaty, sex-drenched, incredibly hot mess at four in the afternoon. "I don't think I can even walk anymore."

Ollie gathered her in close, smirking at her handiwork.

"Luckily, you don't need to," she placed a kiss on her lower abdomen, making Lara twitch and grab for her just in case that kiss wandered. She tugged Ollie up and pulled her down against her body.

"What am I going to do without this?" Lara whispered into her ear. "What the fuck, Ollie, what have you done to me?"

Ollie kissed her, then kissed her again, her heart clenching. Lara hadn't once said anything like this, not one single thing that would suggest she was going to miss Ollie when she was gone. Now that she had, her tone full of longing and confusion, Ollie felt like she was in pieces. She had nothing. All she could do was to kiss her again.

"Lara," was all she could whisper back. "Lara Bennett. How could I have known you would *destroy* me like this?"

. . .

They clung to each other for so long, without words, that they eventually fell asleep in each other's arms, only to wake up in the pitch black night, hungry, disorientated, and a little sad. That night they stayed up by the campfire, telling each other all kinds of mixed up stories about their lives.

Lara told Ollie about her only clear memory of her mother, kissing her goodnight before bed, maybe somewhere around the age of four. *She smelled good. I remember that.*

Ollie told her about the PTSD-lite she was experiencing from her job, how she still struggled to sleep at night without tiny faces popping into her memory. *It's the faces I've probably forgotten that are the worst part,* she told her. *No one should forget a child's death, but I know I have.*

Lara told her what it was like when Tilly was a newborn, Lara completely overwhelmed and sideswiped by terrified love. *I barely knew who I was but I knew that for her, I would find out.*

Ollie just about died laughing, swearing blue that Lara was entirely inventing her claim to remember a twelve-year-old Ollie making *a self-righteous, twenty-minute speech about the dangers of smoking marijuana* during school debates, though honestly it did sound kind of familiar.

. . .

She retaliated with her newfound conviction that Lara's hostility toward her in their teens was purely down to desperate, latent desire for her sweaty, ponytailed, gangly self. *Or was it because you were an insufferable arsehole?* Lara wondered aloud, though with the way her eyes danced, Ollie was adamantly convinced her own theory was for sure the truth.

That night when they went to bed, the sex was furious, like it was their last chance, like they had to somehow get their fill, as if they could each brand themself onto the other's heart through her skin until walking away wouldn't even matter.

Ollie nearly got whiplash when Tilly got dropped off after school on Friday and their camping trip became one big silly sleepover, toasting marshmallows, Lara and Ollie both trying to remember the dumb ghost stories they'd all told each other as kids, fresh sheets on the air bed, Tilly happily snuggled between them talking a mile a minute until almost midnight.

In the morning Lara huffed at them in fake-exasperation as Ollie and Tilly spent forty minutes chasing each other around the campsite with a discarded snake skin, each trying to hide it in creepier and creepier places to make someone jump, mostly Lara as she took the lid off a pot to try to cook breakfast and shrieked so loudly the two of them nearly wet themselves.

"So funny," she said drily as she opened the door of the car to drive them home and found the snake skin curled around the centre of the steering wheel like it was napping.

· · ·

"Are you coming home with us, Ollie?" Tilly said on the way back. "You said ages ago you would come and cuddle Moonbright. I promise you're going to be *obsessed* with her."

Ollie and Lara exchanged a sideways look and that was how Ollie found herself sitting on her arse in the world's most stylish chicken coop, a large fluffy golden hen in her arms and Tilly trying to make her memorise the names of what had to be forty different chooks of every colour and stripe and fluff level.

Ollie would have thought it could be weird, spending an extended amount of time with both Lara and her daughter - god, where to put her hands all the time, just for a start - but when she'd said everything she'd meant *everything* and so she and Lara cooked dinner together again, bickering easily and teasing warmly, Lara even stealing a quick kiss while Tilly was absorbed painting scenes of their camping trip at the dining table. They all ate around the table together, played boardgames and cackled with laughter, Tilly high on all the extra attention before she was sent, complaining, to bed, hugging Ollie goodnight on the way.

That night they went to bed, chastely, both wearing underwear and t-shirts, Lara wrapped tightly in her arms, thighs entwined, kissing and gazing at each in some kind of hazy desperate wonder until Ollie felt like she might die. It was possible that she didn't let go of Lara all night; she'd never know, because she slept like a goddamned baby.

Even though it was Sunday morning, Tilly was up bright and early and Ollie looked over wide-eyed to Lara.

. . .

"Shit, should I be sneaking out or something?" she whispered, alarmed.

"It's fine," Lara told her, calmly. "I mean, she knows."

"Knows *what?*" Ollie was flabbergasted.

Lara rolled her eyes.

"That I *like* you," she told her, making Ollie feel oddly flustered and hot. Had Lara ever been that direct? "That adults who like each other sometimes like to spend nights together. That you're leaving soon. That it's all happy and all sad and all okay." She kissed Ollie and got out of bed.

Ollie got dressed and joined them in the kitchen, making the coffee while Lara fed the chooks and Tilly danced between them both and all Ollie could think about were Lara's words.

Was it okay?

Was any of this?

She had no goddamned idea anymore.

Chapter Twenty-Nine

Myrtle Jenkins was not a fast driver. She was methodical and careful and very few other drivers seemed to appreciate that; there was always some young idiot tailgating her. This morning though, her foot was on the gas.

"Get out of my *way*," she groaned as she peered through the windscreen of her little Nissan at the tractor sputtering along the road ahead of her. "Come on, come on, come on!" This was torture! Finally they reached the long straight stretch of road past the bridge and Myrtle floored it, passing old Jack Mackey who waved apologetically as she fanged it past him, almost tempted to give him the finger.

She wasn't usually in such a hurry to get to her weekly Mah Jong game with the girls. Oh, it passed the time, kept her brain active, got her out of the house and gave her a break from Alfie. But it was so *competitive*. Not the Mah Jong part. But socially. Every Thursday morning they all got together, always the same seven women - and

Doug - and over their boards they told each other stories about their week. And the thing was, no matter what anyone else had to say it was always Dottie Parsons who stole the show.

Dottie just had that kind of life. Her children all lived in exotic places like Dubai or Tasmania. Her husband Bob volunteered for the SES and always knew the grisly details of every tree fall or flood. And *then* her granddaughter was born premature and every week she had an update on a new milestone the little girl was beating. Honestly, it was terribly unfair. Even the same week that Alfie had a close encounter with a red-bellied black snake in the garden, Dottie trumped her with a recounting of the time bloody heroic Bob found a brown snake coiled up in the downstairs toilet. But this morning, Myrtle had a *tale* to tell.

She hit the main road and had to slow to fifty. She was tempted to speed through the town; honestly there were so few residents out and about it seemed silly. But Myrtle was on record in the Silverboom Post complaining about hoons - got her picture in the paper and all - so it wouldn't do her reputation any good to be seen speeding. She gritted her teeth and slowed down to forty-five. She looked around her as she cruised, but the only people she saw were Shirley's nephews Connor and Reuben noodling along on their bikes.

Then, she slowed down even further. Because there was Lara Bennett and where there was Lara, a tale always followed. Lara was lingering outside her store, even though it was well past the time she should have opened shop. Honestly, the woman just made up her own rules as she went along, it was entirely aggravating. And who was that with her? Viola Gabrielli, *again.* Myrtle wondered if Lara realised exactly what the town was going to start thinking if she kept hanging around a known *lesb-* oh good *lord!* Lara had just kissed the Gabrielli girl on the mouth!

Well. Look at *that,* Myrtle thought, thrilled, as she watched the kiss continue in her rearview mirror. Today was going to be the best Mah Jong game in history.

"Wait, *what?*" cried Dottie, twenty minutes later, her eyes round and rapt, just hanging on Myrtle's every word, apple cake forgotten on the table before her.

"And that's not even the real story," Myrtle told the girls. And Doug. Oh victory was *sweet.* "There's a police investigation over at Chloe Perkins' place!"

"Hang on a minute, when you say kissed her, do you mean *kissed* her?" Sylvia butted in.

"Of course she meant *kissed* her," Dottie jumped in. "What other way could she have meant it?"

"Well, young women can be affectionate with one another without it being something suspicious-"

"Suspicious? They're having *sex,* Sylvia, not robbing a bank."

. . .

"I *said* there's a police investigation!" Myrtle used her teaspoon to bang on the table like a judge's gavel. They weren't getting it. "At Chloe's place. I'm talking crime scene vans, police divers, the lot. An *investigation*. I drove right by it this morning. You've never seen such a circus."

"Drugs?" asked Barbara with relish, taking a large sip of her eleven a.m sherry.

"With divers?" Dottie frowned. "Who'd hide drugs in a dam? No one wants soggy marijuana."

"No," Myrtle agreed. She took a deep breath and comprehensively won Mah Jong forever. "I think they're investigating a *murder*."

Chapter Thirty

Ollie awoke in her own bed, slightly disorientated for a moment. No warm body beside her, unless you counted the dachshund that had somehow found his way behind her knees. She tried to stretch and he imitated her, contorting his small entirely odd body and stumbling up over the covers to lie down again with his head on her chest. Ollie huffed out a sigh, but also found herself gently patting his silky soft ears. Was she... *attached* to Rocco? Surely not.

Ten days. That was how long she had left before it was time to board the plane back to Melbourne. Yesterday morning she'd spoken with Cherie, who'd called her again as she'd been just about to sit down for lunch out on the deck, watching a trio of black cockatoos shrieking and spreading their huge wings in the old fig tree. Cherie had asked if she was ready to come back to work and Ollie had stared wide-eyed over the vines, her stomach clenching. Cherie couldn't ask her directly if she'd sought the help she'd suggested and Ollie didn't tell her that she hadn't. She'd been too busy running full tilt into a beautiful woman instead. There'd also been other minor things to contend with, like her Nonna's death, her family's wholehearted overtaking of her life, reconnecting with old friends and wandering through the rainforest, remembering how to breathe.

Was that help? Did it count?

Was Ollie ready?

She had to be.

"Shit Rocco," she whispered to him. "You're only small. I'm pretty sure you can fit in my carry-on luggage."

She paused on her way down the hall, standing for a moment to look into her Nonna's bedroom. The hospital bed was gone, replaced once more by the neatly made single bed her grandmother had slept in for decades. Portia was curled up at the foot-end, alone. Ollie's eyes filled with tears. She came over and gently petted the ageing moggy who squinted her yellow eyes and purred.

It was another glowingly sunny morning when she took a plate of toast out onto the deck. Matty was already sitting in his favourite spot, a loud man taking a quiet moment, his eyes gazing out on miles of green. She nodded at him and he tried to trip her up as she walked past. Ollie was too fast, reflexes honed from a lifetime of being the youngest sibling, and she swatted him instead.

. . .

They sipped in companionable silence, watching a pair of emerald doves busybody their way around the grass together. She thought about Lara, probably in her stupidly pretty kitchen right now, sipping her own coffee while trying to organise Tilly out the door. The two of them had come for Sunday night dinner again the other night, now that the extraneous Gabriellis had finally retreated from whence they came. There'd been several sets of eyes on the two of them as Ollie couldn't stop herself from holding Lara's hand, wrapping an arm around her shoulder, dropping a kiss into her hair. Unlike Sadie and Nico though, no one went out of their way to tease them. Ollie supposed that was probably something to do with the look on her face. If Lara came again this weekend, it would be for the last time.

"Jesus, did somebody die or something?"

Matty and Ollie traded appalled glances as Nico pushed his way out the screen door.

"Sensitive as always, mate," Matty sighed.

"I just didn't picture you two as the silent meditation type." Nico plonked himself opposite them. "Doing a spot of mindfulness are we? Downward dog?"

"Just enjoying the peace and quiet." Ollie shot her brother a look. "At least, we were."

. . .

"Not much more of that for you," Nico observed. "Don't know how you live in Melbourne," he shuddered. "Nightmare."

"Oh yeah," Ollie said drily. "Amazing food, fantastic night life, beautiful parks, incredible culture... not that you'd know what that was."

Nico grinned at her.

"Ribbonwood Pub does a great steak," he said easily. "Couple of good mates, a beautiful woman, what the fuck else do you need?"

Ollie opened her mouth to retort and she found it closing again. For fuck's sake. Sometimes Nico had a point.

"Got you there," Matty pointed at her. "You going to be okay?" His voice came out low and gentle.

Ollie glared down at her coffee cup.

"Yep," she said shortly. She leaned back in the sunshine, closed her eyes and thought of her favourite cafe on Lyon Street, the new wine bar that had opened half a block from her house, the gourmet pizza joint that now delivered twenty-four hours a day. UberEats, street festivals, food vans, arthouse cinema. The NGV, the MCG, Midsummer Pride. She thought of everything she loved about her life there. Eventually she realised it had all faded from her brain as she listened to the bird chorus.

By mid-afternoon Ollie felt a bit like she was going to burst right out of her own skin. What did you do with ten days left, when you couldn't figure out how you were supposed to say goodbye? She imagined herself back in Melbourne, texting Lara from the tea room at work. She couldn't imagine not speaking with her, hearing updates on her day. But that wouldn't be right. Would it? Should they cold turkey it? Close the door gently on their way back to their real lives, a chapter closed? She couldn't fathom it either way.

She grabbed her hat and went for a walk around the winery. The vines were starting to get leafy and lush and the sun was baking down on her bare limbs, adamantly tanned now despite her precautions.

"Ollie!" Her mother's voice rang out from the distance and her head snapped up. There was something off in her high-pitched tone.

When she looked up, she saw her mum with Pia, coming down a row of vines together. Pia stopped still and grabbed an end post, doubling over in pain. Ollie ran.

"Fuck." Pia gritted her teeth, her face sweaty. "Oh my god."

"Oh wow." Ollie took her arm, her smile spilling out and her anxiety spiking simultaneously. "She's on her way?"

. . .

"I thought it was just back pain," Pia groaned. "So I tried to walk it off. Then this," she gestured down. Her shorts were soaked through with her broken waters.

Ollie and her mum helped Pia gingerly make her way down the row, but they'd barely taken five steps when Pia gripped them tight for balance and panted through another contraction. Ollie whipped out her phone to look at the stopwatch. Another few steps and it was happening again. Less than a minute apart.

"Hey mum," Ollie said, trying to keep her voice light. "Want to call an ambulance?"

"*Fuck*," Pia gasped. "No fucking way."

Ollie handed her mother her phone and she very smartly walked away as she called ooo. Ollie and Pia made it as far as the old fig tree and out of the baking sun before she dropped to her knees, an unholy sound coming from her as everything about her began to push, like it or not. Ollie's heart began to race, her hands shaking. She concentrated extremely hard on keeping her voice level as she ordered her mum into the house for every towel they had and some hand sanitiser.

"Hey," she said, approaching her sister, "this might be a bit weird for all of us, but-"

.　.　.

"Oh for fuck's sake Ollie!" Pia glared at her as she panted. "This is my third baby and you're a doctor. Do what you gotta do."

"Okay," said Ollie a second later, her voice so calm she scared even herself, "I can feel the head," she announced.

Pia nodded ferociously, then dropped down onto her hands and pushed again, her face filled with fury and determination and Ollie got down beside her. Her mum rubbed Pia's back, making soothing sounds; she'd been there for every other grandchild, but never in a goddamned *paddock*. Ollie's fingers went numb with sudden terror. She wasn't in any way an obstetrician but she'd done a rotation in birth suite as a resident. She could already count the ways this could go wrong. *Shoulder dystocia,* her mind raced, *cord wrapped around the neck.* Her vision blurred, *postpartum haemorrhage,* her sister bleeding out in the fucking grass before her eyes, Ollie helpless to do anything to stop it.

She heard a voice calmly counting out loud to ten, coaching her sister through each push and realised it was her own.

"Good work, honey, almost there," said Dr Gabrielli encouragingly, while Ollie tried not to pass out.

Barely two minutes later, she was clutching a slippery baby and quickly pulling it up to her sister's chest. The baby was purple. *Normal,* Dr Gabrielli reminded her. *Perfectly normal.* The little hands were moving, Pia sobbing, Ollie rubbing the baby's back briskly with a towel, the small mouth opening, cord still pulsing, the skin slowly turning pink before her eyes as her lungs breathed in oxygen for the first time, a baby's cry.

"Oh my fucking *god!*" Her brothers were suddenly there. "Someone call Jimmy-"

Ollie looked down and realised she was already massaging her sister's belly, trying to help it contract, looking at the blood on Pia's thighs, trying to calculate, a towel under her, damp but not soaked. Time seemed to jump sideways and a paramedic materialised from nowhere.

Pia straight up refused to go to hospital.

"My sister's a doctor," she said, her eyes flashing. "I know how to look after a damn baby and you just said my vitals were all fine. Pretty sure women have given birth in paddocks since the beginning of time."

"And *died,*" Ollie pointed out before she could stop herself. The entire family looked at her, horrified.

"Ollie." Pia eyeballed her directly, a solidly older-sibling expression on her face. "Tell me like my sister who's done a thousand years of training. Do I need to be admitted to hospital right now? Does she? Or can we just call it a damn home birth and go cuddle up together in the peace and quiet while we get to know Alessandra?"

. . .

Everyone gazed at the tiny baby, now latched firmly to a nipple, appetite clearly identifying her as a Gabrielli.

Her dad - who Ollie hadn't even noticed arrive - starting sobbing.

Between them all they got Pia and Alessandra up to the house, tucked in a bed, Ollie calling Pia's midwife to come check them out as a compromise, James running in the door like a man having a heart attack, wrapping his arms around his wife, crying in shock and joy and despair all in one.

They all tiptoed out to give them some space. Ollie washed her hands, stared at her startled face in the bathroom mirror, then dizzily found herself back down in the garden under the fig tree. The bloodied towels were all gone, nothing to say anything monumental had just happened there except a little flattened grass. Her knees practically gave out and she sat down, hard.

"What am I *doing?*" She looked down at the place her niece had just arrived onto the planet, Gabrielli blood on Jinibara soil, everyone's sweat and tears, love and fear, grief and joy all combined until Ollie didn't know whose feelings were whose, whose hand it was that had come down to gently rest on her back as she rubbed her sister's belly, whose tears had soaked her shoulder, whose hand had gripped hers when the ambulance arrived.

She thought of her Nonna's last breath, of her mother looking older every Christmas, the tears streaking down her dad's stubbled cheeks. She thought of fairy crowns made of daisies and dandelions, of the gentle fuzz of soft newborn hair on the niece whose very first breath she'd gotten to see. She thought of a huge bonfire, surrounded with women who might snipe at each other in public but who had each other's backs no matter what. She thought of Lara, the heat and sweetness of her kiss as she leaned out her front door yesterday morning to say goodbye, the laughter in her eyes as Ollie kept trying to leave and kept finding one more reason to kiss her again.

"What am I *doing?*" She gripped her own shoulders and squeezed, her eyes gazing up into the enormous fig tree, the entwined branches, the shade it had provided for generations before her. She squeezed her eyes closed, Melbourne and Ribbonwood flipping like polaroid snaps through her brain.

She was in the farm ute before she even knew she was going to do it.

Her heart raced as she drove the twists and turns of the back roads, not even a grind of the gears now, fully acclimatised. She couldn't get there fast enough, cursing the tight bends and single track road, Lara's voice repeating like a soundtrack. *What am I going to do without this? I like you. I don't let people in my bed. You're so fucking beautiful. What the fuck Ollie, what have you done to me?*

When she reached the house the afternoon was fading into early evening, sunset hitting and reflecting pink light off the glass, soft warm glow spilling from the windows, Lara's car in the carport. She was already opening the door when Ollie pulled up - the ute was hardly subtle - and she looked surprised. Surprised and beautiful, a gleam in her eyes as Ollie stumbled up onto her porch, staring at everything she could ever want.

. . .

"Can't stay away, huh?" Lara smirked at her, a question in her eyes.

"No," Ollie breathed. She tugged Lara just outside her front door and kissed her with intense softness. "Lara," her voice was almost a whisper as she pulled back just enough to speak. "I can't even begin to describe the day I just had but... fuck, I've figured it out, all of it. I... can't leave," she told her, still slightly shocked at the words spilling out her mouth, trying to reel back from any big confessions but still meaning every damn word. She met Lara's eyes and caught the startled expression in their blue depths. She raced on. "I can't leave Ribbonwood. Everything I've ever wanted is here. I'm not going to go back to Melbourne; I don't want to do it.... I don't know what this means for us, but I want to stay and figure that out."

"What do you mean you're not going?" Lara had gotten very still. "You live in *Melbourne,* that's where your life is. You can't just stay here-"

"I can." Ollie shook her head. "Lara... Pia just had her baby, I helped her birth right there at home." Lara blinked at the segue and she tried to explain. "My family... they're *everything.* I don't want to miss out on their lives." She let her hands run down Lara's arms. "And," she met her eyes, "I don't want to miss out on this."

"Ollie." Lara stepped back, Ollie's hands suddenly holding air. "You're emotional, it's clearly been a big day." Her eyes were large, wary. "Everything with your grandmother... your job... it makes sense." She shook her head. "But you don't belong here. We both know that."

Ollie started to feel cold. Lara's limbs were stiff, her expression absolutely the opposite of thrilled.

"I'm not... I'm not trying to push you for something Lara," she said. "I just want to give us the time to work this out- to give it a chance and see where it could go."

"We don't need time for that," Lara told her, her face shutting down completely. "This is everything it was ever going to be, Ollie. A fling."

Ollie stared at her for several long seconds. She saw the slight tremor in Lara's fingers.

"I don't believe you," she said slowly. "I know it's more than that. We both know it's more."

"No." Lara shook her head. Ollie caught the tears shining in her eyes. "I don't *do* what it is you're asking for. I don't want a relationship, that's not who I am or what my life looks like." A tear spilled down her cheek and she wiped it away, roughly. "I'm never going to do that again," she whispered.

"*Lara.*" Ollie's heart was cracking. "Those are two different things. What your marriage was and what we would be-"

. . .

"The only reason I let you talk me into this in the first place was because you were leaving." Lara's tone grew short. She took a sharp breath. "Ollie, you're... god, you are a once in a lifetime thing, believe me I know that." Her blue eyes glimmered with tears. "But this only happened because you were just passing through."

Ollie stared at her, unable to believe how fast her hopes were crumbling. This couldn't be happening. She could almost see Lara's defences rebuilding; she had to break through, make her *see*.

She took a step closer again.

"Lara-"

"Soccer." Lara put her hand out imploringly, her eyes scrunching tightly closed and Ollie froze still.

"I'm sorry?"

"It's my safe word." Lara's voice was low as she opened her eyes. "Please just stop, I need you to stop."

Ollie stood very still, her hands at her side, her eyes on the ground. When she looked up, Lara had stepped away, her hand already on her front door handle though her eyes were still fixed on Ollie's face.

. . .

"Lara," Ollie said. "I'm always going to respect what you want." She could barely find her voice. "But this is goodbye, you know that right?"

Lara watched her for a beat, her face pale. Then she moved. Her hands were in Ollie's hair and she was kissing her, long, tender, slow. Ollie kissed her back, so convinced this couldn't be it, that Lara felt everything she felt. She could taste it in her kiss, in the longing, the feeling she was so sure could one day be love if Lara would just give them a chance. She kept her eyes squeezed closed as Lara let her go. When she opened them it was on the front door closing. She heard the faint *click*, as Lara locked it behind her.

Chapter Thirty-One

A week went by and then two.

Lara put one foot in front of the other. She got her child out of bed and off to school. She put clothes on, did her hair, applied eyeliner with careful precision. She opened the store, made small talk with tourists, restocked the shelves. She kept going, just like she always had.

She was brittle though, so focussed on holding her own shit together that for once she had no time to take care of anyone else's nightmares. Chloe kept calling her, over and over and Lara found that she couldn't make herself pick up. She had nothing left. Not even for sweet, traumatised Chloe having another anxiety meltdown. She texted Esme instead, asking her to check in on Chloe. And then *Esme* started calling her. Lara didn't answer her either. She just needed five goddamn minutes to herself and the world just wouldn't let up.

. . .

Tilly was still furious with her, showing a truly advanced level of grudge holding for her age. Lara had kissed Ollie Gabrielli goodbye for the last time and stepped shakily back into her house to find her daughter glaring at her, small hands fisted at her sides.

"I hate you!" she'd screamed and ran into her room, slamming the door behind her. Lara had followed in confused misery, wishing like she'd wished a thousand times before, that single parenthood came with a pause button you could hit when your life was crumbling down around your ears.

"Honey." She'd opened her daughter's door to find her hugging her knees on the bed, tear-stained and angry. "What's-"

"She wanted to stay!" Tilly had accused her. "You didn't let her!"

"Oh, baby." Lara's voice cracked. "That wasn't a conversation for you to-"

"Why not?" Tilly had demanded. "Me and Frankie had a plan. Sadie would marry Nico and you would marry Ollie and we would be sisters and Aria would be our cousin and we'd get to keep Rocco and be a family and you *ruined it.*"

"Sweetheart." Lara's heart started to break for her child. If there was one desperately sore spot in her life as a single mother of an only child it was this. "Oh, love..."

. . .

"I *hate* you," Tilly cried again. "Leave me alone."

Lara had dropped a kiss on her child's soft silky hair, told her she loved her, that everything would be okay, and then she made herself leave. She'd sat outside her daughter's door, her arms wrapped around her middle, trying to hold herself together. Something vital had sprung a leak somewhere inside her, spilling out feelings everywhere that she didn't fully comprehend, and wanted to even less.

Two weeks later she still felt that way. Sadie was almost as mad at her as Tilly was, although somewhat more mature about it. Lara lay awake at night, trying not to think about the emptiness of her bed, of the arms that weren't holding her, the kiss that wasn't driving her insane. She'd gone a long time without any of it. She would go without it again and be just fine. The feeling was kind of like a drug withdrawal, she figured; she just had to wait it out until Ollie Gabrielli was out of her bloodstream.

Ollie was truly gone now, so Lara didn't have much choice in the matter. For all Ollie had said about her family, in the end she'd gotten on her flight. Sadie had told her, even though Lara hadn't asked. It only made it even clearer to Lara that she had, without a doubt, made the right call. Ollie had thought Lara was worth staying for and Lara had proven she was wrong before she'd gone and made some crazy decision like staying in fucking Ribbonwood forever. Thank god Ollie had seen the light. Back to Melbourne, back to her real life.

Lara wanted nothing more than for Ollie to be happy. She could see her so clearly in the big city, living a sophisticated, cultured existence, the brief fling with a woman from her little country home town already a cute footnote to what would be a long and fulfilling life.

As for Lara, she'd be alright eventually. She'd known from the very beginning that this pain was coming; even one night of Ollie Gabrielli in her bed had been a lot. The problem was that the pain she'd been anticipating had been the pain of a tough goodbye, Ollie getting on a plane and leaving her behind, contact maybe cut, maybe slowly drifting out, Lara left staring up at her bedroom ceiling and missing her, but knowing everything was as it should be.

Instead, the pain that had arrived in the end was an entirely different beast to contend with. The shock of Ollie actually prepared to want more, the sick feeling of being the one to put that devastated look on her face. The knowledge that Ollie was walking around out there thinking Lara had rejected her when the truth was so much more complicated than that. It wasn't something she could put into words, not in a way that would make sense to someone like Ollie Gabrielli with her huge loving family, her big expansive life and her past romantic heartbreaks that were all cute little things like *a girl cheated on me this one time.*

Even Sadie hadn't gotten it when she'd sat Lara down and demanded to know *what the actual fuck* Lara thought she was doing?

"I'm never going to marry anyone ever again," Lara told her. "I'm never having another kid. I don't want to be someone's wife, or to have to answer to someone else. I don't want to live in some little claustrophobic bubble, cooped up in a house together. I want to be *myself.*"

. . .

Sadie had stared at her.

"Does Ollie want to get married?" she asked. "Did she say she wants kids?"

"Of course she does." Lara rolled her eyes. "Look at her family."

"Literally, did you ask her?"

"Are you hearing me though? I'm not ever going through that again, and I won't put Tilly through it either."

"Lars." Sadie grabbed her forearm. Lara stared. They weren't really the touchy-feely kind of friends, not unless Sadie thought things were really dire. "Can we keep in mind here that the last time you were in a relationship it was because you were coerced into marrying your abuser?"

"It wasn't that black and white," Lara said automatically.

"It really pretty much was though," Sadie said matter of factly. "Did you ever consider that maybe your parameters to measure this shit by might be way fucking off? I mean think about it, how does Ollie make you feel?"

. . .

Lara swallowed hard. She wasn't going to go there.

"Like she's someone I would end up reliant on," she said flatly. "If I let her. And I don't want that. What if it fails?" She stared at Sadie. "I don't want to model that for Tilly either. I want her to be able to be self-reliant, so that she's never in the position I was in."

"Self-reliant," Sadie said softly. "Is that what you call it? Don't you think there should be a little room in there, to not have to be so alone?"

"We're all alone," Lara told her with a frown, "when it comes down to it. Better to accept that than to find yourself relying on someone else and have your whole life fall to pieces. People let you down, Sadie, it's just human nature."

Sadie had stared at her for a long time.

"Fuck babe," she said eventually. "That outlook is seriously bleak."

Was it? Lara hadn't been trying to be bleak, just brutally honest.

She didn't think Ollie was out to trap her or would treat her badly; it was abundantly clear who Ollie was. Ollie was a good, kind, deeply beautiful person, who was far too inclined to overlook Lara's pitfalls. A life with Lara Bennett - the town outcast - with a reputation, a salty mouth and a wagon full of baggage? In Ribbonwood? Was she insane?

Lara could see exactly how it would play out. Sexual attraction, even the over-the-top fiery kind they shared, had its limits. Eventually Ollie's sex-hued glasses would come off and she'd see Lara for who she really was, outside of a pair of admittedly excellent tits. Lara might also be solidly influenced by Ollie's attractiveness but she knew full well, that if she let herself dream for even a minute that Ollie was really hers, there'd be no coming back from it. To love Ollie and watch it become unrequited would wreck her. And Lara refused to be wrecked. Not after she'd already survived so much.

The store bell chimed distantly in Lara's ears. She was so lost in her thoughts she didn't even notice who it was who'd entered, until they were standing right there in front of her.

———

Ollie was wearing a jacket. It was the first time in almost three months that she'd needed anything warmer than a light shirt. *For fuck's sake Melbourne;* it was December for crying out loud. Probably in a fortnight it would be forty degrees and the entire town would be suffering heat stroke, but right now, as she turned into Sydney Road, the wind sliced through her like a blade of ice.

Out of curiosity she pulled out her phone and checked the temperature. She snorted at herself. It was twenty degrees. Shit, she really had acclimatised to Queensland. She tried to blame the wind chill factor but that was a stretch.

. . .

This part of Sydney Road was ridiculously busy at just after five-thirty in the afternoon. The traffic was at a standstill and the footpath heaved with people heading home, to after-work drinks or early dinner. It felt overwhelming to her - the noise and busyness of it all - though she'd only been home a couple of days. Home? Well, that felt complicated to claim, on several levels.

She was on her way for a belated catch up with her friend Chelsea, finally having called her from the departure lounge, desperate for the distraction and the patient ear of someone who knew her well, yet was somewhat objective about everyone else involved in Ollie's story. She'd given her the outline, but now Ollie was going to meet her for dinner, to wallow in the details that were keeping her up at night.

She was half a block from the bar when her phone vibrated in her back pocket. She frowned. It was Nico. They weren't really the phone catch-up kind of siblings.

"Hey," she said. "Is everything okay?"

"Ol," he said. "Something has happened."

"What?" Every single one of Ollie's senses prickled. She stood stock still in the middle of the footpath, people huffing and flowing around her. Nico took in a deep breath.

. . .

"They found a body, out the back of Chloe Perkins' place. Reckon it's her old boyfriend, Dale Winchester."

"Shit," said Ollie. She wasn't really sure why Nico was telling her this. She'd only met Chloe a couple of times and Dale never.

"Ol," he said again, his voice sounding strange. A sick feeling hit her, before he even said the words. "They reckon Lara did it. She's been arrested."

Chapter Thirty-Two

Lara sat in the interview room at the Silverbloom Police Station and shivered. She wasn't sure if it was deliberate but the air conditioning was turned up so high she felt like she was freezing to death. Her fingers were white, but whether that was from the cold or from stress she didn't know.

She was alone. The cop - the older one - had left nearly an hour ago, after Lara - who might be something akin to terrified, but who also wasn't an idiot - had refused to say anything at all. The room she was in had opaque safety glass windows, a table and chairs bolted to the floor and a plastic bottle of water for her to drink. She wasn't sure if the door was locked or if the cameras were on. She figured she was being watched one way or another. So she did nothing.

She couldn't stop shivering and she really needed to pee. She was pretty sure she might be about to throw up. She stayed stock still and tried not to give them anything at all, which only made her think of a prey animal. What kind of strategy was this? So far she didn't have another one. All she wanted was to go home.

The door opened and the cop - Chris something, she was pretty sure, because of course they were all fucking called *Chris* - walked in.

"Come on Lara." He looked thoroughly annoyed. "What are you playing at?"

She frowned.

"I'm afraid you're going to have to be a little more specific," she said drily. *Jesus christ, don't taunt the police Lara.*

"There are two goddamned lawyers out here, both saying they represent you. You're entitled to *a* lawyer. So which one is it?"

"What are you talking about?" Lara wasn't playing at anything. She'd used up her one phone call to get hold of Sadie and tell her that shit was hitting the fan and to pick Tilly up from school this afternoon. *No matter what, keep her safe. Don't let her worry, okay?*

The cop eyeballed her. He looked familiar somehow, but she couldn't place him.

He held up a post-it note and squinted at it.

. . .

"There's a Danielle Nguyen, says she's a senior partner at Audrey Coleman's firm, specialises in criminal law. Apparently she'll represent you pro bono. And then there's a Steve Rossi, also a senior criminal lawyer, says the Gabrielli family has hired him and apparently you shouldn't worry about a bill there either."

Lara blinked. Her eyes got hot.

Cop Chris tapped his foot. God, she was so sure she knew him. Years disappeared and a flash of the scent of beer hit her, men's voices from her living room shouting at the football on the television. She swallowed, hard.

"Audrey's one," she said after a minute, forcing her voice to come out steadily. She wasn't about to let a Gabrielli pay a single bill for her, especially not if Audrey's boss was willing to help her for free.

"Fine," he said. He disappeared and a couple of minutes later, an expensive, extremely competent looking middle-aged woman walked into the room. To the detective's distaste he was promptly organised into letting Lara use the bathroom, bringing in a cup of instant coffee and adjusting the room to a comfortable temperature. Lara was not a hugger but if Danielle had offered her a hug too, from this woman she'd probably have taken one.

Lara, now instructed, answered the detective's questions. No, she hadn't killed Dale Winchester, no she didn't know who had. No, she wasn't conducting deep conspiracies to murder and maim men, saying *he'd sleep with the fishes* was a goddamned joke. Yes, Lara was capable of dark jokes about men actually, most women were.

"What did you mean when you said to Eva Sinclair - in regards to her partner Dan Evans -" he checked his notes, *"we're going to find a way to make him pay?"*

"I meant we are literally going to find a way to make him pay. *Child support,*" she emphasised. "And a fair division of assets. He left Eva after four years and a child together to go do FIFO, then decided he was bored of his life with her and wanted to shack up with someone else." The cop just looked at her, nonplussed, and Lara just barely resisted the urge to roll her eyes. "He didn't tell her that though," she explained. "He literally just stopped answering his phone and blocked her access to the only family income they had, while she was stuck out in the bush with no car and no childcare. When she called around - his boss, the local police - freaking out and searching for him, he pretended he didn't even know who she was."

"And how exactly were you planning on *making* him pay?" The cop narrowed his eyes. "What was the plan, Lara?"

Lara glared at him, actively willing him to burst into flames.

"I found a contact up at the mines. And I have a friend who's a lawyer." She tried not to look at Danielle, unsure if this was going to backfire on Audrey somehow. "She drafted a letter outlining his responsibilities and threatening to take him to court if he didn't do the right thing. The contact made sure he got the letter, since Dan has been pretending he has no address."

The cop made some notes. Danielle gave her a carefully encouraging nod while he frowned down at his laptop.

"You were overheard to say to Ms. Sinclair in regards to Chloe Perkin's partner, Mr. Dale Winchester: *I hope I never have to go to that extent again. It was messy. But Dan won't even know what hit him.*" He looked up at Lara to see her reaction. She tried not to give him one. "You can see how that would be of interest to us," he watched her face, "being that Mr. Winchester was reported as a missing person by his mother back in March of this year, just over eight months ago. The body we recovered from the dam at his ex-partner's property is in a deteriorated condition but I'm told the cause of death was probably due to the great big dent someone gave him to the back of the head." He sat back in his chair as if his case was closed. "Ms. Sinclair was heard to say you *got rid of him.* So tell me, Lara, did Dale even know what hit him?"

Lara stared back at him, her chin high.

"I don't know," she repeated. "I wasn't there."

"I can see how maybe things could have gotten a bit out of hand, a bit *messy* as you put it. Maybe you just meant to warn him off. He didn't take it well, things got heated." He didn't ask a question so Lara didn't answer one. "Chloe Perkins wanted him gone didn't she?"

. . .

"Wouldn't you? He beat and raped her."

"So you took matters into your own hands? You didn't, say, assist her to get some help, make a police report perhaps?"

"You have to be fucking kidding me." Lara gave him the iciest glare she was capable of. "Since when do you lot give a shit about *domestic violence*," she bit out. "Just a guy torturing his girlfriend, not really a crime is it?"

Danielle gave her a warning glance and she tried to wind herself back.

Cop Chris kept his expression perfectly bland but Lara could see the hint of red to his throat now.

"Did you conspire to-"

"*No*. I didn't harm him and I didn't ask anyone else to either. I have no idea what happened to him, though I promise you it couldn't have happened to a nicer guy."

"I'm going to take a minute to confer with my client," Danielle interjected. The detective gave her a long level look but got up and left the room. "Lara," the lawyer said firmly as she turned to her.

"This tough girl shit isn't going to help you here."

"I'm not going to cry," Lara said, the words coming out slightly ferociously. "I'm not going to play the little terrified woman or get hysterical or beg to go home. I'm not *doing* that."

Danielle stared at her.

"That's not what I'm asking you to do," she said gently. "I'm asking you to answer the questions, without commentary. Without deliberately antagonising the police detective who might decide they see fit to charge you with murder and send you to a remand facility, awaiting trial."

Lara swallowed hard. She nodded.

When the detective came back into the room she tried to hold her shit together. Why was it so hard to let go of her defence mechanisms without falling apart altogether?

"Tell me what you meant when you told Ms. Sinclair that things got *messy* with Dale Winchester."

"Well," Lara said, fighting hard to keep her voice even. "I flirted with him. I made him think I was interested. Strung him along, made him think he had a chance."

. . .

"Why?" the cop prodded.

I was just getting to that! Lara snapped internally. She kept her face still.

"One day I texted him, told him to meet me, told him it was urgent." The detective watched her closely. "I told him you'd contacted me." He blinked. "I told him the police were onto him, the drugs he was dealing, the shit he was up to. I said you were wanting me to wear a wire, ask him questions about the guys he got the drugs from. He freaked out." She looked at him. "And then he left town."

"When was that?"

Lara sucked in a breath.

"Sometime in March," she said quietly.

The room was silent. The detective looked at her for a long time.

"It got messy."

"Not like that." She tried to keep breathing.

"How did it get messy, Lara?"

. . .

"He kissed me," she said. "I didn't want him to."

"You hit him. It just happened-"

"No," Lara denied. "I just flirted with him some more, managed his ego for him, told him to go before he ran out of time. Then I got the hell out of there. It just... it scared me." She felt sick as she admitted it. "I knew what he was capable of. And even though I met him in public, there wasn't really anyone around. And even if there were..." She didn't finish the sentence. *Even if there were, do you think they'd go out of their way for Lara Bennett if she were cornered by a man? After all, she'd always been asking for it.*

Cop Chris made some notes. Then, without a word, he got to his feet and left the room. Lara stared at Danielle and tried not to panic.

"Remand facility?" she asked, her voice coming out high and tight. She felt like she was running out of oxygen. *Oh god, Tilly.*

"It would be highly unlikely," said Danielle soothingly. "They have nothing but incredibly circumstantial evidence."

"There's *no* evidence." Lara sucked in a deep breath and then another, her throat starting to close up. "I didn't do this. I want to go home." *Don't cry, don't cry, don't cry, don't cry-*

. . .

Danielle was just opening her mouth to speak, her hand gentle on Lara's arm when the door swung back open.

"You're free to go," said the detective. "But I want you back here tomorrow at eleven a.m sharp for further questioning. Don't leave town," he instructed her sternly.

Danielle drove her home, talking calmly about it being completely fine, about how the cops clearly had nothing, but Lara could only hear the words *charge you with murder* and *remand facility* whirling on repeat in her brain. Why bring her back the next morning if not to formally charge her? Were they just getting all their ducks in a row? Did they have something they could twist to somehow look like evidence? After all, Dale had touched her. Were there... fibres? Hairs? That kind of thing happened, didn't it? That cop... she didn't trust him, there was something so supremely confident in his face. Had he been mates with Josh? Lara was pretty sure had. He didn't like her, either way. Lara hadn't been likeable.

She let herself in through her front door with shaking hands. She picked up her phone. She was about to call Sadie, to get Tilly here, to hold her daughter in her arms and never *ever* let her go. *Remand facility.* Then she stopped herself. She was a mess. She would scare the shit out of Tilly. She had to keep it together. She wanted nothing more on this planet than to see her daughter, to hug her tight, to make sure as hell that she knew that she was loved, that she'd be okay-

Lara called no one. She switched her phone off instead. She drifted around the house on autopilot. She unstacked and restacked the dishwasher. She went to hang the washing out but then thought *remand facility* and put the clothes in the dryer instead. She went out and topped up the food and water for the chooks, checking everyone was locked up safe. She looked at all the fresh vegetables waiting in the crisper and slowly made a huge pot of thick rustic stew. She ate a bowl without tasting it and put the rest into containers to freeze. There'd be something nutritious in the house then. *Remand facility.*

Lara curled up in the corner of her sofa and pulled a blanket up to cover herself. She was still so cold. She thought of her daughter, then made herself stop. She thought of Ollie. Arms around her, laughing eyes. Gabrielli family dinner. She thought of Sadie sitting across her kitchen table from her. She thought of bonfire night. All of it, evidence that her life had mattered.

Somehow though, this was where she'd ended up. Holding herself together. Alone. Terrified. Self-reliant.

She stayed that way all night.

———

When Danielle and Lara presented themselves to the Silverbloom Police Station the next day, Cop Chris walked them into another interview room. This one actually had tea and coffee-making facilities and the clear pane of window glass looked out onto the trees. He gestured for them both to take seats.

"You'll be pleased to hear that we're not pursuing any charges against you, Ms. Bennett," he told her. His face was tight and his annoyed expression incongruous with his words.

. . .

Lara felt her vision go fuzzy. For a few seconds it was like her ears were ringing.

"What?" she found herself asking. "Why?"

"Chloe Perkins turned herself in last night. She's been questioned before but this time she confessed to the crime. Self-defence, she said."

"*No!*" Lara cried before she could stop herself. Tiny, frail Chloe Perkins who'd been through so much and who'd tried so hard to warn her. Had she done this to save Lara? "She can't go to jail." She stared at the cop, as if there were a way to argue him out of this. This would never be justice.

"Well," he said, "I suspect she won't. While we were taking her story, Esme Walker came down to the station. She also confessed to the crime." Lara stared at him, her heart racing. *Esme?* "She said she'd found out what he'd been doing to Chloe and was so overcome with rage that she followed him out the back of the property and whacked him with a shovel."

"But... *Esme* wouldn't-"

"This morning, there were three other women waiting for me when I arrived," he fixed her with a firm gaze. "Robyn Lowe informed me she'd seen Dale Winchester selling meth to school kids so she'd lost all control, tracked him down and hit him with her car." He paused and looked down at his notes. "Kylie Burgess said Dale had tried to sexually assault her but she kneed him in the groin, then hit him with a tree branch for good measure." He watched Lara, as tears began to slide down her cheeks. "Jessica Webb-"

"Jessica?" Lara couldn't breathe. Jess had been Josh's fiancé right up until he'd set his sights on Lara. Teenage Lara had been terrified of the weeping, intimidating, beautiful older woman who'd once called her a *slutty little schoolgirl* in public. Adult Lara still couldn't meet her eyes.

"Jessica Webb told me that Dale came after her in some kind of unprovoked drug rage and she'd used the knife he'd been wielding to stab him in the chest." He looked up and rolled his eyes. "I mean, that one doesn't even fit the mechanism of injury, but she also said something about how she should have protected you *back then*, so I figure that one is an obvious outright lie."

"I don't understand," she whispered. There were tears coursing down her cheeks now. She wiped them away but they just kept coming.

"Nico Gabrielli came by not long after that." He looked at her. "Confessed he'd bought marijuana off Dale on several occasions. Said Dale had been *acting wiggy* for months, telling Nico he'd gotten himself into some messy situation, owed money to the wrong guys. Said he seemed scared. By the time Mr. Gabrielli was done, I had a line of bloody women out the damn door, all coming to tell me they'd killed Dale Winchester."

. . .

Lara wept.

"What I'm hearing," Danielle summarised softly, "is that my client is free to go."

"Well, you see my problem," he said with a sigh. "I've got eight different women all prepared to sign statements that they, personally, murdered a man, as well as someone else prepared to get charged with drug possession to let me know another solidly good reason for why Dale Winchester might have wound up dead. No jury in the world is going to be able to convict beyond a reasonable doubt. I don't know what your client has done to deserve this, but yes," he looked Lara in the eye, "she's free to go."

When Lara walked out, it was out into the light.

Chapter Thirty-Three

Three days later Lara was walking down the street feeling cold again. The sun was shining, the afternoon light a particularly beautiful golden blue, the kind that made trees greener and flowers brighter. And still, she'd had to put on a jacket.

As she walked, she thought of all the ways she'd finally lost control of bonfire night. It had always been *her* thing, her place to organise, to build connections in a way she could control and feel safe. The night she'd been let free she'd been home with Tilly - filled with joy at every glimpse of her daughter, the beautiful mundanity of getting to sit next to her on the couch, sharing a bag of chips and wondering what to make for dinner - when she'd heard the first car arriving.

Within half an hour everyone had shown up, completely uninvited, all piling into her house to hug and kiss her, to laugh and weep and haul her out the back of her own damn paddock where Sara was already setting the twigs alight. It was no longer Lara's bonfire night, but their bonfire night; not Lara's role to take care of them all, but for them all to take care of each other, her included. For fuck's sake would Lara *ever* stop crying? *Jesus christ.*

Chloe arrived a little later, tentative, unsure of her welcome, and Lara wrapped her arms around her tightly. She wanted to tell Chloe that no matter what the hell had happened out the back of her property she was safe here, and loved. But as she was hugging her, she glanced over Chloe's shoulder and found herself meeting Esme's eyes. Esme nodded at Lara, just once. Then she turned away and started chatting to Gina Webb and Lara was suddenly not quite sure if she'd imagined what she'd just seen in Esme's eyes. An image flashed through her mind, Esme Walker, the gentle demure tuck shop lady, raising a shovel in her hands. She blinked. She glanced at Esme again and almost laughed at herself. *Nah.*

Chloe was safe. No one was going to jail. And Eva announced that night, as the fire danced, that Dan had consented to signing both a financial agreement and a child custody plan without anyone needing to be dragged through the court system. Now she could see a way through to getting a job that could keep the roof over her child's head and start to rebuild their lives.

All was right that night, under the stars in Ribbonwood.

And it would stay that way. Until the next time.

. . .

Now Lara stopped beside a forest green letterbox on a gate post outside a little house in the inner north of Melbourne. Taking a deep breath, she opened the small gate and walked up the short path to the door. She tucked a stray wisp of hair back behind her ear and steadied herself. And then she knocked. Silence followed. Lara stepped back, hesitating. There wasn't so much a front porch as just a slight alcove, but on it stood a big pot of red geraniums, a bright spot against the tiles. There was a solid chance that no one was home, but she knocked again anyway.

She heard footsteps coming up the hall toward the door and her heart rate skyrocketed. The door opened and Lara felt *shocked* - even though it was she who'd come all this way, to knock on this specific door - to see Ollie Gabrielli suddenly right there in front of her.

Ollie's mouth fell open. Her hair was scooped back in an appealing half-mess of a ponytail, soft grey track pants that probably cost three hundred dollars, a vintage Le Tigre t-shirt, bare feet. Her arms were bare too, her eyes wide. Lara maybe loved her.

They both stared at each other for a long moment.

"You're wearing jeans," Ollie said, her voice sounding far away. "I don't think I've ever seen you with your legs covered before."

"Well, yeah, it's fucking freezing here," Lara pointed out, gesturing vaguely behind her at the cold city beyond Ollie's front gate.

. . .

"It's probably twenty-three degrees," Ollie disagreed.

"Like I said," Lara repeated, unable to believe she'd been derailed into talking about the weather at a moment like this. "Fucking freezing. *No one* should have to live here." She felt herself frown. "Especially not you."

Ollie sunk her teeth into her lower lip at that.

"What, exactly, are you doing here?" she asked quietly.

Lara couldn't take her eyes off her. Her skin looked so warm, her lips soft. She could remember, viscerally, the scent of citrus in Ollie's hair.

"I've never pursued anyone," Lara said carefully. "Not once. My whole life I've only ever been pursued." She looked at Ollie's dark eyes, thought of the light in them when she laughed. She wasn't laughing now. "You scared the shit out of me Ollie," she told her. "Wanting to stay. I only let you in because I thought I could control it... that I could have you, without risking everything." She swallowed, glancing down at Ollie's bare feet. Something about them felt absurdly vulnerable. That was enough to make her keep going. She gazed up at Ollie's face. "I was wrong," she said, struggling not to let her voice crack. "I can't control it. I am risking everything. But I know now that I can take that risk," she swallowed hard, "and that I want to."

. . .

It had hit her, sitting around the bonfire, surrounded by the women who'd risked their freedom for hers, the women who knew, even when Lara hadn't, that she was worth it, that she was good inside. That maybe - just *maybe* - Lara deserved Ollie Gabrielli after all. That perhaps Ollie would in actual fact be incredibly lucky to get to spend her time with the Queen Bee of Ribbonwood. That maybe Ribbonwood was a goddamned beautiful place to live, especially if you were loved well.

And, if it all went to shit, Lara would never find herself alone. She knew that now, all the way to her bones.

"What are you saying, Lara?" Ollie's eyes were soft, but she wasn't exactly throwing herself into Lara's arms.

Lara straightened.

"I've never pursued anyone, but I'm pursuing you," she said, her voice firm, her eyes on Ollie's. "I know that you left... and maybe you might think I'm too late to ask you to come back. But if you think that, it would only be because we are both fucking *idiots* who are always going to be better together than we are apart."

Ollie burst out a small laugh. Okay, sure, maybe that wasn't the most romantic of lines, but Ollie had always known what she was getting into here. Her *eyes*, Lara couldn't stop staring at the light that was dancing in them now. Oh fuck, how had she gone without this for even a day? Before Ollie could say anything, before Lara even knew she was going to do it, Lara was kissing her, fingers slipping into her hair, surprised intake of breath against her mouth. She felt Ollie's hands firm on her hips, pulling her in and Lara was smiling against her lips and *fuck* was she crying *again?*

Ollie kissed her and kissed her and Lara was fucking drowning.

"Shit." She made herself pull back. "Sorry. I didn't even wait to let you say anything." She let her hands drift from Ollie's shoulders to the waistband of her pants and *oh fuck* she was so warm and Lara was way ahead of herself. "I'm way ahead of myself." Lara scrunched her eyes closed. When she opened them again she made herself look at Ollie. "You went back to Melbourne," she added, with a small frown. "Your life is here. I know what *I* want but I also know it's not as straightforward as all that-"

"I'm not sure I've heard you ramble before," Ollie interrupted. "Are you *nervous?* It's fucking cute."

"I'm not *nervous,*" Lara bit back. "Why would I be nervous?" She looked at Ollie, at the smirk on her perfect smug mouth and just managed not to kiss her again. "I fly across the country begging women to give me another chance basically every other week," she told her. "I'm just super *casually* asking if you would still consider uprooting your entire fucking life for me, so, no: I'm not nervous at all."

Ollie watched her flail for another three excruciating seconds.

. . .

"I want to show you something," she said.

Lara blinked. It wasn't quite the affirmative answer she was looking for.

Ollie took her hand and pulled her inside her house.

"Nice digs," Lara said, hugging herself, very unsure where this was going. There were old polished floorboards, off-white walls, a long narrow hallway. Ollie pulled her all the way down to the living room, afternoon sunlight throwing squares of gold from the window to the opposite wall, a big comfy couch, a table and chairs, some pot plants, and a *mess*.

Ollie's possessions seemed to be strewn everywhere. Haphazard piles of books and crockery, folded towels, sheets and utensils were tumbled across one side of the living room. On the other was a much neater stack of cardboard boxes. *Records*, one was marked in extremely precise permanent marker, *Misc kitchen appliances*, said another. Lara stared.

"Why would anyone need that many extension cords?" she managed, looking at a truly epic pile of tangled cables.

Ollie laughed.

. . .

"I was always coming back," she said. She was still holding Lara's hand. "Whether you'd have me or not. I meant it." She turned to look at Lara, a splash of gold light hitting her features. "There's a whole world in Ribbonwood I don't want to miss out on. Even if it meant I had to spend the rest of my life unable to purchase my own ginger gummies since I couldn't set foot in the general store without bumping into an ex-lover," she said, her teeth sinking into her lower lip again, just barely holding back her smile. "It's that kind of shit that makes a place home."

Lara gazed at her in wonder. At least seventeen feelings hit her at once. Ollie was coming back. Ollie was looking at her like *ex*-lover was absolutely not what she wanted to be.

Without letting go of Ollie's hand, Lara walked backwards and bumped *herself* up onto the dining table, tugging Ollie in between her legs. Ollie bit her lip and watched her intently. Her hands rested on Lara's thighs, thumbs stroking just slightly, the same way they had the very first time they'd gone to bed together. This time there was a lot more clothing in the way, Lara reflected, already annoyed by the denim between Ollie's hands and her skin. Still, she couldn't stop her smile or her racing heart.

"Do you think you could still feel as nostalgic about Ribbonwood if we downgraded that drama to current lover?" Lara asked her, leaning back on her hands and looking up at her. "Maybe as of, more or less, right now?"

Ollie pretended to consider for almost a second and then gave up.

· · ·

"Oh fuck yes," she said, the words barely out of her mouth before she was kissing her.

———

Later - much later - stupid jeans long gone, darkness fallen, low golden light from the lamp at the bedside, Lara lay in Ollie's arms, tangled in the sheets, her head on her warm shoulder.

"Hey, quick question," Ollie said to her, stroking her hair. "Did you happen to kill a guy?"

Lara tilted her head up to look at her, eyes narrowed.

"Did you deliberately wait until after you'd gotten laid to check if I was a murderer?"

Ollie laughed. Then her face suddenly turned serious.

"I wanted to be there for you," she said. "I actually got as far as buying a plane ticket."

"You did?" Lara frowned.

. . .

"Yeah," Ollie confessed. "Then I realised it was Lara fucking Bennett I was dealing with. That if I tried to ride in on a white horse to save you, I'd have just been another damn thing you had to manage and you'd probably never have spoken to me again."

Lara thought about that for a moment, Ollie's fingers running through her hair, turning her to liquid.

"It's like you've met me," she said after a while.

Ollie laughed again. Then she wrapped her arms around her to hold her tight.

"I hope you appreciate me abandoning you in your time of need, because it was the hardest thing I've ever done and I'm quite sure I'll never manage to do it again."

"I think," Lara said softly, "that maybe next time I get arrested for a terrible crime, I might just be okay with that."

"That means a lot," said Ollie. She didn't let go of her though. "Are you okay?" she murmured.

"Yeah." God it felt good to be held. "You did help though," she pointed out. "You hired that lawyer."

. . .

Ollie eased back just enough to smile and roll her eyes.

"No," she said, "I didn't. That was my mother. Well, both my parents actually, but mostly my mother."

"Oh for *fuck's sake,*" Lara was crying *again.*

Chapter Thirty-Four

One year later

"I've figured out what I want for Christmas," Tilly announced from the back seat as the car wound its way up through the trees in the sunlight.

Ollie felt Lara's warning gaze on her from the passenger seat as she drove.

"And what's that?" Lara answered her daughter, a note of caution in her voice.

"Aria told me that Rocco's mum had another litter of puppies-"

. . .

"Absolutely not." Lara stopped her.

"But it would be Rocco's baby brother or sister!" gasped Tilly, already gearing up to argue her case. "Think how much he would love it!"

"Honey, I love you but you're not getting a *puppy* for Christmas-"

"What do you think Ollie?" Tilly's eyes were beseeching from the back seat.

Ollie opened her mouth.

"Do *not* answer that, Ollie Gabrielli," Lara stopped her quickly.

"Uh, what your mum said?" Ollie deliberately made her voice extremely tentative and Lara poked her in the thigh.

"See, mum? Ollie agrees with me-"

"I did no such thing!" Ollie quickly defended herself. She glanced sideways at Lara and found herself smirking against her will. Lara looked thoroughly needled. She also looked hot as hell: a simple shift dress, those leather ankle boots she'd bought when they'd been in Melbourne together, hair tousled, those legs. Lara caught the look in her eyes and shook her head like she couldn't even *believe* Ollie right now. Ollie could see right through her to the smile she was biting back.

"You're trouble," Lara said, her voice low, underneath Tilly's trenchant argument and Ollie let her eyebrows rise just enough.

"You're *in* trouble," she shot back and Lara just shook her head, the smile slipping out.

Her hand reached over and squeezed Ollie's thigh.

"And that's the reason I think we should get a puppy," Tilly concluded her backseat lecture. "To teach me responsibility."

"At which point did you realise you'd given birth to a tiny lawyer?" Ollie asked Lara as they reached the main road and Ollie indicated right.

"I suspect this is all for your benefit," Lara told her, then frowned at her daughter in the rearview mirror. "You do know that even if Ollie is a pushover, *I'm* still your mother, right? We don't have time for a puppy."

"He could stay at Ollie's place when I'm at school and you're at work!" Tilly was on a roll now. "He'd be such a good work-from-home dog. He could jump on your video calls," Tilly enthused to Ollie. "The sick kids would love it!"

. . .

"Notice how she's not even addressing any of this to me?" Lara's eyebrows were solidly raised now. "This is what happens when you can't say no."

"Who could say no to that face?" Ollie met Tilly's eyes in the rearview and they grinned at each other.

"Me," Lara said plainly.

Ollie pretended to look appalled and Tilly was still arguing her case when they pulled up at the mechanic's shop. As soon as they were out though, Tilly caught sight of Audrey and Sadie half a block down.

"I'll meet you there!" she shot out and raced down the street to catch up with Frankie and the two eldest of Audrey's kids. They were all on their way to hang out for a lunch at the pub together, right after they'd dropped Ollie's car off for a service. Now that Ollie was a real Ribbonwood resident, she'd ditched the damn farm ute for a vehicle of her own. The Subaru was the perfect city-country blend car, but the suspension had already taken a solid thumping.

"Morning," Audrey had abandoned the kids to Sadie and strolled up to say hello, so Ollie chucked Lara the keys to book the car in as she greeted her old friend. "Are you just going to stand by for that?" Audrey shot her a look as they watched Nate Kerr looking thoroughly pleased at himself for making Lara laugh as she looked up at him in the sunlight.

Ollie smirked.

"Are you kidding me? I've never paid so little for car repairs in my whole life," she said smugly. Nate Kerr glanced sideways as if knowing he was being talked about and Ollie gave him a threatening *I'm watching you* gesture, pointing two fingers between her eyes and his with a excellent glower. He laughed out loud and stepped back, his hands out, *I'm innocent.* Lara dropped the keys into his palm, smirked at him, then her eyes met Ollie's as she walked back to join her, a sparkle in her gaze.

"You're welcome," she said, her expression mischievous and Ollie made a show of grabbing her hand and tugging her firmly away from the burly mechanic. Lara laughed, her fingers squeezing hers as they walked down the street in the light.

"I don't know how you two can carry on like that and still feel like couple-goals." Audrey looked at them in disbelief.

Ollie laughed.

"It's almost," she said, "like Lara knows to whom she actually belongs," she smirked at the woman she loved.

· · ·

Said woman looked at her, her eyes narrowed.

"It's almost," Lara retorted, "like Ollie knows that I belong to my damn self. But," she added, her expression getting soft, "that for some reason I choose her anyway."

"Spew," said Audrey. She was smiling though. "God, it almost makes me want to believe in love again."

"It has its perks," Lara said. "On occasion."

Ollie grinned at the studious nonchalance in Lara's voice as she let the word *love* drift out into the wide blue sky. It was still something they teased each other about. She remembered the day the word finally got used, almost six months ago now, when she and Lara were taking a break from an extended Gabrielli family gathering and taking a walk around the winery together.

"Hey how come you never call us an *olive oil dynasty?*" Ollie reflected. "Is it because it sounds less sexy?"

Lara snorted, glancing at her sideways.

"You never let a single thing go, do you?"

"Not when you insist on being so damn hilarious," Ollie told her.

. . .

"Oh please, my point still stands," she rolled her eyes. *"Poor Ollie, nothing but beauty and brains and athletics prowess and the warmest family who thinks the sun shines out of her arse and owns a fucking winery."*

"It worked for me though didn't it?" Ollie pointed out. She made puppy eyes. *"Please take your clothes off Lara Bennett, for I am suffering."*

"Yes, that's exactly what happened." Lara gazed skywards as if for strength.

"You couldn't resist me," Ollie added smugly.

"In my defence it had been a really long time since I'd had sex and there you were."

"You, Lara Bennett, *love* me." The words came out her mouth before she could stop them.

Lara went still. Ollie did too. Oh shit. This was exactly what she'd promised herself she'd never do: push Lara anywhere she wasn't ready to go.

. . .

"Fuck," Ollie interjected. "That wasn't what I meant. Come here." She grabbed Lara's hand and started walking again, annoyed at herself for breaking the ease of their day, for just maybe ruining things between them, just as they were getting comfortable.

Lara stopped immediately, dropping Ollie's hand. Ollie felt slightly seasick. Lara's eyes were wide, her expression set.

"Actually," she said slowly. "I do."

"Hm?" Ollie wasn't sure she'd heard her right.

Lara huffed slightly.

"I *said* I fucking love you, Ollie Gabrielli."

Ollie's jaw dropped.

"Are you announcing you're in love with me or giving me a good telling off?" she asked, incredulous and dizzy with joy.

"Both," Lara told her, sounding slightly exasperated. "You've been looking at me like you love me for approximately forever but you never *say* it. You're such a chicken shit."

· · ·

Ollie laughed out loud.

"Are you fucking kidding me?" she demanded. "Do you know how hard I've been working, not saying *I love you* every goddamned day for the last half a year?" Lara blinked at her. "I've been taking it slow. For you."

"Well *stop*," said Lara impatiently, biting her lip. "Say it."

Ollie pulled her in and kissed her, then kissed her again.

"So," she said, "it turns out I love you too. Wildly."

"You'd better," Lara told her, her smile finally slipping out. Her eyes sparkled with a hint of tears.

"Look at you," Ollie was smiling too. "You're so pretty when you're all in love and shit."

"Please stop talking," Lara said, the words soft against Ollie's mouth.

Ollie did.

Epilogue

Well. Who in Ribbonwood would have expected that twist? Lara Bennett a late in life lesbian! It strikes some women that way, Dottie Parsons told everyone. You could go half your life, everything hunky dory and then, *bam*, wake up one day a lesbian. At least, that's what she'd heard that from a friend, that is.

Stephen Westerson said that was garbage. It was hardly surprising that Lara had switched to women, after all she'd already been through all the damn men in this town.

Kimberley Evans said that wasn't it either. Lara had always been a schemer. She simply couldn't let go of the chance to snag a single doctor no matter who they were; she was an equal opportunity gold-digger that was all. *Oh for god's sake,* said Esme Walker, *that's enough of that rubbish. Have you got any idea how profitable that damn store is? Lara Bennett probably has more money than god at this point. She doesn't need to dig anyone else's gold.*

. . .

Now *that* was the real problem. Suddenly, Lara Bennett defenders were everywhere. Ribbonwood was split right down the middle; it was worse than the covid vaccine! One minute you were innocently remarking to your neighbour that Lara was really quite brazen, kissing a woman all over town, obviously knowing full well how much everyone's husbands liked watching that kind of thing, and the next minute your neighbour - Robyn Lowe, of all people -would snap, *oh for fuck's sake Stacey, have you honestly ever seen two people more in love? The truth is right there for anyone with half a brain to see it.*

It was quite out of control. All of a sudden there were people everywhere more than willing to stop you in your tracks and swear on their mother's grave that Lara Bennett was, in fact, *the very best thing that had ever happened to Ribbonwood.* Albert Sanderson shook his head gravely from his perch on his bar stool. He'd had no idea there was such a scourge of lesbians in town but suddenly half the women in Ribbonwood were going on and on about how much they bloody adored her. Converted them all with her feminine wiles no doubt, damn unnatural when you thought about it. Of course Albert Sanderson always did had have a bit of dirty mind so no one paid him too much attention.

He had a little bit of a point though. Even Nate Kerr had been spotted recently wearing a t-shirt with the word *Ally* in great big rainbow font across the front like he was fronting a bloody Mardi Gras float while he changed your tyres. Everyone, it seemed, was taking a side, but one side in particular seemed to be growing.

. . .

Maybe it was something to do with the fact that Lara's doctor was Francesca Gabrielli's youngest child, a prodigal daughter returned from the big smoke down south, all the way home to Ribbonwood. Once Francesca had made up her mind about something there was no changing it.

Not only was her son engaged to Sadie O'Malley - *a cross-cultural marriage, you know* - but as far as Francesca was concerned, Lara belonged to the Gabrielli family every bit as much. You couldn't go to the Silverbloom chicken auction without finding Lara at her side, smiling and playing every bit the dutiful daughter-in-law, her own daughter jumping up and down excitedly beside her like another grandchild to the mix. It was quite clear Francesca was holding out hopes of adding a *same-sex wedding* to the Gabriellis' extensive social calendar but despite the gold-digging accusations no ring had yet appeared on Lara Bennett's finger.

Some said she'd never marry again and as the years went by that seemed more and more likely. Ollie Gabrielli didn't seem to care one whit; you'd see the two of them down at the Ribbonwood Pub, laughing and gazing at each other like no one else existed, Ollie even pulling her out on the dance floor to whirl her around and kiss her right on the mouth like they really were newlyweds, rings be damned. Some weekends you'd even find Lara cheering on the side-lines as Ollie singlehandedly resurrected the Ribbonwood women's soccer team. It felt quite strange to see Lara Bennett all carefree and excited about something in public, but perhaps she was just passionate about women's sports (another point in the *maybe she's actually gay* column if you were still in the business of trying to work that one out.)

. . .

Amber O'Brien said lesbians were supposed to do a thing called U-Hauling which made Myrtle Jenkins open her eyes very wide and tell her to *mind the children for goodness sake*. Amber said no, actually, it just meant they moved in together almost instantly, no men to put the brakes on things, you know how it is. But Ollie and Lara didn't even seem to do that, Ollie keeping that little house on Vine Street for years, though the rumour was she really didn't use it for anything other than the odd bit of work these days.

It's the daughter I feel sorry for, Myrtle shook her head. *Imagine trying to have a boyfriend with those two watching your every move.* Lara was still over protective as far as she was concerned and Ollie had been seen giving Chris Wiseman's youngest boy a solid lecture when he'd said something surely innocent and cheeky about fourteen-year-old Tilly, who was now almost as pretty as Lara had been at that age, though thankfully nowhere near as *precocious*. Tilly had just rolled her eyes complaining about how embarrassing her parents were. *Don't you think it's actually pretty nice,* Eva Sinclair argued, *that after Lara had to grow up with no mother at all, her daughter gets to have two of them?* Myrtle was a bit annoyed about that point, especially because suddenly she'd gotten something in her eye and had to scurry off to fix it.

So fine, perhaps Lara really had changed for the better, *or maybe,* pointed out Chloe Perkins, *maybe Ribbonwood has?* Of course Chloe would think that. It was commonly believed that no matter the result of the inquest, Lara had been the one to push Dale Winchester into the dam that night. The thing was, Dale Winchester was an incredibly nasty piece of work, so if that really was the case it might be the one time Ribbonwood was actually united in thinking Lara had perhaps done the right thing for once. *Tread carefully,* women warned their husbands, *or I'll send Lara Bennett after you.*

. . .

One thing was for sure: Ribbonwood had once held Lara on the outskirts and now she seemed firmly in the centre of it all. The general store became such a meeting point for residents - a social hub it seemed - that Lara got annoyed by the deadlock around the counter and branched out the business to include some tables and chairs out the front of the store and a coffee machine and pastries just inside the door. It was Jessica Webb's daughter she hired to staff it, because of all the miracles on earth she and Jess seemed to be friends these days. *What times,* Dottie Parsons shook her head in wonder.

Lara Bennett. Some said she was a witch and others some kind of a town goddess. Either way she'd become a bit of a Ribbonwood legend. After all, there's nothing a small town likes more than a real life redemption story.

Afterword

Ribbonwood deals with a range of interpersonal and intimate partner violence. If it has raised any issues for you, please take care and seek assistance.

I've written male perpetrators in this book, and statistically speaking that's accurate.

Queer relationships though, are absolutely not immune from abuse. Recent Australian statistics show that 3 in 5 (61%) of LGBTQ+ respondents surveyed had experienced intimate partner violence. So that's *most* queer people; it could be you, or it could be your friends. These experiences can be further compounded by stigma and are complex because not all interpersonal violence is physical.

If someone you're in a relationship with isn't treating you with kindness, if you feel fearful, if you're on eggshells all the time, please reach out to your support systems, to advice lines, wherever you feel safe to seek out information and help.

Afterword

You deserve to feel safe and respected, especially at home.

Acknowledgments

Ribbonwood was a passion project for me, something akin to getting lost in a hurricane. Some stories happen slow, this one poured out fast. I lost sleep over it. It kept me going when I was running on fumes and then it drove me quite honestly nuts. It's a glimmer of a time and a place full of new hope and freedom and I hope it means something to you too.

I'd like to thank all my early readers, including Jo Havens (thank you for your incredible constructive feedback and encouragement, I appreciate you deeply), Erica Lee (your support has been wildly amazing!) Evren.D (as always!) Karen. F, Mary.S, Kate.J, and critique partner Sarah.G. Thank you for this team effort that made the end product far better than the first draft!

Thank you to Elizabeth Luly, J.E. Leak, and all the amazing sapphic authors I've chatted to along the way. I appreciate this community so damn much.

Thank you to literally everyone in the sapphic bookstagram world! You are all extraordinarily wonderful humans who I appreciate more than I can say. @SterlingSapphicReads, @nonbinaryknightreads, @Bookshelvesandtealeaves, @sapphicsread, @sapphic_bookworms, @thesapphicnarratives, @jessreadswithpride, @lez.be.readin.ya.89, @sapphic_book_club, @bookwork.247_, @sappho_atheneum and so very many others. I appreciate the hard work you all do, uplifting sapphic authors and helping us find our readers. You're all superstars.

To every single reader who's reached out to me to tell me that something I wrote meant something to them; to the readers who sent my book to someone else, or who took it along for book group; to the readers who told me their wife loved it; to the readers who sent me a photograph of my book on a beach or on a shelf. You're the reason I keep writing anything at all. Appreciate you endlessly.

Thank you to Cath Grace for this spectacularly perfect cover; it's almost like you've been to the hinterland and love it as much as I do? Having a local artist do this cover was a dream, even if we disagreed about what a fig tree was...

As always to my sisters; this one is a love story to whanau and to home, as much as it is anything else. I appreciate the incredible work you do in your lives to learn and survive and grow. Here's to thriving in the light. You're everything.

To my son: four years old?! This book is about motherhood, the highs and lows and doing it alone, but it's impossible to feel alone when you give such excellent hugs.

Moira.K. Fuck babe. What a year. I couldn't be more damn proud of you. You're brave, strong, creative, talented as hell and now you're unstoppable. Thank you for your words of wisdom, your encouragement and as always for stepping into the unknown with your face towards the sun.

Melissa.H. "Ask yourself: what would my great grandmothers, who didn't get choices, want me to do?" *Bro.* I couldn't ask for a wiser voice in my head.

To Cat. "I fucking love you" might be the best declaration I've ever heard in my life, especially from someone who doesn't swear. Gosh, I love you too x

The Grace Notes Trilogy

Falls From Grace

Grace Notes: Book One

Savannah Grace is a huge star in Nashville. At least, she was. Her hit band *Twice Struck* topped the country music charts for almost a decade until her high profile marriage to her bandmate and co-writer publicly exploded. Now she's fading from the spotlight and her own life, just trying to keep her head above water.

Brynn Marshall is a little lost. Dropping out of med school made her the black sheep of the family and now she's floating around LA trying to find a sense of purpose. When she falls down on her luck, her best friend - indie musician Noah Lyman - refuses to let her wallow. After all, he's just got his big break: co-writing with a megastar!

When Savannah enlists Noah to help her break out of country music and make a name for herself for once and for all, what better way to do it than to spend the winter in her secluded vacation home in the woods of Vermont? And what better way for Noah to help out a friend than to pretend he's bringing along his wife?

After all, what could possibly go wrong?

Graceless

Grace Notes: Book Two

Savannah Grace is on top of the world. She's back to selling out stadium tours and winning Grammies *and* she's just arrived home from her honeymoon after marrying the love of her life...nothing could burst this bubble.

Except, of course, her estranged family.

When her younger sister Cassidy shows up on her doorstep, in need of help and thoroughly - inexplicably - pissed off, the whole household gets turned on its end. Where did she spring from and why the heck is she so damn *mad?*

Savannah's nanny Lane has grown all the way up, from a cute punk kid to a classic heartbreaker, a long trail of short flings in their wake. They don't have a second to waste on Cassidy; after all she's rude, ignorant, hot-tempered and kind of a brat. It's just...does their boss's little sister have to be so *hot?*

Of course things could always get worse. Cassidy has one plan and one plan only: for her sister to turn her into a star.

Saving Graces

Grace Notes: Book Three

Rosalie Carlson is the person everyone turns to in a crisis. She's kind, calm, caring, and a social worker, after all. She's got it all together... except that her personal life is kind of a disaster. Things can get a little hectic when your complicated best-friendship is with a megastar like Savannah Grace.

When twenty-six year old Kinsey moved to Nashville, it was in the hopes of finding a creative partner and making it big. When she meets Cassidy Carver, musical sparks fly. It's a chance meeting with a beautiful older woman however, that truly knocks her off her feet.

Rosalie's gorgeous - and there's no denying the intense chemistry between them - but she refuses to consider even a single date with a young musician. Besides, Rosalie's given up on love altogether, so what would be the point?

Fighting this level of temptation is always a losing battle, but after one red hot minute they go their separate ways. It's just lucky there's no connection between their different worlds and no way they'll ever cross paths again...

About the Author

Ruby Landers lives in Meanjin (Brisbane) Australia. As you're reading this she is either typing a million daydreamy words a minute, giving someone a thousand-yard stare while secretly working out a plot twist, having a deep conversation with anyone four-legged, bargaining with an expert toddler negotiator, or dreaming of quitting her day job. Either way, there'll be coffee.

You can follow her at

Instagram @rubylandersauthor

Made in the USA
Las Vegas, NV
07 February 2025

17727322R00236